Goa

Goa

Blood of the Goddess
I

Kara Dalkey

TOR®

A Tom Doherty Associates Book
New York

This is a work of fiction. All the characters and
events portrayed in this novel are either fictitious or
are used fictitiously.

GOA

This book is printed on acid-free paper.

A Tor Book
Published by Tom Doherty Associates, Inc.
175 Fifth Avenue
New York, NY 10010

Tor Books on the World Wide Web:
http://www.tor.com

Tor® is a registered trademark of Tom Doherty
Associates, Inc.

Library of Congress Cataloging-in-Publication Data

Dalkey, Kara.
    Goa / Kara Dalkey.
        p.   cm. — (Blood of the goddess ; v. 1)
    "A Tom Doherty Associates book."
    ISBN 0–312–86000–5
    I. Title.   II. Series: Dalkey, Kara. Blood of
the goddess ; v. 1.
    PS3554.A433G63   1996
    813'.54—dc20   96–1405
                                                          CIP

First Edition: August 1996

Printed in the United States of America

0   9   8   7   6   5   4   3   2   1

Goa

PROLOGUE

I do not envy you, O seeker of Truth. Yours is a goal unattainable. The hills you wish to climb are made of glass.

You say I must be a cynic or a boor; but no. I am only a humble *vina* player. My *dharma* it is to beguile the ear, not offend it.

What of mystics, you argue, who empty their minds and deprive their bodies? Do they not perceive Truth? I say no; a mystic does not see Truth, he attempts to be Truth, or rather his small part of it.

Now, you say, I quibble like the brass merchant in the bazaar. But I speak to a purpose. Know you the tale of the seven blind men and the elephant? It is a story quite dear to me, as you might guess from my own sightless orbs. In any case, I heard an interesting version of it from a Buddhist monk who was passing through Bijapur. If you are not in a hurry, sit and I will tell it you.

So. There were seven blind men, each thought to be wise, brought to an elephant. Each man was placed beside a different part of the creature and asked to tell, by sense of touch, what manner of beast it was.

The first blind man ran his hands along the tail and said, "Ah, this beast must be a small snake." The next, who touched the trunk of the elephant, said, "No, it is a very big snake." The third man felt the thick leg and said, "You are both wrong. This creature must be very like a tree." The fourth man had hold of an ear and said, "No, no, it has wings like an enormous bat!" The fifth wise man attempted to encircle the belly with his arms, exclaiming, "It must be a horse of great girth!" The sixth had placed his hand on the elephant's broad forehead and said, "No, brothers, we are deceived. This is no animal, but a wall!" The seventh blind man was given the beast's testicles to hold, and said, "You are all wrong. This is but two gourds in a leather sack."

Some versions of this tale end with the blind men cudgeling each other to death over their disagreements. But the Buddhist monk chose to end it another way: He said the blind men became so perplexed by their differing answers that they could not believe it could be the same animal. So each man kept his hand on the part he had first touched, sliding his other hand along the elephant's body until it met the hand of another. By doing this, the blind men discovered that although each part was different, together they joined to make one thing. And although they were still unable to perceive the complete shape of the creature, the blind men could all agree that it must be a marvelous beast indeed.

I do not speak just to fill the air with my breath, or to help you spend your time with pleasant emptiness. I would have you remember this tale as you continue your journey. A mountain is viewed but one side at a time. See all that you can, but know that it is never All. May you walk in the shadow of the Divine Will, stranger.

Gandharva
Musician to the court of
Sultan Ibrahim 'Adilshah II

I

🌿 OAK: The most puissant of trees, most royal and holy.
The ancients thought it the first of all trees. Even now, there
are some who pour the blood of sacrificed animals on oak
roots for its blessing. Oak wood is thought the embodiment
of strength and endurance, and is oft burned in sacred fires.
Twigs of oak are used in the gathering of medicinal herbs. A
ship built from that tree known as the blood oak, however,
is ill-fated and will meet with disaster....

SEPTEMBER 1597, AMINDIVI ISLANDS, LACCADIVE SEA

Thomas Chinnery looked up at the sound of distant thunder. No clouds darkened the sultry sapphire sky above the masts of *The Bear's Whelp*. He blew on the wet ink of the letter he had been writing and stood. From the ship's railing, he could see the palm-lined shore of the small island where they lay anchored. He saw no man with a pistol. Their companion ship, *The Bear*, was moored to the west, but the sound had come from the east and north.

"Penning another letter missive to your lassie, Tom?" he heard behind him, and he winced. The Scotsman, Andrew Lockheart, was a fellow wool merchant with Master Bathwick, purported to be an experienced traveler and rumored to be a rogue. He also seemed strangely determined to press his friendship upon Thomas.

"In truth, I am not, sir. It is a report to my master the apothecary Geoffrey Coulter of London. From whence came that roar?"

Lockheart's black-beard–framed lips pulled into a sly smile. "Methinks 'twas a wealthy dame, crying 'Take me for I would be thine.' "

"You speak in riddles, sir."

"Think you so? Look to the tops of yon trees, Tom, where she waves her kerchief to catch our eyes."

Thomas gazed where the Scotsman pointed and saw the tip of a mast, flying a pennant with the colors of Portugal, moving south toward their end of the island. "By'r Lady," he whispered. "Not again."

A sailor in the *Whelp*'s rigging cried out, "A galleon! Nay, two! Riding heavy!"

Men were already running down the shore, having dropped whatever provisions they may have been gathering. They leapt into the beached skiffs and oared them like demons back to the ships. Captain Benjamin Wood appeared on the foredeck, his red hair streaming in the wind. "To the sails, men! The Good Lord sends quarry into our blind. If we catch the breeze, we'll catch Lusitanian game. Hoist anchor! To the sails!"

"Our men have scarce recovered from our last encounter," sighed Thomas.

"Greed is a most potent physic, m'lad, and brings life to the limbs of many a man. In mind of that, mayhap you ought to go below. Your potions and herbs shall doubtless see more use 'ere long."

"Nay, our able men are few. I will ask the bo'sun for a sword and lend my arms to the fight."

Lockheart frowned. "Bravely said, lad. But should you not save yourself for your master's work?"

"If we are defeated for want of men," said Thomas, "I will have little chance to factor for my master."

"True. But Dame Fortune smiles. Yon ships are scarce fit to meet us. And Cap'n Wood has a canny plan."

"How know you that?"

"Because I gave it him." With a wink, Lockheart bounded away across the deck to assist on the ropes. Thomas went to a hatch between the masts, where a boy was hauling up swords from the hold below. Even those sailors who sprawled weak with the scurvy roused themselves to distribute the weapons and mugs of ale.

The navigator posted himself at the whipstaff and pulled it hard to port. The mainsail unfurled with a ponderous crack, and turned to catch the northerly breeze. Slowly, the *Whelp* pulled out into open water. The *Bear*, some lengths behind, came away from the island at an angle more southerly.

Thomas quaffed his allotted mugful of sour ale in one gulp. *'Tis medicine given afore the wound. Physic to numb the senses to what must follow.* He could hear the constable shouting orders belowdecks, and the rumble and clatter of culverins being readied. The smaller lombards and rail pieces on the main deck were being loaded with what little shot remained. Thomas traded the ale mug for a cutlass and a large, battered wheellock pistol, and went to stand by the railing.

Masters Allen and Bromefield, the merchants in charge of the voyage, strode past Thomas, faces dark with dudgeon. He heard them argue with Captain Wood, who would have none of it.

'Struth, thought Thomas, *I ne'er thought I'd become more pirate than 'pothecary. If I'd wanted plunder to be my living, I'd have 'prenticed myself with Admiral Raleigh.*

As the *Whelp* emerged out from behind the island, Thomas got his first look at their prey. Running down the wind, in true aim for a broadside, came a gaudy gilded little galleon of only thirty tons or so. Looming behind it, however, was the biggest Portuguese carrack Thomas had ever seen; over a hundred feet long and a thousand tons, with a main-mast taller than any natural tree, and her sides bristling with cannon.

We're done, thought Thomas.

At a shout below, the *Whelp*'s four port cannon greeted the newcomers with thunderous voices. Through the acrid smoke, Thomas saw a gash appear in the galleon's sparsail and wood splinter on her bow just above the waterline. The crew of the galleon were astonished at the appearance of the *Whelp*, and rushed about the decks like frightened ants.

"Caught 'em napping," said Nathan, the ship's carpentry apprentice.

"So 'twould seem," said Thomas. "And that may be all that saves us." The *Whelp* was passing east of the galleon and the enormous carrack turned eastward as well, as if to come between the galleon and the *Whelp*.

"A rich one," said Nathan, his eyes still on the galleon. "A private merchantman, mayhap with rubies and emeralds for his ladies in Lisbon."

"Aye," grumbled Thomas, "and a mighty escort to see him off." He could see that half the carrack's sixteen port guns were set and manned, and more gun ports opened as he watched.

The stern lombard of the *Whelp* fired a parting shot at the passing galleon. The crew made ready on the sails to come about to give the port culverins another chance to fire. Like a waterborne mountain, the carrack neared, towering over them.

The *Whelp*'s guns fired again, and by good aim or good fortune one ball split the topspar of the carrack's foresail, sending canvas and rope raining down on her deck. A cheer rose up from the English sailors.

But as the carrack passed astern, her culverins responded. It rained cannon shot and Thomas threw himself down on the deck. The ship shuddered and acrid smoke swirled around him.

"I am hurt!" Nathan groaned.

"Damn you, Captain Wood," Thomas growled as he crawled to Nathan's side. The boy's shirt bore a bloody rent. "Be still, Nate, else you will tear the wound."

"I am still well enough to fight." The boy winced as he sat up. "I'll not give up my share of the takings."

"There are things worth more than gold and rubies," said Thomas, tearing the boy's shirt for a bandage.

Another volley sounded, but not from the carrack or the *Whelp*. Thomas peered over the railing and understood what Lockheart's "canny plan" had been. The *Bear*, behind and to the south, was now well positioned for a broadside on the carrack.

The *Whelp*'s crew were fighting with the sail lines to bring the ship around again. The carrack and the galleon would be caught between the two smaller, faster English ships. *A pretty trap indeed*, thought Thomas, *if we are not sunk first.*

A shot from the carrack's foredeck took off the *Bear*'s bowsprit and part of the upper forecastle. Two elegant little bronze cannon on the galleon's aftcastle belched fire . . . and the Portuguese carrack lost her mizzenmast.

"They fire upon their own escort!" said Nathan, clutching his side. "Have they gone mad?"

"Or have we mistook their relation?" mused Thomas. "I know not." Lockheart appeared at Thomas's right elbow, gazing out at the scene. "Do not tell me, sir," Thomas said to him, "that the galleon's madness was part of your canny plan as well."

The Scotsman's mouth twitched into a rueful smile. "The Good Lord doth help those who help themselves, 'tis said."

Across the water, the crewmen of the galleon and the carrack shouted at one another. The carrack tightened her sails and hauled away, passing the bow of the floundering *Bear*.

"She runs!" said Nathan.

"Leaving her charge, if so it was, behind," said Thomas. "What wondrous cowardice."

"I would wager," said Lockheart, "that yon carrack was not protector but pursuer. See the scars upon the galleon's filigree? 'Twould seem the carrack had got a shot or two at her afore us."

"Do you mean, sir," said Nathan, "that we have been someone's rescue?"

The galleon's elegant bronze cannon boomed again, the balls taking off some of the railing near where they crouched.

"Aye," said Lockheart, daring to raise his head once more. "And he's as grateful as a tiger freed from a trap."

The *Whelp* and the *Bear* fired together on the galleon, making a tangled mess of her masts, rigging, and sails. Neither English ship was in a condition to give chase to the fleeing carrack, so they closed on the hapless galleon. The crew of the *Whelp* threw out grappling lines and drew up beside it. The crew of the galleon, many of them turbaned Arabs and dark-skinned Hindus, glared back silently from the morass of canvas, wood, and rope.

"Think you can fight in that, Nathan?" said Thomas.

"With the best o'ye," the boy said.

"Brave lad," said Lockheart. "What of you, Tom?"

Years spent in Master Coulter's shop mixing foul-smelling ointments and potions had not prepared Thomas for hand-to-hand butchery. But it had taught him to see an unpleasant task through to its end. "If I must."

Lockheart clapped a broad hand on his shoulder. "May the Fates look kindly on you, then."

"Do you surrender?" shouted Captain Wood to the captive galleon, "or will you be boarded and taken by force?"

An unearthly yell rose from the Arabs and Hindus. The Portuguese sailors cut at the grappling lines with their knives.

Boarding planks were thrown from the *Whelp* to the rails of the galleon and the English sailors scrambled across. Thomas muttered oaths beneath his breath and followed, pistol in his left hand, cutlass in his right.

As he ducked beneath a fallen sailspar, a curved knife thrust out in front of his throat. He beat it away with his cutlass and charged forward, but the foe had vanished. Thomas found himself standing in a bewildering tangle resembling a fogbound forest. Masts canted like fallen trees and ropes caught at his ankles like vines. Powder smoke stung his eyes. Shadows of men on the sails confused his vision. Shouts and screams surrounded him. Now and then, a pistol ball whizzed past like an angry bee.

An Arab leapt before him, sword at the ready, eyes glaring. Thomas stepped back, raising his cutlass as his opponent slashed at him. It warded the Arab's blow, but Thomas tripped and fell back into a mass of rigging and sail. The Arab smiled and jumped closer to take advantage of Thomas's fall. Thomas raised his pistol.

A shout rose above the others. It was followed by a long declaration in a language Thomas did not understand. A profound silence followed. The Arab lowered his sword with a scowl and stepped away.

Captain Wood, somewhere behind him, called out, "Desist, men! They have surrendered!"

Thomas sighed deeply with relief and peered through a slash in the sail beside him.

The Portuguese and Arab sailors were laying their swords down on the deck, glaring at the ship's forecastle. The Hindus were pressing their foreheads to the deck in prayer. Thomas craned his neck further and saw, standing on the forecastle, a tall, slender woman. She was dressed in a sari of crimson silk that glimmered with threads of gold. Her skin was a light brown, but her eyes were an astonishing blue.

Here is a rare marvel. Can this be her ship, that she can command these men? Might she be the daughter of a wealthy merchant? And why did the carrack pursue her?

The woman bowed to Captain Wood and spoke to him, one of the Hindu sailors acting as interpreter. Although the captain nodded, chin in hand, he seemed to be having difficulty understanding. After a few minutes, the captain waved off the interpreter and escorted the lady onto the *Whelp* himself.

With her departure, an unseen spell was broken on the deck of the galleon, and men began moving and speaking again. Slump-shouldered, the galleon's crew divided themselves; some to try their luck reaching safety in the galleon's two tiny skiffs (mainly the proud Portuguese and Arabs), others choosing to sail with the *Whelp* and the *Bear*. Meanwhile, the English sailors opened the hatches to the galleon's holds, beginning their plunder.

Thomas pulled himself out of his nest of rigging and made his way toward the aftcastle. *I may as well seek my fair share. Master Coulter will be wanting some profit from this unhappy voyage.* At least he would not be much in competition with the other sailors, since gold and silks were not what he sought.

As he neared the aftcastle, Thomas felt a tugging on his breeches. A black-braided Hindu knelt beside him, desperately pleading in his soft, liquid language. Some of the *Whelp*'s crewmen emerged from the aftcastle door, carrying wooden chests and jars that smelled of aromatic resins and spices. The Hindu gestured at them as he spoke.

"What do you want, man?" said Thomas. "I cannot stop them."

Lockheart came out of the doorway with an armful of colorful silks and cotton calicoes.

"Know you, sir, what his wight is saying?" Thomas asked.

Without stopping, Lockheart called back, "He says take what you will of the cursed cargo below. They are better off rid of it."

Thomas stared after the Scotsman's broad back. *Betimes I wish he would not jest so. Though it is possible the Hindu had no love for whom he served.* Thomas said some words that he hoped would be calming to the man and stepped into the doorway. He felt his way down a narrow stair into the dark lower decks. He turned and entered a passageway filled with sailors shuffling past, each with arms and pockets laden. In the dimness, Thomas saw an empty passage leading farther aft and he headed for it.

"Ye need not trouble yourself that way," called out one sailor. "We've searched. It's bare."

Thomas nodded, but proceeded nonetheless, preferring the quiet hallway to the rapacious crowding of the main passage. He continued past the ruddershaft and found that the corridor ended at a diamond-paned window at the stern. Just below him would be the master stateroom for the captain or ship's owner. Crew's quarters would be forward of that, and stowage the deck below. Thomas leaned against the window, gazing back the way he had come.

As his eyes adjusted to the light, he noticed a door to his right, carved with emblems of hunting and a border of eight-petaled roses. Thomas pressed on the ivory latch handle and opened the door. It led into a room containing a long table and several heavy chairs of carved oak and leather. A few porcelain bowls lay on the table, but the room was unoccupied.

Thomas entered, shutting the door behind him, grateful for a few moments of peace. He sank wearily into one of the chairs and closed his eyes.

He heard the scraping of another chair against the floor and he sat up again, eyes wide. No one else was in the room. *Can this ship be haunted with the shades of those so recently dispatched?* The scraping came again, but now he placed the sound beyond a wall to his left. *But that should be the rudder-shaft chamber.* A glance around the room told him it was smaller than the length of the passageway outside.

The wall to his left had a deeply carved wainscoting, again depicting scenes of hunting. He noticed a carved bird seemed to protrude just a little more than the boughs and leaves surrounding it. Drawing his pistol from his doublet, Thomas silently approached the wall. He twisted the bird as though it were a knob and a door opened inward. Swiftly, he stepped in.

It was a tiny room, in which an elegantly dressed man sat at a desk. He wore a black velvet doublet, slashed sleeves trimmed with gold, and a wide ruff of fine, stiff linen, edged with lace. He had a neat, pointed black beard, and dark eyes that seemed wary but not afraid. In his right hand was a quill pen and his left was poised over the lid of a wooden box.

"Leave that be," said Thomas, waving his pistol at the box. He feared it might hold a weapon. He hoped the fellow understood him.

The bearded man slowly withdrew his hand and smiled a thin-lipped smile. He said something in Portuguese that might have been a polite deferral. Thomas wished Lockheart were near; the Scotsman seemed to know every language on earth.

"Up from there. Slowly." He gestured with the pistol.

The bearded man put down his pen and stood. He began to come around the desk, toward Thomas. Thomas raised the pistol, hoping he would not have to kill an unarmed man.

"Ey, good work, Tom!" Sully, the first mate, appeared in the doorway behind him. "I see ye caught our sorcerer."

"Sorcerer?" The word, in Thomas's experience, could mean anything from a man who summoned devils, to Her Majesty's astrologer, to one who had too great a fondness for cats. Even apothecaries such as his master, Geoffrey Coulter, were occasionally accused of sorcery by clients and clergymen.

"Aye, he's wanted by the Inquisitors in Goa, we've learned. 'Tis why the carrack was giving chase."

Thomas could see nothing in the tiny room that suggested the black arts. "Is this his ship, then?"

"Aye, so Cap'n Wood wants him treated respectful."

"What of the lady who stopped the fighting?"

"Well, now there be many a question wanting answer, isn't there? Have ye got anything valuable off this one? Maps or pilot's logs perchance?"

"We had only just met."

"Eh, belike he'd not give 'em ye. Shall I take this wight off yer hands or do ye want the glory of bringing him in yerself?"

"You may take him. I would search somewhat more."

"Good hunting to ye, then. Come along, senhor, and meet Cap'n Wood's hospitality."

The Portuguese sorcerer glared at the first mate and uttered cold, precise words.

"Your curses shall not work on me, sir," said Sully. "I am

an English seaman and I have heard the worst curses there be. Come along."

Thomas stepped aside and allowed the first mate to firmly escort the gentleman away. As soon as they were gone, Thomas went to the desk and looked it over. Beside the fallen pen was a sheet of parchment. Only a few words were written on it, but Thomas did not recognize the script. He turned to the wooden box.

It was the length of his hand and the breadth of his palm, made of a dark wood. On the top were carved geometric patterns. Thomas pushed aside the brass hook latch and opened the box.

Inside, upon a bed of black and gold silk, lay a flat, stoppered bottle of iridescent glass. On the inside of the box lid was a folded piece of paper. Removing this, Thomas saw carved on the inside of the lid a staff around which two serpents were entwined—a caduceus. Thomas opened the folded paper and saw several lines of script. The uppermost was in Greek, and Thomas blessed his schooling, for he could read it. "A serpent's bite to one who breathes. A serpent's skin to one who does not."

A riddle, or perhaps a curse, thought Thomas. The other lines of script he could not read, though the second he recognized as Arabic. He folded the paper and put it back under the box lid. *Could this be a magical potion? A drug? Curative or poison?* Thomas closed the box and put it within his doublet. *If it be medicine, I should learn of it. Others may choose their share of the day's bounty. This will be mine.*

II

🦋 HAWTHORN: This small, thorny tree bears pale flowers in midsummer and red berries in autumn. 'Tis said Our Lord's Crown of Thorns was made from the boughs of this tree, and thus it is credited with much power against sorcery. Keeping hawthorn in the house will protect from ghosts and lightning, yet 'tis also said that hawthorn in the home brings ill luck and death....

SEPTEMBER 1597, PORTUGUESE COLONY OF GOA

Father Antonio Gonsção, Special Envoy from the *Conselho Supremo* of the Grand Inquisitor of Lisboa, stood at a window of the Santa Casa. To his relief, the scene before him did not undulate like the sea.

Below the window lay the Praça do Catedral, a broad square like that of any European town. Across the square stood the Cathedral of Santa Catarina, its façade embellished with sculpted saints, its twin square towers rising modestly toward Heaven. Twin stone dolphins spouted playfully in the plaza fountain. To the west of the square was the Misericordia, the hospital run by the Jesuits. Balconied, two-story houses with roofs of red tile surrounded the rest of the plaza. In the distance, fine estates with orchards and gardens dotted the hillsides. In appearance, the view could almost have been that of any prosperous port in Portugal. But for certain differences; differences disturbing to Gonsção.

The plaza was filled with people; *mestiço fidalgos*, wearing velvets and lace, strolling with one boy behind to carry a sword, another to carry a parasol, yet another bearing a cushion. The lordly ones bowed to one another, doffing their caps with grand, sweeping gestures. This was as much competition as courtesy, for woe betide the man whose bow was not low enough, or hinted of mockery. Ladies rode in gilded palanquins borne by slaves with skins of no Iberian hue. Arabs, Jews, narrow-eyed men from far Cathay, Persians, Hindus, in addition to all manner of Europeans, passed below, walking to and fro on the Rua Direita, coming and going under the black stone Arco de Vicereis that faced the Mandovi River.

The air was redolent with the scent of tropical flowers, colorful birds squawked in unfamiliar song. It was all too bright, too varied, too alive; Gonsção's senses felt under attack.

He remembered a woman, the daughter of a neighbor on the street where he had lived in Lisboa. As a boy, he had admired her dark-honey hair and sweet face. But years later she was brought before him for judgment, dressed in a garish gown of red and purple silk, accused of prostitution and witchcraft. Goa reminded him of that woman; beauty painted over in harlotry, corruption festering beneath all.

The Portuguese settlers of Goa had been encouraged to intermarry with the natives, in the hope of producing mass conversions. But instead, the True Faith had taken only a precarious hold on the souls of Goa, so beguiling were the surroundings and foreign influences. Heresy and heathenism ever surfaced like sirens of the deep. Only the Santa Casa, the sacred Inquisition, stood as a bulwark to the tides that would engulf the faithful. And even that holy institution had, it seemed to Gonsção, developed cracks. *And I am sent to shore up its piers. I have been too long at sea*, he mused with an inward smile. *Even my thoughts smell of fish.*

He heard footsteps approaching and he turned from the window. It was Domine Rui Sadrinho, the Inquisitor Major. He was tall and very thin, perhaps of forty years. The face above his well-trimmed black beard was mottled and pocked with scars of some past pestilence. Gonsção inclined his head to him. "Domine."

"Good morning, Padre. I trust you have recovered from your long voyage? Are your accommodations pleasing?"

"They are quite comfortable, thank you. And I am glad to say that the ground has stopped swaying as I walk. But tell me, Domine"—Gonsção tugged at the neck of his heavy white Dominican habit—"is it always so hot here?"

"Indeed, Padre. Always."

"Even when it rains?"

"Most particularly when it rains. Then it is hot and damp."

"And at night?"

"Then it is hot and dark, Padre."

"And the mosquitoes, Domine—"

"Are with us always as well. The Devil is busy in this part of the world. Pests and pestilence abound here."

As is writ in your face, Gonsção thought, and then chided himself. "So I have been told. But why assume it is the Devil's work? A plague may be an act of God."

The Inquisitor Major looked startled, then wary. "Surely our Lord is more merciful than that."

No, I am not trying to entrap you, thought Gonsção, *yet*. He attempted a disarming smile. "An idle musing only, Domine. I will bear this climate with patience, if I must."

"I think you will find that our Santa Casa has ameliorating comforts to offer, Padre. This building, I will point out, was the palace of the 'Adilshah of Goa, before our people arrived. We have saved some of his furnishings—they are in the residential wing. This chamber used to be his throne room."

The *Mesa do Santo Officio* indeed still retained some semblance of its former majesty. The long, high-ceilinged hall was lined with false archways which were decorated with delicate arabesques, and hung with tapestries striped blue and citron. Dominating the east wall was an enormous wood crucifix. A stepped dais filled the center of the hall. On the dais stood a long table surrounded by armchairs upholstered in red silk brocade. At one end of the table stood a simple folding stool.

"I can arrange for you to have a tour of the building, if you wish," Sadrinho went on.

"Thank you, but I am not here as a pleasure traveler, Domine, and my appointed task weighs heavily. I should like to begin my inquiries as soon as possible. Grand Inquisitor Albrecht views your troubles here with great concern. Your letter touched him deeply."

Sadrinho gazed at the floor. "We are pleased the Grand Inquisitor has a care for so distant an outpost of the Santa Casa."

"It is the sheep at the far edge of the herd who is most earnestly looked after by the shepherd, is it not?"

Again, the Inquisitor Major seemed wary. "It did surprise us that he would be so generous as to send a special envoy to . . . assist us."

Ah. Was your letter a list of excuses, then, and not a request for help? "Ever since Governador Manuel Coutinho returned in shame to Lisboa, the Grand Inquisitor has been concerned about relations between the Santa Casa and Goa's colonial government."

Sadrinho sighed. "In the past, the governors have tended not to heed us."

Gonsção nodded in sympathy. "Wealth and power blind men to thoughts of faith."

"Sorcery and heathen rites are more than blindness, Padre."

"True. Sorcery is a serious charge. The fact that first Coutinho and now, this year, Viceroy de Albuquerque have been sent home accused of it has greatly disturbed the Grand Inquisitor."

"It is the atmosphere of this place, Padre. It breeds heresy like flies on rotting fruit. But your arrival is timely. We have uncovered some of those involved in the pagan cabal which corrupted Coutinho."

"Ah, excellent. What sorts of men make up this cabal?"

"One was an Arab doctor named Zalambur. Regrettably, he was found dead, poisoned, before we could put the question to him. We suspect he took his own life. But we do have his mistress as a guest here. We will be interviewing her again this evening, if you would care to watch."

He offers it as though it were entertainment. "That might prove quite . . . informative, Domine. Were there others involved?"

"Yes. A Portuguese alchemist and sorcerer by the name of Bernardo De Cartago. He has attempted escape from Goa by ship, but I believe he will be returned to us soon. And there is another who may be with him; a woman who is the most mysterious of the circle, but perhaps the most influential. She is known to us only as Aditi, though I have also heard her referred to as *Manasadasa*, which means Servant of the Serpent Goddess."

"A title of ill omen."

Sadrinho shook his head. "Not to the Hindu people.

They hold the serpent as a symbol of wisdom and immortality."

"Our Lord once also said, 'Be ye wise as serpents,' but I do not think he meant us to worship or serve them."

"Did He?" the Inquisitor said with a fascinated gaze.

"It is in the Scriptures, Domine. Book of Matthew. Surely you recall your religious studies. I note you have some knowledge of native beliefs."

With a half-shrug the Inquisitor said, "In our work, one learns things. As to the woman, it is the name Aditi that gives us cause for concern. It is the name of a Hindu sky goddess, but also has the connotation of liberation. It is rumored this woman has the support of the Marathas."

"Marathas? What are they?"

The Inquisitor's eyes widened. "Ah. But I forget, you are new to this region and do not know its politics. The Marathas are among the most wealthy and noble Hindu families here. They are of a high warrior caste, and their cooperation is crucial to Portugal's hold upon Goa, yet it is known they have strong ties to the ruling families of Bijapur."

"I see. So these corruptions may have more to them than the spread of heathen practices." Gonsção nodded. "You have made good progress on this, Domine. The Grand Inquisitor will be pleased. Tell me, how are relations with your new governor, Dom Francisco da Gama? Does he bring honor to the name of his illustrious grandfather?"

"He has done nothing to stain it. And he is respectful of the Santa Casa."

"I am glad to hear it."

"Please pardon me, senhores," called a young, dark-skinned boy at the door across the hall, his Portuguese accented with a musical lilt. "His Excellency Archbishop Alexio de Menezes and Captain Pedro Ortiz have arrived and crave your audience."

Sadrinho said to the boy, "Very good. We will see them." The boy bowed low and departed.

"This is indeed timely," said Gonsção. "I had hoped to meet with Archbishop de Menezes soon."

"And Captain Ortiz should have good news for us concerning the very subject we have been discussing. Come sit, while we await our visitors." Sadrinho gestured toward the red chairs on the dais.

Gonsção ascended the platform and eased himself into one of the chairs. Resting on the long table was a silver bell and two books. One was a leather-bound missal, the other was a small, vellum-bound tome.

Gonsção idly picked up the little book and examined it. He read the inked title on the spine, then turned to Inquisitor Sadrinho, allowing a trace of his consternation to show. "This book, Domine. Why is it here?"

"Which? Ah. *Os Lusiados*. Brother Timóteo must have left it. He is young, and absentminded sometimes."

Gonsção opened the cover and glanced at the first page. He noted the date written there in Roman numerals. "Domine, this is the original publication, of 1572."

Sadrinho frowned. "Yes? What of it?"

"Do you not know about this work?"

The Inquisitor looked wary again. "It is an epic poem by Luis vas de Camões. I thought it was much respected in Lisboa."

"So it is. Among scholars. Have you read it?"

"No. I am told some of it was written here in Goa. Brother Timóteo prizes it because his grandfather, Garcia de Orta, the famous herbalist, knew Camões. In fact, Camões lived in his houschold for a time, and wrote a few verses for the introduction to de Orta's book on oriental drugs and simples."

"Ah. Interesting. It is understandable that the boy would treasure this book, then. But this is an unexpurgated version,

Domine, and contains many . . . paganistic verses. How old is Brother Timóteo?"

"Thirteen years, Padre."

"Only thirteen? A dangerous age. You see, this poem is a false history, Domine. It describes the voyages of da Gama as if they were Homeric myth. It is peopled with the pagan gods and demons of ancient Greece and Rome. Look here." Gonsção opened the book at random. "On this page, the poet writes of Mars and Jupiter on Mount Olympus, siding with da Gama's cause to thwart the wine god, Bacchus. On another page, we have da Gama speaking to Prometheus and Apollo as if they were true powers to be prayed to. And here, the poet writes a long passage concerning Venus, and her Isle of Love."

Sadrinho raised his brows. "I had no idea."

"I am not sure this Brother Timóteo would yet have the wisdom or education to . . . understand this work in its proper context. I strongly suggest, Domine, that this book be placed in a vault until the boy is older."

The Inquisitor nodded. "I understand. It shall be done."

Gonsção slid the book down the table to him and Sadrinho's long fingers stroked the vellum cover with what may have been regret.

It would seem the rumors reaching Albrecht's ears are true. This Santa Casa is lacking in discipline. They care more for their comforts and possessions than their holy work.

"Brother Timóteo will be disappointed," said Sadrinho. "His grandfather was much loved as a healer in Goa, and we are fortunate Timóteo came to us. He is one of our better acolytes, and even serves as an advocate to our guests. He has a way with them that is better than any scourge."

"Admirable. I should like to meet this young wonder. If he is a lover of poetry, I can recommend to him the work of Diego Bernardes. The collection *Various Rhymes to Good Jesus*

I have often found inspirational. I have a copy with me I could lend to him."

With a sour smile, Sadrinho said, "I am sure he will be pleased."

"I assure you, Domine, the verses are not as vapid as the title implies."

"As you say, Padre—Ah, here come our visitors."

The far doors were open. The page had stepped in and announced, "His Excellency Archbishop Alexio de Menezes, and Captain Pedro Ortiz of the *Santa Rosa*."

The Archbishop entered: a grey-haired man of mild appearance on whom the scarlet robes and cap seemed gaudy. Behind him, aromatic of garlic, oranges, and fish, came Captain Ortiz, a small, wiry man. His green satin doublet and slashed slops were stained and patched. The gilt scabbard at his side had been highly polished, however, and his deep bow was genteel.

The Inquisitor acknowledged the Archbishop and the captain with a nod. Gonsção rose from his seat and descended the dais. Clasping his hands before the Archbishop, he said, "This is an honor, Your Excellency. May I congratulate you on your appointment as First Primate of the East. It is an honor well deserved."

The Archbishop seemed startled. "I thank you, Padre. I have heard good things of you as well. My appointment was an unexpected blessing. I hope I may prove worthy of the post."

"I have no doubt you will, Your Excellency. And good afternoon to you, Captain Ortiz. I am Padre Antonio Gonsção. The name of the *Santa Rosa* is spoken of with praise throughout Lisboa. I pray you be welcome."

The captain looked back and forth between Gonsção and Inquisitor Sadrinho. "I thank you and give you holy fathers good day," he said in a rasping voice. "May the Good Lord bless you this day and always." The hands that clasped his velvet cap were pale.

Visitors to the Santa Casa are often uneasy, thought Gonsção, *yet I expect his news is not good.*

He accompanied the Archbishop and the captain to the table. De Menezes sat some distance from Sadrinho, and the captain remained standing. Gonsçao sat near the Archbishop, which seemed to annoy the Inquisitor Major.

Sadrinho turned his scowl on the captain. "It is our hope, Captain Ortiz, that you bring us evidence of such blessing. I trust that Bernardo De Cartago is now held in the Aljouvar."

Archbishop de Menezes sighed and looked down at the table. Captain Ortiz stiffened his shoulders, his cap twisting in his hands. "I regret, Domines, that he is not. We have damaged his ship, but we were unable to capture it."

"You did not capture him," said Sadrinho, slowly. "We had expected better of you, Captain Ortiz."

Eyes defiant, Ortiz responded, "I did not expect the sorcerer to conjure English ships out of nowhere in his defense, Domine!"

"English ships?"

"I think," said the Archbishop, "that you should hear the circumstances, Domine, before you judge. The presence of the English has been confirmed by other travelers coming into Goa."

Sadrinho stared at the Archbishop, then returned his gaze to the captain. "So. Explain."

Captain Ortiz began with a quick bow. "The *Santa Rosa* came upon the sorcerer's galleon near the Bassas de Pedro. It was heading south. We gave chase, as ordered. As we passed the Amindivi Islands, we were nearly upon him. It was then that the English ships appeared, coming out from behind the island of Kiltan. My men worked hard to bring out all our guns, but the English were prepared for us. They sailed between us and the sorcerer's ship, firing their cannon. Their ships were smaller and faster. They had many more chances to fire on us.

"We did what damage we could, and brought down masts on the English and sorcerer's ships. But I ordered the *Santa Rosa* to continue south, rather than let it fall prize to the English. If it will console you, I am certain Senhor De Cartago is either dead or an English prisoner."

"You ran," Sadrinho said softly. "I had not thought you a coward, Captain Ortiz."

The captain's nostrils flared. "Domine, while I was honored to do a service for the Santa Casa, my ultimate duty is to my men and to His Majesty, King Philip. Perhaps you forget that the *Santa Rosa* belongs to His Majesty's fleet."

"Perhaps you have forgotten your duty to God."

"I am told, Domine, that service to the king is service to God. Or do you mean this House is higher than the royal throne?"

Well argued, thought Gonsção, *if not wisely. This man is no coward.*

Sadrinho's face paled. "We believe that service to one is service to both. You would seem to have failed us all. Fortunately, we have a room available in which you may contemplate your error." He reached for the silver bell.

"Wait, Domine," said Gonsção.

"Padre?" A muscle in the Inquisitor's cheek twitched and his eyes narrowed.

" 'Blessed are the merciful, for they shall receive mercy.' "

"Is that from some Jesuit tract?"

So that rumor is true as well. He is quite ignorant of Scripture. "No, Domine. Those are also the words of Our Lord. From the Holy Book."

The Archbishop murmured, "Matthew: verse five."

"So. What is your point, Padre?"

"Captain Ortiz, are you a good Catholic?"

"With all my heart, Padre, God hear and defend me."

"And you accept all teachings of the Mother Church?"

"All, Padre, from birth until death."

"Domine, this man is no heretic or apostate. Your quarrel with him is a civil matter. If you must seek grievance against him, you must bring it to the attention of Governador da Gama. He has the authority to decide if Captain Ortiz has properly served the king."

Sadrinho worked his jaw, but said at last, "Very well. You may go, Captain Ortiz."

The captain bowed low to Gonsção. "God has surely granted you wisdom, Padre." Turning to the Archbishop, he added, "If I may have your blessing, Your Excellency." He knelt and kissed the Archbishop's ring.

De Menezes laid a hand on the captain's head. "If it will aid you, you have my blessing. Go with God, my son."

Captain Ortiz stood again, acknowledging Sadrinho with a sweep of his cap. "I will place myself in the hands of Governador da Gama immediately."

Inquisitor Sadrinho nodded solemnly as Captain Ortiz strode out. As soon as the doors closed, he glared at Gonsção. "How dare you—"

"Grand Inquisitor Albrecht," said Gonsção, "sent me to observe this Santa Casa, and correct deviance where I saw fit. You know we must keep a very clear line between matters of faith and matters of civil justice. I understand this sorcerer is important, but men of Captain Ortiz's skill are needed against the Dutch and the English. Portugal cannot afford his loss."

"If this bungling is typical of the captain's skill," growled Sadrinho, "then I weep for Portugal."

"Ortiz may have done more for you than you assume. You

do have *familiares* among the merchants and fishermen here, do you not?"

"Of course. What of them?"

"Damaged ships cannot travel far. If the *Santa Rosa* brought down the masts on the English ships, they will have to find safe harbor for repairs. If the *familiares* can tell us where the English were last seen, we could estimate where they have gone to ground. A few small coastal vessels, sent in secret, might accomplish what a mighty carrack could not."

Sadrinho blinked. "Ah. Yes. I see. Perhaps that could be done. I will make inquiries at once. Pardon me, Your Excellency." With a nod to the Archbishop, he rose to leave.

"Domine," Gonsção called after him.

"Yes?"

"Please have the ledgers for this past year prepared for my inspection."

"The ledgers?"

"I believe my letter of introduction stated clearly that I was to be presented with any materials I require."

"Ah. Perhaps in a couple of days, Padre. When you have recovered from your journey."

"I was chosen for my industriousness, Domine. I would see the ledgers this afternoon, if I may."

"Ah. I will see what can be assembled on so short a notice."

"Thank you, Domine. Perhaps you could have that young advocate, the one who likes poems, bring the ledgers to me."

Sadrinho sighed. "As you wish, Padre Antonio. After the mass in Santa Catarina's."

"Excellent. And while you are at your services, please remember me in your prayers."

"I will, Padre. Be assured, I will."

After the door closed behind the Inquisitor, Archbishop de Menezes turned to Gonsção. "You are bold, Padre Antonio. That quality is much needed here, although the Inquisitor Major may not be appreciative of it."

"I cannot say it was unexpected, Your Excellency. Few who achieve power are spared its corrupting influence. We must remember the Inquisitor in our prayers as well."

"Indeed," said the Archbishop with little enthusiasm. "This appearance of the English," he said, leaning forward and steepling his fingers on the table, "I find it most disturbing."

"If it will ease your mind, Your Excellency, as I was leaving Lisboa, I learned that His Majesty was assembling a new armada. That is, in part, why I wished Captain Ortiz released to the Governor's care. He will be needed. I think we need not fear English piracy for much longer."

"That is good news, Padre. Yet I cannot help remembering the fate of our previous armada."

"Please, Excellency, give our *adelantados* some credit for learning from past mistakes."

"Some say the storm that destroyed the armada was an act of God."

"Our Lord defend English heretics? Careful, Excellency." Gonsção playfully wagged a finger. "You stray perilously close to heresy."

"Forgive me," said de Menezes with a smile. "I will say two hundred prayers to Santa Maria for penance."

"Kindly add a few for me." Gonsção stood, smoothing his white robe and scapular.

The Archbishop also rose. "If I may ask, why did you want the de Orta boy to bring the ledgers to you? Because of his famous grandfather, the herbalist?"

"Domine Sadrinho told me Brother Timóteo is an advocate, despite his youth. Who better could tell me about the guests who are brought to the Santa Casa and how they are treated?"

"I see. Very wise."

"There is something you might do for me, Excellency."
The Archbishop seemed uncomfortable. "If I can."

"I wish to learn everything possible concerning the trial
of Governador Coutinho. If you could see that I am given the
records of the trial, that would be most helpful."

"I will see what I can do, Padre. But, I confess, my influence in the Santa Casa is modest at best."

"I am confident of your capabilities, as is Cardinal Albrecht."

"You honor me too much." As they walked together toward the doors, de Menezes added, "It was a curious case.
Coutinho was of good Christian family, without a whiff of the
scandal of heresy. Yet something lured him, convinced him
into apostasy. Something he accepted as proof of pagan beliefs."

"Very curious. And distressing that his faith proved so
easily corruptible. We must delve into this mystery as deep
as we can. Where the Serpent of Evil rears his head, more lies
hidden in the earth."

De Menezes smiled. "It will be refreshing having you
here, Padre Gonsção."

III

PIMPERNEL: This plant is also called Herb of Mary, or herb of the pig. It has flowers of crimson or gold, which close when storms approach. They open in fine weather, and thus are called "poor man's weatherglass." It is said that to hold the pimpernel gives one the second sight. Pimpernel turns away witchcraft, and sorcerers do shun it for it brings them to reveal their secrets....

To Master Geoffrey Coulter, Apothecary, London, from his apprentice and factor, Thomas Chinnery, written in the month of September, in this Year of Our Lord 1597—

Sir, I find I must begin this letter anew, as my last has been ruined in yet another piratic raid ordered by Captain Wood. I know not whether this will ever reach you, but I must not lose hope.

We have reached the coast of India, but do not marvel at our speed. The manner of our voyage is not what was at first intended. Sir Robert Dudley had commissioned this expedition to seek a trade route to Cathay westward, through the Straits of Magellan. I cannot think but had we proceeded in this manner, Fortune would have been more kind.

Instead, our fleet met up with Admiral Raleigh in the Canaries, and his boasts of the riches to be found along the African coast and in the Arabian Sea, and his warnings of the perils that lie westward, convinced Captain Wood and much of the crew that we should take the easterly route. "Better the devil known," they said.

The merchants Masters Allen and Bromefield were in a fury but there was little they could do. But our way has been no easier than that of our predecessors. The *Benjamin* was lost in a storm off the Cape of Good Hope. Full half the crew have fallen ill with the scurvy or other ailment. By the Grace of God, so far I have been spared from sickness.

Mayhap to ease the merchants' ire, or to increase his glory and wealth, Captain Wood has seen fit to give chase to every Portuguese galleon we encounter. We have become more privateers than merchantmen. In these battles, we have prevailed, but not without cost. As I write, we are harbored to the north of Calicut, attempting to repair damage done in our last skirmish. The *Bear* wants new masts and the carpenter says the trees of this region will not serve.

Although we may yet reach Cathay, we have few stores remaining with which to begin trade. I have had to use forty-seven pastilles of your chamomile-poppy compound for ease of the sick and wounded among the crew. Full half the herbal stores are gone, in particular the garlic, birthwort, angelica, and valerian. I have managed to spare the powdered mummy and unicorn horn as yet, as well as the *confectio alcarmas*, but I may perforce need them if no other source of medicament is found.

I fear it may not be possible to replenish these supplies between here and Canton. I am told that such goods may be found in Pegu, but they would be of uncertain quality.

I beg you to forgive my profligacy with those goods that were to be our means to trade and wealth in the East. But I have become the foremost healer aboard, as our ship's doctor did himself succumb to a fever but two days ago. While I have no miss of his bleedings and leeches, I find I long for his company in this heart-offending work.

We had hoped some men might proceed on foot to Calicut to solicit aid, but we cannot spare the hands from repairs. And there is fear that if rumor spread concerning our location and weakened state, we might find ourselves the target of brigandage. . . .

Thomas lifted his quill from the letter, his hand shaking with weariness. From his perch on the steps leading down to the crew's quarters, he could hear the moans and restless movements of sick and wounded men. Beyond the bulkhead, water lapped against the ship's side and anchor ropes creaked at the pull of the tide. The air was humid, stifling, and thick with the odors of rot, both of wood and flesh.

On the pallet nearest him lay Nathan, the carpenter's apprentice, his face pale. His cannon wound was festering and there was little Thomas could do for the boy. *His fate lies with a greater power than mine.*

A blot of ink fell from the quill point onto the paper as heavy footsteps clumped down the stairs behind him.

"What ho?" boomed Lockheart. "Another heartsong to your lassie? Do not drown your girl in affections, me lad, or she'll find a less slobbery puppy to pet."

"You have a canny sense, sir, of when you can most easily disturb my correspondence." Thomas was not, however, entirely displeased to see the stocky Scotsman. Lockheart's blustery good humor, while baffling, made even hope seem possible.

And although his letter was not addressed directly to her, Thomas hoped Anne Coulter, his master's daughter, whom he had long admired, would read the letter and know he was well.

Lockheart settled his bulk awkwardly onto the stairs. "I've the ears of a bat, Tom. I heard the scratchings of your pen from afar."

"With ears so fine, how do you not deafen yourself with your own voice? Mindful of which, I pray you speak more soft. Disturb me if you must, but allow these poor wretches some peace."

"Your pardon," Lockheart said in a quieter rumble. "I trust you have also written your mother? Mothers are wont to be o'erwrought with care and need much reassurance."

"I have no mother, sir. She died at my birth."

"I cry you mercy. My condolement, then."

Thomas shrugged. "Perforce, I did not know her. There was no one to mourn." Thoughts came to him unbidden of a childhood filled with sad, lonely hours, a succession of nursemaids, some kind, some indifferent, some worse.

"You must write to your father, then, if he is your sole parent."

"My father takes little interest in my affairs."

"Surely that cannot be! Are you his only son?"

"That I know of."

"Then he must hold you more dear than you know of. Oftimes, even the most distant-seeming sires have a keen interest in their sons."

Thomas paused, remembering how, from the deck of the *Bear's Whelp*, he had spied his father's unsmiling face among the crowd on the dock as the ship pulled away. "Mayhap. My father had once encouraged me to join a voyage to Naples, but Master Coulter had said a voyage to the Far East would come to more profit. I now wish I had taken my sire's advice."

"There you are," said Lockheart.

"You may have the right of it. But Master Coulter has

been more parent to me than any other in this world, he and his good wife."

" 'Tis good when men treat their help kindly. But from your speech and manners, I took you to be of gentle birth when first we met. What caused you to become apprenticed?"

Thomas laughed. "Gentle birth? Distantly, at best. My father had well-born connections on the Continent, and he once boasted that my mother had the blood of Italian kings. But 'tis a thin and winding thread that binds me to any nobility. Such small richness of blood carries little wealth and few prospects. Mind you, if the tales told of the lust of Britain's kings past has any credit, full half the souls of England can doubtless claim royal descent."

Lockheart grinned. "I had not thought it so, but there must be some truth in what you say, lad."

Groaning inquiries rose from the pallets in the gloom around them.

"Peace, all is well," Thomas said in answer. To Lockheart, he added, "We disturb their rest, sir. Let us go abovedecks to speak."

"A wise thought. Let us ascend before the unwholesome air in this hold makes maggots of us both."

"There are those of my master's art who believe that thick, stinking air acts as a barrier to disease. I can but only think such men have never gone to sea." Thomas blew gently on his letter to dry the ink, then folded it and tucked it back in his doublet. He stood and followed Lockheart up the creaking steps into the bright daylight.

A cool breeze, redolent of saltwater and exotic flowers, washed over Thomas. A golden-winged sunset filled the western horizon, fading to deep blues and indigo toward the east. Off the starboard rail lay a turquoise lagoon, fringed with sandy beach and palm forest.

"Here is a scene more meet for merriment," said Lockheart. He was wearing a stained, sleeveless jerkin of iron-grey leather, artfully slashed to reveal a blood-red velvet lining, laces open down to the peascod. Visible behind the lacing was a silver medallion on a chain.

"I see you would begin a new fashion," said Thomas.

"Think you so? This garb is more comfortable than the ruffs and mandillion cloaks our Master Bromefield prefers."

"But he is a wool merchant, and 'twould not do well for him to display clothes that require less of his cloth."

Lockheart wagged a finger. "Then he has not the heart of a tailor, who knows one can always demand more on the cut of a garment than on its weight."

Thomas laughed, his spirits daring to lift a little. He sat down on the deck, back against the starboard rail.

Lockheart thumped down beside him. "So tell me, how fare the men below?"

"To be honest, poorly. I've few salves and ointments left, and nothing to ease their pain. Do you think it true that medicaments may be found in Calicut?"

Pursing his lips, Lockheart said, " 'Tis possible. But to acquire them without calling attention to the purchase, 'twould be the rub."

"Could it be done quickly?"

"If three days' travel, plus two days to find and purchase the goods, plus three days return be quick, then aye. With God's blessing and all else being well, of course."

Thomas nodded. "You paint the picture too well." He gazed out past the railing at the luxuriant palms and wondered what fruits and sap and healing herbs might lie within that jungle. *If only I knew what to search for. Any source of balm or pains-ease would be of help.* His arm bumped against something bulky in his doublet. He pulled out the wooden box he had found on the captured galley.

Lockheart's brows rose. "What have you there, lad?"

"I took it from the galley we raided. It belonged to the Portuguese sorcerer." Thomas opened the box and pulled the paper from inside the lid. "Within this box is carved a caduceus, the sign of Aesculapius, whom the Greeks worshiped for his powers of healing."

"Ah. I see you know your classics."

"My sire provided me some education, sir. 'Twas my hope that the contents of the bottle in this box might be medicinal in some way."

"You have not yet tried it?"

"It was in the keeping of a sorcerer, remember. I do not know if it is trustworthy. On this paper are some inscriptions. I can piece out the meaning of the lowest, the Greek, but the upper ones are in scripts unknown to me."

"Lend it me," said Lockheart, holding out his hand.

Reluctantly, Thomas gave him the paper. To his relief, the heavy-fingered Scotsman unfolded it with care.

"Here is a wonder. The first phrase is writ in Arabic, yet its meaning is biblical. 'I am the Resurrection and the Life.' "

"That gives hope. The next line is Arabic as well, is't not?"

"A good surmise, laddie, but 'tis Persian."

"Know you that tongue?"

"A moment." Lockheart examined it closely, as if it were a strange insect. "These words are from another holy book, the Qur'an of Islam."

"Are they? What is their heathen message?"

" 'He brings forth the living from the dead, and the dead from the living. The lifeless earth is quickened by him.' "

Thomas scratched his cheek. "These all speak of life brought forth from death. Mayhap it is a most potent medicine."

"Or the physician who employs it must pray for its efficacy."

"Since man knows not how medicines do their work, perhaps prayer is the most efficacious part of healing. But what is the next line?"

Lockheart again examined the paper. "It is, I wot, Sanskrit."

"What tongue is that?"

"Many ancient Hindu holy books, I am told, are writ in this script."

"Yet more sacred words on life and death, I'll wager. Can you read those words as well?"

Lockheart opened his mouth, paused, then grinned. "No."

Thomas sighed. "I still am not convinced I might in safety use this. The Greek line, I know, speaks of serpents and skin."

"Mayhap it means naught pertaining to the contents of the bottle. These may be the idle scribblings of one practicing his letters."

"Hm. I think not. The sorcerer had this box beside him when I encountered him. He was loath to be parted from it."

"If the Greek speaks of serpents, perchance 'tis snake venom."

"Then it could be either poison or physic. Theriac is a medicine we used in Master Coulter's shop. It contains the flesh of vipers; 'tis a common curative. This may be somewhat of that nature."

"May I see the bottle?"

Thomas paused. "I shall want it returned." He scooped the iridescent glass bottle out of its silken bed and handed it to the Scotsman.

"Fear me not. A pretty thing, this." Lockheart gently

tugged on the cork stopper. It emerged with a tiny pop. Lockheart tipped the bottle until a fine brown powder spilled into his palm. Licking his thumb, he dipped it into the powder. He rubbed the mysterious substance between thumb and forefinger, sniffing from a cautious distance. He stared a moment out to sea, deep in thought. Frowning, Lockheart put his palm over the bottle mouth and poured what he could of the powder back into it. Then he carefully wiped his hand on his breeches to remove the rest.

"What think you?" said Thomas.

"I think our wonderings wander down the wrong path."

"Is't not medicine or poison?"

"Those phrases I read were from holy works, Tom. Mayhap this is not physic for the body, but for the soul. Or a means to the downfall of souls. If I am any worthy judge, the dust in this bottle is dried blood. And much blood have I seen in my day." He stoppered the bottle and handed it back to Thomas as though it burnt his hand.

Thomas took it, feeling a chill. "Blood of man or beast? What might a sorcerer do with it?"

"What might he not do, Tom? As the Good Book sayeth, 'The blood is the life.' The blood of vermin can enhance a witch's potion, whilst blood of a man might be used 'gainst him. The blood of a saint, well . . . if our sorcerer's art be white, it might bring about miracles; if black, great evil may be done."

"This may be a relic, then?" If it was papist, Thomas knew his soul would be safest if he threw the bottle into the sea at once.

Lockheart shrugged. "I surely have not the skill to tell."

Thomas gazed down at the little bottle. *Which evil more endangers the soul; papist relic, heathen talisman, or satanic charm?*

"Howsomever," the Scotsman went on, " 'tis possible our sorcerer may merely have used it as spice in his stew."

Despite himself, Thomas laughed. "Sir, never do I know when you jest."

"Fret not on it. Oftimes, nor do I."

Footsteps approached and Thomas looked around. Master Bromefield strode toward them across the deck, his velvet cloak flapping behind him. Thomas thought he resembled a tavern-sign portrait of old King Henry VIII, only thinner and more care-worn. He wondered what exaggerated sense of honor led men such as Bromefield to wear such heavy garments and a stiff linen ruff even in this hot clime. Perhaps, as Special Envoy to the Great Emperor of Cathay from Her Majesty, Queen Elizabeth, Bromefield never knew when he might be called upon to impress someone.

Thomas returned the bottle to its box and slipped it back into his doublet as the heavily sweating Bromefield came up to them.

"Sir," Bromefield said to Lockheart, "our captain extends his heartiest apologies and would have you return for the last questioning of our captives." Bromefield wore an expression of distaste, and Thomas wondered if the master merchant disliked more the message or the task of messenger.

"Fair words, fairly given, sir," said Lockheart. "You may relay to the good captain that I shall return anon."

"I will, sir." Bromefield turned to leave.

"One thing more," Lockheart said. "I will bring Master Chinnery as well, for he has questions of his own to ask." As Bromefield frowned, he added, "Forget not, 'twas he who discovered our sorcerer. Methinks he has earned the right."

Bromefield sighed, as if the world had passed beyond all reason. "Very well, if Captain Wood is of agreement." He turned, cape swirling, and stalked away.

Thomas raised his brows at Lockheart. "Wherefore this apology?"

"Our captain, as you have doubtless noted, has moods changeable as the gales off Cape Horn. For reason I know not, he chose to direct a stormy blast at me. Well, he has made his suit most prettily. Come, Thomas. Let us receive it like the gentlemen we are." Lockheart leapt to his feet.

Thomas followed him. "What is to become of them, the sorcerer and the lady?"

" 'Tis what our captain now ponders."

"I wonder that so many of their native crew stayed to serve with us, and did not take the offered freedom."

"The Portuguese are hard taskmasters, lad. No doubt they hope for better in our care."

Thomas and Lockheart passed several of their new crewmen, who sat picking oakum from old rope with which to repair leaks, others sewing on torn and tattered sails. Thomas felt disquiet at having so many dusky foreigners aboard, yet so many of the *Whelp*'s original crew were disabled that help was needed from any quarter.

Lockheart led Thomas onto the poop deck, which was now furnished with a table and some chairs. Captain Wood slouched at the head of the table, a frown on his ruddy, leathered face. To the captain's left sat the Portuguese sorcerer, alert and erect, his manacled hands resting on the table. Masters Allen and Bromefield stood warily to the captain's right. The mysterious Hindu lady was nowhere to be seen.

Captain Wood nodded curtly at Lockheart, then at Thomas. "Master Chinnery. How fare my men?"

Truth won out over diplomacy. "Not well, sir. They suffer fevers, infections, and want of medicine. Not many will recover."

"As I feared." The Captain stared down at the table and Thomas was surprised to feel some sympathy for the man.

"Thomas," said Lockheart, "allow me the honor of introducing Senhor Bernardo De Cartago of Goa. *Senhor, com licença, apresento Senhor Tomás Chinnery, médico e alquimista.*"

The prisoner raised his fine brows and nodded respectfully to Thomas. He then directed a question in Portuguese to Lockheart, who answered with a brief affirmative.

"Sir," Thomas said softly to Lockheart, "I am truly neither physician nor alchemist. Is't wise to call me such?"

"He'll think better of you for it. And how better to describe what it is you do, eh?"

In Latin, to Thomas, the sorcerer softly said, "It is proper, then, that I tender my apologies to you. I understand a high price was paid for my rescue."

"What says he?" Captain Wood grumbled at Lockheart.

"The gentleman expresses regret at our losses, sir."

Master Bromefield frowned. Thomas wondered how well the envoy knew his Latin.

The captain looked over at Thomas. "Master Lockheart, our sorcerer guest also calls himself an alchymist, does 'ee not?"

"Aye, and a scholar, sir."

"Ask him if he might have healing skills or medicines that might be of use to our Master Chinnery."

Thomas blinked in surprise. *The captain knows my purpose 'ere I speak it.* His estimation of the man rose again.

Lockheart rattled off an inelegant stream of Portuguese.

"Sir!" Bromefield protested to the captain. "Think you to endanger our souls by use of this man's evil methods? Is't not better we should die unblemished than to take aid from the Devil?"

Leaning heavily on the table, Captain Wood rose from his chair and faced Master Bromefield. "Sir. Will these ships reach Cathay, think you, sailed with naught but the souls of sainted men? Will blessed shades reef our sheets and Heaven-sent ghosts man the gun ports? Will the angels pull the ropes and cherubim bail the bilge water? I'll warrant ye, damn few of the men below are e'en now unblemished with sin. Yet their life and labor are my God-given charge. Think you not 'twould be better service to them, to Her Majesty, and to God to do all to help them live? In a longer life, more prayers may be said and more sins forgiven. And, blemished though they may be, will our journey not see a more profitable end with the help of living hands?"

Bromefield, his jaw working back and forth, grumbled, "Let it be on your conscience, then, sir. God forgive you. God forgive us all." He glared meaningfully at Lockheart.

Captain Wood grunted and sat once more.

The sorcerer spoke to Lockheart some moments in Portuguese.

Lockheart cleared his throat. "Senhor De Cartago says he has little with him in the nature of common medicine. However, he has some knowledge of the plants that grow in this region. He will impart this to us if we will permit him passage with us to Pegu."

The captain scratched his scraggly red beard, then nodded. "A fair request. I will give it thought. Now, Master Chinnery, I am told you have a query for our guest."

Thomas felt his throat go dry. *How might I ask without alarming the captain or Master Bromefield?* "You have already asked it for me, sir. I also wished to know if he had medicament to offer. But I will ask him once more." He turned to De Cartago and spoke in Latin. "Are you certain, *Magister*, there was nothing on your ship that would heal or ease pain?"

De Cartago paused, staring at Thomas, who noticed a corner of the wooden box poking out of his doublet. The sorcerer tilted his head, an odd glint in his eye. "None, *Magister*, save that offered by Ouroboros." He steepled his hands before him such that his curled fingers and thumbs created a circle.

Thomas sensed he was being tested. The word

"Ouroboros" was vaguely familiar, but he could not remember from where. Rather than betray his ignorance, Thomas nodded to the sorcerer. "I see. Thank you."

"Do you speak Greek?" asked De Cartago.

"I do. My father had me tutored extensively in that tongue."

"Domina Aditi will find that interesting, *Magister*. You might speak with her. I, myself, have no Greek. Perhaps, if there is time, you might teach some to me."

"Perhaps," said Thomas, hiding his bewilderment.

Lockheart turned to him, a smile spreading on his face. "Of course. 'Tis fated, lad!" He clapped him on the shoulder.

"Come, come, Master Lockheart," said Captain Wood. "What has our man said?"

The Scotsman responded before Thomas could answer. "No medicaments has he, sir, but 'twould seem we have at last found someone to speak to our lady passenger."

"Have we now?" The captain raised his bushy brows at Thomas.

"The lad has his Greek and 'twould seem that is the tongue to charm our lady's ear."

"Damn you, Lockheart!" Bromefield exploded. "Wherefore did you not tell us she spoke Greek? I myself went to the Merchant Taylors' School and have some Greek grammar. I could have spoke to her."

"Sperr your gob, sir," growled the captain. "If ye cannot cool yer blood, Master Bromefield, I'll have you tossed in the drink to do it for ye. Master Chinnery, are you fluent in Greek?"

Thomas nodded. "I am, sir. I have mastered the Clenardus grammar, and have read Aesop, Plato, Demosthenes, and Homer."

Captain Wood turned to Bromefield. "Did the Merchant Taylors' School teach you those?"

Bromefield sucked in his breath and puffed out his chest. "As it would seem I possess no skills of use here, I shall join my partner on the shore, who is at this moment engaged in the proper purpose of this expedition, sir, which is the designment of trade in the East." Bromefield turned on his heel and strode away, glaring at Lockheart as he left.

Thomas felt himself in a bewildering fog, not unlike the time he, by accident, ingested a drop of poppy syrup in his master's shop. There was clearly more to Lockheart's presence on the voyage than the selling of good English wool. "Forgive me, Captain, if I have caused offense."

Captain Wood waved a meaty hand dismissively. "Pay it no mind, boy. 'Tis this suffocating air. I would have you speak to this Lady Aditi as soon as you may. We have learned from her only that she is well connected and may bring a high ransom. Discover how much and from whom and how it may be accomplished. Learn if this expedition may see some profit yet. Go your ways."

As they descended from the poop deck, Thomas asked Lockheart, "You are a man of so many tongues, sir, I am surprised Greek is not one of them."

"In truth, it is, though mayhap I have it not as well as you."

"Then wherefore did you not tell the captain so?"

"You wish to learn the contents of the box, do you not? Methinks our sorcerer is directing you toward the one who might give you answer. These philosophs may have labyrinthine ways, but they oft are generous with a fellow traveler."

"In truth, I wish you had not presented me as a fellow alchemist."

"Wherefore not? See what it has already gained you? What's the harm?"

"I fear to be found out. He is e'en now putting me to the

test. That name he mentioned—Ouroboros—do you know it?"

"Methought it was the name of a worm."

"His hands made a circle. Ah! Now I remember. Master Coulter pointed it out to me on a jar of medicinal clay he had bought from an alchemist from Saxony. 'Tis not a worm, but a serpent, biting its tail."

"Aye, alpha and omega, world without end." Lockheart raised his brows. "And imagery of snakes again. This mystery leads us down a serpentine path indeed."

"So 'twould seem. Let us hope we find no teeth at its end to bite us."

IV

ELDER: This small tree brings forth sweet-scented flowers in springtime, and black berries in summer. It has wood that smells foul. 'Tis said from the elder Judas did hang himself, and that it is the wood from which our dear Lord's cross was hewn. The red elder berries are sprung from the drops of our Lord's blood. The elder is ever a tree of sorrow and death. To bring elder branches into the house is to become host to the Devil, and neither cradles nor ships should be made of its wood....

Brother Timóteo clutched the worn, leather-bound Bible to his chest. *The poor lady does not understand*, he thought with sorrow. He approached the woman who lay gasping on the stained pallet. "Senhora," he said, hoping his voice sounded gentle and forgiving. "Senhora, why do you let yourself be tormented?"

The dungeon was silent, save for the woman's ragged breathing and the incessant dripping of water in some dark corner. The woman wore only a once-fine silk undergarment, now filthy and torn. Sharp wires bound her to rough, hard wood planks. She had suffered the *potro*, the torment of water dripped from a jar down a linen rag that is placed over the tongue and into the throat. She had been given a few moments' rest, but still struggled for air as if drowning. She turned her pale face toward Brother Timóteo as he came to her side, but her dark eyes seemed not to comprehend him.

"Senhora?"

"No!" she breathed. "No more water, I beg you." Coughing, she rolled her head to one side and fluid spilled from her mouth.

"I do not bring the jar, senhora. Fear not. I bring hope. Do not let the Devil harden your heart, but open it to God and to the Domines who question you."

"But I have said all I can!" she whimpered. "There is no more I can tell them. My father . . . please let me speak to my father."

"The Domines are your fathers here, senhora. And God is father to us all. Why will you not tell them the truth?"

A shuddering sigh. "I have told them the truth."

"That cannot be so, senhora, for you are still here and the Domines are returning. They know truth when they hear it. Why can you not see the truth in your heart?"

The woman closed her eyes. "I cannot—I do not know what they want me to say."

Timóteo grasped the woman's cold, trembling hand, tears forming in his eyes. He wished he did not have this task, to witness the pain of the guests of the Santa Casa. Yet he knew it was the most important work he was given to do, to guide their souls into the light. He hated the Devil who caused such suffering, who blinded sinners to their sins. "Please, senhora," he said. "Look into your heart and save yourself. Speak freely, and accept God's forgiveness."

He was interrupted by footsteps on the stone of the passageway outside the cell. The woman raised her head from the pallet, eyes wide. Her hand gripped Timóteo's like iron.

"The Domines are returning, senhora. They bring the jar again."

"No . . . do not let them . . . please, do not let them—"

"Only you can stop them, senhora."

The hinges of the cell door shrieked and three men entered: the two Inquisitors Major in black robes and a stranger in white. Timóteo squeezed the woman's hand one last time and stepped back. If the kitchen gossip he'd heard was true, the Dominican must be the Envoy from the Grand Inquisitor. Lowering his gaze, Timóteo bowed politely and stepped aside.

"Brother Timóteo," said Domine Sadrinho, "does the senhora Resgate wish to give her confession?"

"I do not know, Domine. She must speak for herself." Timóteo gazed at the ceiling and prayed. *Lord, loosen the Devil's hold on her heart. Help her to see the light of Your love. Do not abandon her to darkness.*

"Why do you continue to torment me, Domines?" rasped the woman. "I do not know anything."

Inquisitor Sadrinho replied softly, "Because, my daughter, the torments you face in Hell are far greater than any torment you can receive on earth. The senses of the flesh are fleeting. Hell is pain eternal. What we give you is loving kindness compared to that dealt in Satan's domain. We do this to remind you of that fact. Will you not speak freely with us and thereby escape the horrors of damnation?"

After some moments of silence, Inquisitor Pinto said, "It appears she wishes to spend more time on the Bed of Memory."

The man in white approached the pallet and said, "What is your name, senhora?"

Her mouth moved but no words came out. Timóteo could feel her fear.

"Senhora," said Inquisitor Sadrinho, "this is Padre Antonio Gonsção. He has come all this way from Lisboa to see that you are not lost to the fires of Hades. Such is the compassion of the Santa Casa."

"Padre," she whispered, "please help me."

"Padre Gonsção, this unfortunate is the Dama Serafina Resgate, widow of a prominent *fidalgo*. As I told you, she was known to keep company with the sorcerers Zalambur and De Cartago. Alas, she seems to recall nothing of her time with them, or others of their circle."

"Padre, I beg of you—"

"Senhora," said Timóteo, "please do not waste precious strength asking for that which only you can give. You have been through a terrible ordeal. I pray you, say only those words which will bring you release. Let the Domines be as midwives to bring your soul into a new life, not gravesmen to watch a soul bury itself in sin."

The woman gazed up at him. "Is there no other hope for me?"

"None, senhora."

She sighed. "I swore an oath. Never to speak of it."

"You swore to false gods, senhora," said the Inquisitor. "How can you be punished by that which does not exist?"

"I have seen . . ." She closed her mouth firmly, a new fear in her eyes.

"What have you seen, daughter? Tell us and be free."

She coughed again, eyes shut tight, but did not speak.

"Very well." Domine Sadrinho nodded to Inquisitor Pinto, who raised the jar over the woman's face, letting the wet linen touch her cheek.

"No!" Her eyes opened wide and she struggled against the wires that bound her.

"Please, do not force us to do this, senhora."

As the linen strip touched her mouth, she cried out, "Yes! Forgive me. I will confess!"

Inquisitor Pinto immediately pulled the cloth and the jar away from her face.

"Bernardo, Harun, forgive me," she whispered.

Timóteo's heart leapt in joy. He fell to his knees. *"Graças a Deus!"*

"A wise decision, senhora," said Inquisitor Sadrinho. He stepped to the head of her pallet and gently stroked her damp hair. "What would you say to us, my child?"

"Domine, I . . . I have sinned."

"Yes." The Inquisitor Major stroked her arm slowly with the back of his hand. "Continue. Describe your sin."

"We . . . I was a part of . . . meetings. Ceremonies. In worship of the goddess."

"And who was with you in these meetings?"

"My lover, Harun. A woman named Aditi. Others . . . I do not know. It was dark. We could not see each other's faces."

"So. What did you do in these pagan rituals?"

"Sri Aditi told us the goddess lives among mortals in India. That she has the power to give life and death."

"You were lied to, senhora. Only the Lord God gives life and death, and life eternal thereafter."

"As you say, Domine. Only God. But she offered proof."

"Proof? You mean she used illusion to trick you. Did she show you idols?"

"Statues. There were statues. . . ."

"And does this goddess have the head of a hippopotamus or other bizarre creature?"

"Snakes . . ." The woman seemed to be drifting into delirium. "There were snakes."

"What is the name of this goddess?"

"Her name is strength."

"What acts did you do in these rituals in worship of her?"

"There were prayers . . . and songs, I think."

"Such evasions will not save your soul, my child. Be more

specific. Do not think you will shock us. The Santa Casa is familiar with all manner of the Devil's work."

"Then why must I tell them to you?"

"For the sake of your soul, senhora."

"Some of us . . . drank blood. Aditi said it was the blood of the goddess."

"Indeed? Continue."

"That . . . that is all."

"Impossible."

"No."

"We know all about pagan ceremonies, senhora. It will do your soul no good to hold back. Of course, Inquisitor Pinto can bring back the *potro*, in case your mouth is too dry, or your tongue needs loosening."

Wild-eyed, the woman said, "No, what would you have me say? That we ate poppies, or fornicated with animals?"

"Ah," said Inquisitor Pinto. "Now we are getting somewhere."

The visiting Padre coughed. "Domine, perhaps the young brother ought to see to his other duties now."

"Pardon? Oh. Of course. You may go, Timóteo."

Timóteo bowed and walked to the door, smiling and happy. After her confession, he knew the woman would be bathed and fed and returned to her cell. She would be given plenty of time to recover as she awaited judgment at the next auto-da-fé. She would be excommunicated at her trial, but if a proper sponsor could be found for her in Goa, she would immediately be welcomed back into the arms of Mother Church.

Outside the cell door, he looked up to see that the Dominican Padre had followed him. "That was most impressive, my son," said the Padre. "You are indeed an asset to this Santa Casa."

Timóteo felt his cheeks grow hot. "I am pleased another soul has returned to God, Padre."

"Of course. Has Domine Sadrinho told you that I should like to speak with you at length later?"

"No, Padre."

"Perhaps tonight, when your evening duties are finished. Will you do me the favor of meeting with me?"

"Um . . . most certainly, Padre."

"Good. You are clearly talented and perceptive. You may be of great help to me in my work." With a nod, the Padre turned and reentered the cell, closing the door behind him.

Timóteo found his joy diminished by worry. *What does the Special Envoy want of me? Why does he praise me? I only guide our guests toward the light. Their return to grace is the Lord's doing. Not mine. Not mine at all.*

V

🍃 OLIVE: This much-venerated tree has grown in the East from ancient times. From its fruit comes an oil good as medicine, food, or fuel for lamps. To the Greeks, the olive tree was symbolic of peace, safe travel, and very long life. It was sacred to Athena, their goddess of wisdom. In Italy, an olive branch is thought to ward from lightning and witches. To Spaniards, a magicked olive bough makes a woman ruler of the house....

Sri Aditi, born Dara Naini of a clan of caravaneers in Rajasthan, stared out at the desert of the sea. *So much water, yet no help for thirst. So far a horizon, but nowhere to walk. Death in the midst of life. Life in the midst of death. A paradox worthy of the Mahadevi. Why did I let Bernardo talk me into fleeing with him? I do not even love him. In Goa there were familiar streets and houses where help might be found. What shall I do now?*

The window in the cabin of the English ship was too small to leap out of. No matter; Aditi could not swim. *To be smothered by water, or torn apart by the monsters that lurk beneath? No, if death must come to me, that shall not be the way.* A breeze brought an acrid salt smell from the sea. Aditi stepped back and closed the window.

Voices were approaching her door.

Aditi swiftly stepped behind a table, putting it and a chair between her and the door. She slid the oil lamp into arm's reach and rested her other hand on the hilt of a knife stuck in the waistband of her *gahgrah* skirt. She would try to hurt or kill as many English as she could, or herself, before they had a chance to shame her. They had been courteous so far, but Bernardo had told her what the English were like. She did not expect their kindness to last.

Sailors were lighting the lamps belowdecks. In the dim light, Thomas and Lockheart found the door to the stateroom of Master Bertwick, who had died of the scurvy two months before. Thatch, the *Whelp*'s old, wiry Master at Arms, who was looked upon by the crewmen with mixed measure of terror and respect, leaned against the bulkhead on guard.

"Good even to you, Master Thatch," said Thomas.

"Ah, young Master Chinnery! Good even to ye. Perchance have ye more of that oppium juice? Methinks me tertian fever is coming worse."

"Alas, no, sir, no more. But if we should procure some, you shall know it."

"Well, then, I shall thank ye. What brings ye this bend of below?"

"I am told our lady prisoner is lodged within."

Behind him, Lockheart added, "The captain would have us speak with her as we have a tongue she knows."

The Master at Arms rubbed his stubbly chin with his thumb, eyeing the Scotsman suspiciously. "Aye, there's many a man aboard would ply a tongue with her, and lips and hands as well. But I am charged to see she is not harmed."

"Have a care to your own tongue, sirrah," growled Lockheart. "We are gentlemen, here on the captain's business."

"If you please," said Thomas, bewildered again at how Lockheart seemed to cause enmity everywhere. "I have orders to learn how the lady may be ransomed. And mayhap she knows what medicines we may find in these lands, the poppy syrup in particular."

"Then enter, good Master Chinnery. But if aught goes amiss, call for me." The Master at Arms pushed on the latch and stepped aside.

"I will, sir."

The Lady Aditi was standing behind a small table as Thomas and Lockheart entered. The dim light of the lamp on the table flickered on the gold threads in her scarlet sari, glistening on the dark braid of her hair. One long-fingered hand rested on the table, the other at her waist, near a half-concealed knife. She regarded them warily, but she did not seem afraid. Thomas thought her quite handsome, though her frame was too muscular and her demeanor too proud for his taste. *The blue of her eyes holds more steel than fair skies.*

He felt Lockheart poke him in the back. "Do not stand and gawk, lad. Speak!"

With a small bow, Thomas said in Greek, "Greetings, Despoina Aditi. I am told you know the language of the wise and ancient Hellenes."

Her eyes widened and a slight smile appeared on her lips. Her wary posture eased and her hand dropped away from the knife hilt. She inclined her head. "*Nai.* You must have spoken to Bernardo."

"If you mean Despos De Cartago, you are correct."

"How is it you come to speak this language? Are you a scholar, like Bernardo?"

"I am, Despoina. Although our realms of study differ. I am Thomas Chinnery, apothecary, a purveyor of healing herbs and drugs."

"I see." She tilted her head with a curious smile. "Tamas, is it?"

"*Nai*, Despoina. Is there—"

"It is nothing. Your foreign names are strange to me."

"Ah. May I ask how you come to speak Greek?"

"I was taught it by my nursemaids as a child."

"You had very . . . learned nursemaids, Despoina."

"*Nai*. Who is this one?" Aditi turned her gaze to the Scotsman.

"I am Andrew Lockheart, Despoina," he said with a bow. "A wanderer far from his forest, bearing the holy branch of the Huntress."

Thomas glanced sidelong at him. *What can he be trying to do?* The Lady Aditi bowed in return, but showed no reaction to his words.

"We have been sent by Captain Wood," Thomas went on, "to learn what ransom we may obtain for you and from whom."

"I understand. You may negotiate with the Marathas of Goa. They will willingly pay thousands of *tangas* of silver for my safe release. They also control much trade in this region, and if I am treated well I may have some influence with them on behalf of your merchants."

"What of the Portuguese," said Lockheart, "who pursued you and Despos De Cartago? What might they pay if we deliver you to them?"

She raised her chin, her eyes narrowing. "They are not to be trusted. They would cheat you and pay you in death."

Thomas suspected that it was Lady Aditi who would pay in death, were she turned over to the Portuguese, but he did not mind helping her avoid such a fate. "How might we contact these Marathas?"

"Any Hindu trader you encounter on this coast will accept payment to carry such a message. Beware of pirates, however, for they are also common in these waters."

"We are aware of this, Despoina, but we thank you."

"Why do you wish to return to Goa," said Lockheart, "when you have just fled from there? Do you not wish to continue on to Pegu with Despos De Cartago?"

The Lady Aditi gazed down at the table. "I find I regret fleeing with him. I have no wish to leave India. It is my home. I am ashamed at my cowardice in attempting to escape my *dharma*, and the wrath of the goddess who sustains me." She turned her face toward the window.

Lockheart nodded gravely. "How well I understand. You may be braver than I, Despoina."

Thomas looked at him again. *Does he try to flatter her?* "I have one more question I would ask, Despoina."

"What is it?"

Thomas pulled the purloined box out of his doublet. "I came upon this on De Cartago's ship. There are signs within it that suggest its contents may be medicinal in nature. We have many men sick and injured aboard, and we have no more pain's-ease or all-heals to give them. Can you tell me if the powder within will be of use to us?"

The Lady Aditi stared at the box. Thomas was uncertain because of the poor light, but her face seemed to turn a shade more pale. She paused before replying. "You have opened the bottle?"

"*Nai,* Despoina. We believe it to be filled with some sort of powdered blood. Despos De Cartago implied that you might know of it. Is it a holy relic, or a substance used in sorcery?"

She paused again. "Bernardo told you nothing more?"

"He did not, Despoina."

She gripped tightly the back of a chair. With a sigh, she said at last, "It is not medicinal. You must not use it so, for it may cause harm. It is monkey's blood. Bernardo used it in his . . . alchemical experiments. I would ask that you return it to him, for it can be of no use to you."

"Why, then, was the bottle accompanied with a caduceus if it is not medicinal? And why the paper with holy phrases concerning life and death if it is not a relic?"

"I do not know. Perhaps the box once contained medicines. The blood would only be holy to those who worship Hanuman, the ape-god. Again I say, do not try to use the powder for healing. It will only bring . . . ill fortune."

"Ah," said Lockheart. "A talisman of bad luck, like the paw of that selfsame ape. No wonder the Portuguese were biting at your tail."

Thomas looked down at the box, reluctant to let it go. "For what manner of experiment does Despos De Cartago use this?"

"When you return it to him, perhaps he will tell you. I have no more to say. Please leave me. I am tired."

"Yet one thing more," said Lockheart. "Who is the goddess you spoke of earlier, who sustains you?"

Her eyes became wary again and her hand strayed toward her knife hilt.

Lockheart held up his hands. "Fear not, Despoina. We are not priests come to convert you. I ask only as one curious about the ways of the world."

Her lips thinned in an expression that may have been fear or contempt. She walked to the window and opened it. "Her name is strength," the Lady Aditi murmured, staring out at the sea.

Thomas could not tell if she was answering Lockheart or uttering a prayer. Lockheart opened his mouth as if to ask yet another question, but with a glare at the Scotsman, Thomas spoke first. "Forgive us for troubling you for so long, Despoina. We will take leave of you now."

Lockheart shut his mouth with a rueful smile and

Thomas followed him out of the room. When they had passed out of earshot of Master Thatch, Thomas said, "Think you she lied? About the blood powder, I mean?"

"Like a lioness in the desert, lad, she lieth with her pride."

"Wherefore said you those odd words of a branch and a huntress at your introduction, and those questions about whom she worshiped?"

"I had hoped to learn what manner of sophist she might be, mystic or scholar or sorceress. Now, methinks, perhaps a priestess of a sort."

"What matter, so long as we are able to see her safely ransomed?"

Lockheart frowned. "All knowledge has its use at one time or another, lad. I have made a habit of gath'ring it wheresoever I may. You might well do the same."

"You begin to sound like my Master Coulter, sir."

"Do I?" His frown became a subtle smile. "You flatter me. Ah, well, let us go tell the captain her terms for ransom and then we may join the rest of the crew on the beach. We've not yet finished the casks of fine Spanish wine we rescued from De Cartago's hold."

"I thank you, but I have seen that such spirited revelry oft leads to fisticuffs 'ere long. I should look in again on my patients below, who can take no part in such revels. Will you deliver the Lady Aditi's message to the captain without me?"

Lockheart stopped walking and blinked. "If you are certain that is your wish. A night out of the noisome depths would do you good, lad. It will not serve the ill to have a physician who is out of humor."

"Then, pray, humor me, sir, and leave me to my work. Go you to enjoy our spoils whilst I minister to those spoiled by its getting."

"A touch," Lockheart said with a bow and a grin. "Take care, then, to remain below for the night, as the antics of drunkards are a dismal sight to sober men."

"I will, sir."

"Mind you, eat no pomegranates whilst you toil below, or we'll not see you for half a year."

Thomas laughed. "I will give Lord Pluto your regards, should I see him, sir, as you must give Bacchus courtesies for me."

"Nay, chaste Diana is my muse, and I must play companion to the moon all night. 'Til the morrow, Tom." Lockheart ascended the ladder to the upper deck, disappearing into darkness.

Thomas made his way farther down the narrow corridor, between the masts, to where another ladder led down into the crew's quarters. Thomas descended it, in mind of Orpheus descending into Hell. *Though I seek no true love's spirit here, much I would give to bring one of these unhappy souls into the light once more.*

VI

HAZEL: This small tree bears round leaves and long catkins. In late summer, it brings forth husked nuts named filberts, after Saint Philbert, upon whose feast day the kernels ripen. The hazel is, to the Irish, a tree of knowledge and eating of the nuts therefrom they say make one wise. Those in Wales weave twigs of hazel into their caps, believing it will grant wishes. The best twigs for divining come from the hazel, when cut on Saint John's Eve. A rod cut from hazel wood by an innocent child of true faith will give aid in seeking murderers and thieves....

Padre Gonsção sat in a dim, musty, windowless room. He rubbed his eyes, which ached after many hours of reading in candlelight. The tall stool he sat upon felt hard as stone. Despite his careful stacking, the three enormous ledgers he had been reading continually threatened to fall off the narrow lectern. And the ledgers themselves contained little of what Gonsção had needed to see.

Inquisitor Sadrinho does not invite my success, it seems. Even so, those books he had been given pointed toward the reason. He had checked carefully the record of the last auto-da-fé, held on December 8 of 1596. The lists of those released for civil execution, those kept in imprisonment, and those set free showed that only the richest heretics, who had the most property for seizure, were burnt. Gonsção was keeping a list of those sent to the stake, intending to request the records of their questioning. He suspected he would see the same *familiares* named as those giving condemning testimony.

As expected, he had not been given any record of the trials of Governador Coutinho or Viceroy de Albuquerque. *Both were wealthy men, and in positions that could challenge the power of the Santa Casa. Might the charges against them have been false?* Gonsção was reminded of a case in Lisboa; a man had been imprisoned as a heretic for two years until his accuser confessed to giving false testimony—he had been jealous, as the prisoner had paid court to a woman the accuser desired. *The Santa Casa is like a well-made sword; a powerful weapon as easily wielded for evil as for good.*

A knock at the door startled him. Gonsção closed the ledger and said, *"Benedite.* Come in."

Brother Timóteo entered, bearing another leather-bound ledger, and atop it a silver tray. On the tray were a pitcher of water, a glass, and a bowl of rice with a spiced *ragu* sauce, topped with strips of smoked fish.

"A multitude of blessings upon you, my son. Our Lady of Mercy must have sent you herself." Gonsção indicated that the tray should be set on the floor, there being nowhere else to put it.

Brother Timóteo set down the tray and the ledger carefully. "No, Padre. Domine Pinto sent me."

"Then surely he was inspired by the angels." *Inquisitor Pinto is Dominican, as I am. Perhaps loyalty to a brother of the order may prove of greater strength and value than loyalty within the Santa Casa.*

"Yes, Padre." The boy stood deferentially by the door. He had bowl-cut black hair and dark eyes, and the candle-light gave his brown skin a coppery cast.

Clearly he has some Hindu blood in him, a mestiço *as most*

Goans seem to be. A pity. It will prevent him from any position higher than parish priest. "Stay, Timóteo. I am glad we at last have the chance to speak." Gonsção slid off his stool. "Feel free to sit a while. I have been on this stool too long."

"Oh, no, Padre! I will sit here." With no hesitation, the boy sat cross-legged on the dirty floor.

"As you wish." Gonsção walked around the lectern, finding it more comfortable to stand. "How long have you served in the Santa Casa?"

The boy counted on his fingers a moment. "Four years, Padre."

"And for how long have you been an *avocato* to the guests here?"

"One year and one month, Padre."

"Mm-hmm. What can you tell me about these guests, Timóteo?"

The boy blinked. "I do not know what you mean, Padre."

"Are they educated scholars? Or poor farmers and tradesmen? Or wealthy *fidalgos*?"

"I am not sure, Padre. I pay little attention to such things. They are all sad, frightened people, with aching in their souls. All needing our guidance."

"Yes, I suppose by the time you see them, that is how they all appear. Are they treated well?"

"Those who confess and accept God are treated with all kindness, Padre. But—"

"But?"

Softly, the boy said, "Sometimes I think the guards are too rough with them."

"Well, sometimes rough men must be hired for that task. Our guests are like lost children, and children require stern guidance and discipline to find the proper path in life, do they not?"

Timóteo frowned. "So I am told, Padre."

So his upbringing has been lax. Amazing that so fine an instrument can come from so shoddy a craft-house. "What of the Inquisitors? How do they treat the guests?"

"Oh, the Domines are most kind, Padre. Domine Sadrinho spends much time with the guests, the women especially. Nearly every one of the ladies he has ministered to have made a confession."

Gonsção was uncomfortable with the turn this was taking. "Have you served any of the Nestorian heresy?"

"Um . . . only two, Padre. They were very difficult."

"Yes, that is why they must be dealt with severely, my son. They are so close to the truth, and yet so in error."

Timóteo nodded and looked down at his hands. "One did not recant. He is condemned to the flames the next auto-da-fé."

Gonsção walked over and placed his hand on the boy's shoulder. "Do not blame yourself. I am sure you did all you could."

"I pray for him every day, Padre."

"That is good, my son. Have many Nestorians been brought here?"

"I do not think so."

"I see." *And yet the destruction of that heresy was a major reason for this Santa Casa's founding. The Inquisitors would seem to have fallen away from their purpose.* "Timóteo, you were not an *avocato* when Governador Coutinho was here, were you?"

The boy shook his head.

"Perhaps you have heard something about the case, though. Some mention of his charges, or his confession."

"No, Padre. And if I had, we are told never to repeat what a guest has confessed."

"Of course. Except in certain circumstances. Let me explain. The forces that turned Coutinho and de Albuquerque to sin may be even more powerful and treacherous than those of the Nestorian heresy. These were men of good Christian family, you understand, and not lacking in honor and material wealth. Yet something caused them to turn from God, to take a path that they surely knew endangered their lives and their souls. This is the mystery I have been sent here to solve, Timóteo. That source of evil may still be at work in Goa, and may spread its influence farther if we do not discover it. I have been given this duty by Grand Inquisitor Albrecht, and, through him, His Holiness the Pope, himself. Do you see how important this is, my son?"

The boy nodded, wide-eyed.

Softly, Gonsção went on. "This miasma of corruption may even have infected the Santa Casa itself."

"No!"

"Shhh, it pains me to think it too, and I hope it proves not to be so. But we must be very careful, my son. I must ask you not to discuss with anyone these things we have talked about. Can you do that?"

After a pause, the boy nodded again.

"Good. Now, there is something I need to help me in my task. I need the accounts of the trials of Coutinho and de Albuquerque. Inquisitor Pinto may know where it can be found. Ask him where no others can hear you, and if he can provide it, I want you to bring it to me. Will you do this?"

The boy swallowed hard. "Yes, Padre."

"God bless you. You are a soldier of the Lord in the battle against Satan. Go now, and see if you can find Domine Pinto."

Timóteo stood. "Yes, Padre." He looked toward the door, but hesitated.

"Is there something else, my son?"

"May I ask one question, Padre?"

"Certainly."

"Forgive me, but . . . Domine Sadrinho said that you told him to take *Os Lusiados* away from me."

"Ah. Yes, I did recommend that he do so. Did he tell you why?"

"No, Padre. But . . . he said some things I should not repeat."

Gonsção sighed. "My son, you must understand that Camões's book is possibly part of the very danger we have been speaking of. It could be a corrupting influence to a mind so young as yours."

"But I have read the verses all my life!" Timóteo's eyes were sad, and a touch defiant.

"Then it is to your credit, my son, that your faith remains strong and pure. But you are coming to a dangerous age, when the Devil sends doubts to trouble your mind and temptations to torment your young flesh."

"But the book is just stories!"

"Stories have power, Timóteo, for great good or ill. That is why Our Lord used parables to teach his message to his disciples. But you must be wary of stories other than those in the Good Book."

The boy's mouth tightened and his hands clenched. But at last he gazed downward at his sandaled feet and said, "As you wish, Padre."

Gonsção smiled. "You will have the book back again, someday. Perhaps it will mean more to you then. I am told it is a difficult work, even for those who have studied the classics. All those references to faraway places, obscure deities and creatures."

"But I know about all those things, Padre," Timóteo said. "I have read the *Iliad* and Virgil and other books. They were all in my grandfather's library. And he told me many stories he had read—"

"Shh, enough of that. Clearly, you have more education than many wealthy boys in Lisboa. God has granted you a quick mind, but your learning must now be of a different sort. You have the calling to inspire faith in others, thereby leading them to God. We must see that no ancient pagan tales distract you from such important work."

Timóteo sighed. "Yes. You are right, Padre."

Gonsção patted his shoulder. "You are wise, my son. You are even an inspiration to me. Now go. We have much to do, you and I."

Without another word, Timóteo bowed and left.

Gonsção took up the rice bowl and sat again on the stool, feeling vaguely unclean.

VII

ALDER: This tree has round leaves and aglets of a red hue. The Irish use it for fortune-casting, and to learn the nature of a man's illness, and they are loath to fell the alder. If a bough of alder is cut, the wood will change from white to red, as if the tree were of flesh and blood. Mayhap for this reason the alder was esteemed by the ancients as a tree of resurrection....

Thomas crouched in a boneyard, the close darkness ripe with the stench of rot. He clawed at the damp earth before him like a cur searching for its buried dinner. In the distance behind him, he heard soft wails and moans. *They still seek me. And should they find me—* He dug faster, pulling up tangled roots and jagged stones. His fingers struck something hard and he cleared the earth away. A pale, round thing rose out of the dirt—a skull, still possessing a few limp strands of hair. The skull fixed its empty-socketed gaze upon him and opened its ivory jaws. Thomas screamed "Mother!" and sat up, awake, banging his head on the bunk above him.

He sat for a moment, gasping, heart pounding in his chest. *The nightmares. They've come again.* In the darkness of the crew's hold, his dream lingered in his thoughts, unbanished by wakefulness. *Lord, wherefore am I so tormented?* He rubbed his eyes and wondered what the hour might be. Thomas remembered leaving Lockheart's company and going among his patients, not that there had been much he could do for them. Tiring, Thomas had rested on a vacant bunk. And slept. And dreamt.

The sick, injured, and dying men moaned softly around him, some murmuring prayers or calling out for loved ones.

What right have I to self-pity, when these unfortunates live a nightmare from which there is no waking? Thomas removed a dim lamp from the bulkhead and held it up, surveying his charges.

Here beside him lay Stephen the cooper, whose ribs had been stove in by a cannon ball. Around his neck, Thomas had placed a pomander of hollowed oak gall stuffed with crushed garlic and horseradish to keep fever at bay, to no avail. The man shuddered in troubled sleep.

A thin arm reached out of the darkness. "More pain's-ease, sir? For the love of God, I prithee." It was Howard, the roper, whose legs and chest had been burned and bruised by the very cannon he had fired. For him, Thomas had tried the theory of weapon ointment advocated by the great Paracelsus; Thomas had applied a paste of valerian and mallow to the cannon itself, treating the man with only clean water and bandages. As a result, Howard's wounds were healing tolerably well, but he still suffered great pain.

"Anon," was all Thomas could say. "There will be more 'ere long."

Next was Corbin, whose arms and legs had been shattered by a fallen mast. Thomas had set his bones as well as he could, and given the man an amulet of terra sigilita made of Maltese clay. Thomas did not assault Corbin's dignity by acknowledging his whimpers of despair.

In the bunk beyond lay Pepper, the cook's apprentice,

who lay insensate with fluxion of the bowels. Small doses of mercury mixed with mummy powder had not seemed to help him and he did not respond to Thomas's voice.

He squeezed the boy's shoulder and hurried past. *Dear God, I was never prepared for service such as this. Would that the popinjays who came to our shop whining of the headache could see these men and know what true suffering is.* The blandishments he'd learned for ailing ladies in their frippery had no place in this hellish chamber that reeked of sweat and foul infection. *Wherefore am I their caretaker when I have so little skill to help them?*

Thomas continued the gruesome round, giving what small comfort he could, thinking about what medicines he might concoct out of the few stores that were left.

At last, he came to Nathan, the carpenter's apprentice, whose bunk lay close by the ladder. The boy's face was composed in peaceful sleep. Thomas sat at his side, congratulating himself that here at last was one who was not suffering. But as he watched, he realized the boy was very still indeed, more than is in the nature of sleep. Fear stole over him, and Thomas placed his hand against the boy's neck. There was no pulse.

Thomas bowed his head, with a heavy sigh. *Wherefore this one, oh Lord, who had so much life ahead of him?* Thomas knew he should bestir himself. In this climate, untended corpses swiftly became a danger to the living. *Yet a prayer should be said.* A phrase passed through his thoughts: *"Whosoever believeth in me shall have everlasting life."*

Thomas set the lantern on the steps and pulled out from his doublet the wooden box. Carefully he opened it and unwrapped the silk from the little bottle. His hands began to tremble as he raised up the opalescent bottle, glimmering in the lamplight. Finely etched upon the glass surface, unseen before, was the image of a bird, wings outstretched, rising from a bed of flames.

"Monkey's blood, art thou?" Thomas whispered, his heart pounding. "O precious ape, whose sap comes with words of life beyond life, thou speakst thy message clearly." He remembered the Lady Aditi's warning, yet how earnestly she had asked him to return the bottle to De Cartago. *Might the alchemist have discovered the philosopher's stone of legend? The elixir of life?*

Thomas regarded Nathan's young face. *What harm could it do to one already dead?* Not daring to reconsider, he unstoppered the bottle. "Nate, if this substance be holy, be you blessed by it. If not, may the evil fall upon my soul, not yours. God help me."

He held the bottle over Nathan's face and sprinkled a tiny amount of the powder between the boy's slightly parted lips. He paused a moment, but saw no change. Thomas sighed and put the stopper back in the bottle, the bottle back in its box. He grasped Nathan's cool hand in both of his and shut his eyes. *Lord, if it be Thy will, restore his life. If not, then speed his soul to Heaven.*

There came a tugging at his sleeve. Slowly, Thomas opened his eyes. Nathan had turned his head and was looking at him. "Master Chinnery? Sir, you are hurting my hand."

Thomas realized how hard he had been squeezing and let go. "Nate . . . pray, forgive me. How fare you?"

"Weary, sir. Have I slept much? I had strange dreams."

"Dreams?" *Do the dead dream, then?*

"Aye—there was a beautiful building by the sea, all white columns and such. And a pretty lady. And serpents."

"Serpents?" *Dear Lord, what have I done?*

"But I wasn't afraid, sir. 'Twas a pleasant dream."

"Ah. Let me see your wound, Nathan." Thomas pulled

away the rough bandage binding Nathan's side. Red scars still ran across his chest and abdomen, but they no longer oozed. They were dry and clearly on the mend. "The infection is gone! Say your prayers, Nathan, for God is granting you recovery. I . . . I must go speak with someone."

Thomas placed the box in his doublet and stood.

"Might I return topside tomorrow, sir? I tire of this pallet."

"Aye. We shall see. On the morrow." Thomas took up the lantern and climbed the ladder, breathless with terror and with awe.

He emerged from the hatch into a night darker than the depths below. Few of the lanterns on the rigging had been lit and the stars glimmered bright above the broken masts. There was no moon.

Across the lagoon, revelers on the beach were silhouetted against their bonfires, dancing and gesturing like demons cavorting in the fires of Hell. Astern, one lone sailor stared out at the sea, his hourglass unturned, forgotten. Except for him, the *Whelp* appeared deserted.

Thomas turned and walked swiftly toward the forecastle.

Aditi paced the length of her stateroom, unable to sleep. Her thoughts churned like stormclouds. Again, there came voices at her door.

The burly, dark-bearded one entered and bowed. His face was flushed and his breath shallow and quick. "Despoina. I hope I have not disturbed your rest."

"No. Where is your yellow-haired friend?"

"He is performing other duties. Forgive me, but I must speak to the point, and swiftly. A chance has arisen that must be seized this night or not at all."

"A chance at what? Does your captain not agree to our offers of ransom?"

"He does, but I fear you must know that he is unable to keep any bargains. Our ships are too badly damaged to sail, repairs may take months."

Aditi sucked in her breath. "Ai, by then the *Santa Rosa* may return and more ships with her."

"Indeed, and with so few able men, we are in no shape for another battle."

"Perhaps the Goans will not find us here."

"No, Despoina. It is already too late. The traders who serve us have Goan spies among them. Our location, and De Cartago's presence with us, is already known."

Aditi grasped her upper arms, feeling cold. "What will you do?"

He outlined his plan.

Aditi's eyes widened. "You would do this for us?"

"For me," he said with a self-mocking smile.

"Against your own—"

"No one will be harmed, and with the sorcerer gone, they will be in less danger. Captain Wood has given me leave to bring you together with Despos De Cartago, in order, he believes, to further discuss ransom. Let us hurry, Despoina."

The chance to leave the tiny, bare stateroom was welcome. The thin, older sailor who had been guarding her door fell in behind her as they entered the corridor. Aditi could feel his gaze on her back. She longed to leave the confines of this ship, with its lost and damaged men. She was keenly aware of how fragile the bonds of civilization could be. One misstep, one change in the wind, and she might be set upon like a doe in the midst of jackals.

She was led to a room much like the one she left, but even smaller. Bernardo sat at a table, his hands shackled. Weariness had seeped into the nobility of his face. He greeted her with a regretful smile.

Aditi went to him and placed a hand on his shoulder. "Bernardo. They have harmed you?" She spoke in Marathi.

"No. But I have not rested and have no stomach for their food. It is good to see you, my falcon."

Aditi inwardly flinched at his endearment. "He has told you his plan?"

"He has."

Aditi frowned. "Do you trust him?"

"From what I saw when they questioned me abovedecks, I believe that these ships cannot sail anytime soon. That much is true."

"You know the danger if you return to Goa."

De Cartago raised his hands to his chest. "I am not a fool, Aditi. I am prepared."

Thomas was surprised to see Master Thatch guarding a different door than before.

"Ah, Master Chinnery, I wondered when you'd appear. Your friend is already within and the conf'rence begun."

Thomas blinked, confused. "Your pardon, sir? D'ye mean Lockheart? Methought he had gone ashore. And were you not watching the Lady Aditi 'ere this?"

"So I am, sir, and she is within, with the sorcerer. They are together to discuss plans for ransom. Were you not told?"

Thomas shook his head. "It matters not. May I enter?"

"Certes, and if aught is amiss, do not be close with me."

"I will not." Thomas shoved the door open and stepped in. De Cartago and Lockheart were seated at the table, the Lady Aditi stood to one side. All stared at him like children caught at some forbidden game. As Thomas met Aditi's gaze, he sensed she knew why he had come.

"Thomas?" said Lockheart. "What is the matter? Methought you watched your flock below."

Thomas clenched his fists and his throat felt dry. "A lost sheep has untimely returned." He faced De Cartago, but said in Greek, "I believe I have been lied to."

The Lady Aditi said, "You have used the blood."

"You seem as though you'd seen a ghost, me lad," said Lockheart. "Pray, sit and be comfortable."

"Your words are too apt, sir," said Thomas, sitting. To De Cartago, Thomas said in Latin, "I must know, *Magister*, the source of this powder."

"A moment," Lockheart interrupted. "We come in at the middle. What has happened to make you so frantic and pale?"

In Latin, so the sorcerer could also understand, Thomas said, "You remember Nathan, the carpenter's apprentice? When I examined him on my latest rounds, he lay still, no pulse in his veins or breath from his mouth. I put a little of this powder between his lips. After a short time, the boy awoke, alive and his wound healing. He was unaware that he had been without life."

De Cartago let out a long sigh.

Lockheart gave the sorcerer a speculative glance, then smiled sadly at Thomas. "But there is no miracle in this. I have been a soldier, and seen many a seeming corpse dragged from the field, only to quicken on the way to the bonepit. The boy was not dead, Tom, only sleeping."

"I know what I saw, sir!"

De Cartago said, "Did anyone else witness this?"

"No, *Magister*. It was dark. No one else would have seen."

"So we have only your word of this amazing resurrection," said Lockheart. "Have you had sufficient rest, Tom?"

"After we parted, sir, I examined the men in my care, then lay down to rest. I slept, but awoke from nightmares."

"And you are certain this event was not part of your dream?"

"I know the difference, sir!"

Lockheart reached over and clapped a meaty hand on Thomas's shoulder. "I think you, yourself, have need of a potion more powerful than powdered ape's blood. Abide a bit, and I will bring you some of our guest's good Madeira. Try not to pester them too much with fanciful questions, eh?" With a wink, Lockheart stood and strode from the stateroom. Thomas heard him banter a moment with Master Thatch before his footsteps clumped away down the corridor.

"I gave you warning to not use it," said the Lady Aditi in clumsy Latin.

"But you did not tell me why, Domina, and I was desperate for a remedy. A most powerful remedy it has proved to be, and therefore I must know its nature."

De Cartago watched the door, frowning. "Forgive us, *Magister* Chinnery, for not being forthright with you, but we have taken an oath not to reveal the source of the powder. It is a matter for . . . initiates alone."

"Initiates?" Sighing, Thomas jammed his fingers into his hair. *"Magister,* are you a Christian?"

"I was once. My learning, however, has led me to become apostate. Why do you ask this?"

"To know that you will understand what I ask next. Have I damned my soul, or that of the resurrected boy, by use of this powder?"

The Lady Aditi frowned and held out her slender, long-fingered hands. "You have been fortunate, Tamas, for the Mahadevi has shown you her blessing. But it is not always so. And you will be troubled by what you do not comprehend. If you value your faith, you should return the powder to us and forget what you have seen."

De Cartago raised a hand in gesture to her, but his manacles interfered. He spoke gently to her in a language foreign to Thomas. Then, to Thomas, he said, "What manner of alchemist are you?"

"You have been misled, *Magister*. I am not an alchemist, but an apothecary's apprentice. I use herbs, spices, and all manner of things to heal ailments. I understand we share some knowledge in common, though what we seek through our knowledge is different. I have never before used a substance of such power."

De Cartago raised his brows. "So. My lady is not the only one whose word cannot entirely be trusted."

"I did not choose to mislead you. Lockheart wished you to think me an alchemist, perhaps to gain your trust. Forgive me. Only, please . . . am I doomed?"

"I do not know what to tell you. In your land, those of my former Mother Church are called traitors for their faith."

Thomas sighed. "It is true that my papist countrymen are asked to choose between their faith and their queen. It is a sad state of things. Do you mean, then, that this is the blood of a saint? Is it a papist relic?"

The Portuguese gentleman regarded him a long time and Thomas felt as though he were being weighed in a delicate balance. "What would you believe from me? I, who to you am a heretic, apostate, and seeker of forbidden knowledge? I could tell you tales fantastical of demons who walk the earth in mortal shape; flames that appear in the night through no earthly agency; stones that fall like rain from the heavens. What would you understand of these?"

Thomas did not know whether to laugh or shout with frustration. "You are a skillful magus indeed, *Magister*. You can transmute a discourse all out of its shape. But I cannot let this go. You may not care about the state of my soul, or that of any other Englishman. But I would know this one thing."

De Cartago and the Lady Aditi looked at one another. She shook her head, gravely. De Cartago turned back to Thomas and smiled with sad amusement. "My young lion, there are things, sometimes, a wise man does not tell another. Some knowledge is not to be apprehended by the unprepared mind."

How very like what my father said, when I bade him tell me of the work that kept him so sequestered from my sight, thought Thomas.

"Still," De Cartago went on, as though speaking to a child, "if my opinion means anything to you, I think your soul is no more doomed to Hell now than it was yesterday. But, then, if there is a Hell, I was doomed long ago." He glanced at the door. "After tonight, perhaps, it will not matter what I think."

Bootsteps approached the door and Lockheart came in, bearing three pewter mugs. "Drinks for the house!" he declared, as he plunked them down on the table. "The men on shore shall not have all the festivity. We've·cause enow for celebration." He set one, with a bow, before De Cartago. The sorcerer inclined his head, but did not take up the wine.

Lockheart pushed another toward Lady Aditi. "Despoina?"

She gave it only a quick glance, then turned away.

He put the last mug before Thomas. "If the others are unsociable, at least you will drink with me, eh, Tom? Have you heard any colorable tales?"

Thomas shut his eyes and sighed. "They have told me naught of use."

"Aye, the very tongues of serpents, have they. Well. Sip some of this wine, for I have had a useful thought."

"Have you?" Thomas took the handle of his mug.

"Indeed," said Lockheart, sitting. "Remember you

Bandy Ted, from the *Benjamin*, who fell with the scurvy not two days ago?"

"Aye. He was buried on the beach that very night."

"E'en so. Here is an excellent test of your miraculous powder. Let us try to quicken him."

Thomas envisioned the decaying corpse rising from its sandy grave. "Are you mad, sir? That would be abominable!"

"Hah. For your daintiness, you would deprive a good man of resurrection, would you? To spare your stomach, you would doom him to lie 'neath foreign soil? Or do you fear seeming foolish when naught is stirred but a sand crab?"

De Cartago looked at Thomas and requested a translation.

"*Magister*, he is suggesting using the powder on a man two days dead."

The Lady Aditi exclaimed something and covered her mouth.

The sorcerer stared at Lockheart. "You cannot mean this."

"Think you we will not succeed?"

"More and less than you desire. But surely this is not the time for such an experiment."

"There is a time for words, Senhor De Cartago," said Lockheart, "and a time for deeds."

"Is now that time?" said De Cartago with a level stare at the Scotsman.

"Soon," Lockheart said, solemnity behind his jovial eyes. In English, to Thomas, he added, "There's no more to be learned sitting and jabbering here. Come away, lad."

This last had a tone of command Thomas had not heard from Lockheart. He pushed himself up from the table. With a bow to De Cartago, he said, "Good night to you, *Magister*."

"And to you, herbalist."

Thomas nodded to Lady Aditi. "M'Lady."

She inclined her head, her blue-eyed gaze intense. "Be wise, Tamas, or you will bring destruction around you."

Her words unsettled him. "I intend to, Lady."

VIII

BRYONY: This vine is also called tetterberry, or the Devil's turnip. It has a prickly stem and fleshy rootstock. It brings forth yellow flowers and black berries. Although it makes a useful purgative, the plant is oft thought wicked, for evil men would carve its root and sell it as the more powerful mandrake, deceiving and poisoning the hopeful purchasers. For the rootstock is poisonous in large amount, and the berries are quite poisonous indeed....

As Thomas stood, pondering Lady Aditi's warning, Lockheart flung open the door and Thomas found himself roughly shoved out, blundering headlong into the Master at Arms. Master Thatch began to sputter invective, and Lockheart shouted, "Within, good Thatch! Bestir yourself! Yon prisoners are plotting escape! The sorcerer nearly charmed us into abetting them. In and watch them with your eagle's eye, lest their spells and cantations let them slip away!"

Thomas started to protest, but Lockheart's hand clapped over his mouth.

"Poor Tom is still caught in th'enchantment. I must get him out to fresher air. In, man, before yon witches fly with the time!"

Suspicious, Thatch peered through the doorway. Lockheart kicked him into the room and pulled the door shut behind him, locking the door with an iron key. Ignoring the
pounding and swearing on the other side of the door, Lockheart threw an arm around the bewildered Thomas and led
him down the corridor.

"What has possessed you?"

"The spirit of Apollo, lad, and Pan besides, methinks.
Did you not think it amusing?"

Is the man drunk? He does not smell it. "Nay, nor will Captain Wood, when he hears of it. He will burst from the
apoplexy."

"Ah, now there would be a sight, indeed." Lockheart
climbed the ladder to the main deck and Thomas followed.

"Not if you view it whilst hanging from the yardarm.
Jesu, it is dark! Know you why all the lamps are out?"

"Everyone is ashore, lad. Who needs to see?"

Thomas perceived the shapes of turbaned men huddled
in the shadows of the masts and rails. "De Cartago's men are
still here."

"Eh? Oh, they are Mohammedans. They do not approve
of drink. A sad custom. Come, here is the rope; the boat rides
below."

"You are determined to try this foul experiment?"

Lockheart grasped his shoulder. "Only to ease your mind,
lad. Once it is proved to you that your miracle was but a
phantasm, you may no longer fear for your soul, but join the
festivities and welcome spirits other than the departed sort.
Now, will you go?"

It would seem I must humor this strange mood in him. "Very
well. For once, sir, I pray you are proven right."

"Only once? I pray that I am right most constantly."

"Would it content you if I joined the revels straightaway
and made no attempt to first bring back a lost soul?"

"What, and deny poor Ted a chance at revelry?"

"Methinks 'twould serve him little. Any drink would drain out of a creature of only bones."

Lockheart laughed. "Very well, 'twill content me. But then I would hear no more of this resurrection nonsense, eh? Leave such stuff to the prophets of old, and be about those deeds that are the domain of youth. On, down with you. I will follow."

Thomas looked over the side. Far below, he could hear the slap of water against wood in imperfect rhythm, and see the faint outline of the rowboat bobbing beside the ship. Swallowing his unease, Thomas swung his leg over the rail, grasping the rough hemp rope. Reaching out with his foot, he found a rung, then lowered himself until his whole weight was on the ladder.

"Show some dispatch, lad. Be swift."

"A swift dispatch is what I fear," muttered Thomas as he sought each rung in slow descent. Halfway down, he glanced up and saw Lockheart's dark shape outlined against the starry sky, as if a shadowy fiend of Hell had usurped his form and now urged Thomas downward to perdition.

A loud report, like a pistol shot or wood slapping wood, rang out from the aft of the ship. Thomas heard Lockheart softly swearing above him.

" 'Twould seem Master Thatch has forced the lock," Thomas called up.

"Mayhap. I'll see to it, lad. Get down to the boat. I will follow anon."

Thomas continued his descent, until his foot found the seat plank of the rowboat. He heard a sound above him, and looked up again—something struck him in the face and he fell back into the boat. Sharp pain shot up his shoulders and arms. He flailed about, tangled in rope, disoriented. He paused, and breathed a moment waiting for the violent rocking of the boat to slow.

It is but the ladder, which has fallen on me. It must have come off the rail. Now Lockheart cannot join me, nor can I ascend to give him aid.

Thomas disentangled his arms from the ladder and sat up, listening. The shouts and singing of the crewmen on the beach came faintly across the lagoon. The lapping of water against the boat and ship seemed loud by comparison. Nonetheless, Thomas became aware of other sounds, unusual ones: soft footfalls on the deck above, voices whose rhythm was not English.

Are De Cartago's men trying to take the ship? Thomas looked to the beach and wondered if he should call an alarum. *Nay, they would not hear me. But what can I do? Is the captain amid the revelers or aboard?*

More noises came from the aftercastle, and a splash from the far side of the ship. Thomas thought hard how he might get back aboard. The hull of the *Whelp* loomed above him, an unscalable black cliff. The railing was far too high to toss up the rope ladder. *Ah. The anchor line on the other side of the bow. Mayhap I can climb it.*

Thomas piled the rope ladder into the stern of the rowboat and knelt on the seat-plank. Placing his hands flat against the damp side of the *Whelp*, he pulled himself along the hull, thanking God the water was calm.

As he rounded the prow, the bowsprit above him, an ordinary mermaid in daylight, seemed to be a creature from his nightmares, hungry to swoop down on him. At last on the port side, he scanned the gloom for the anchor line—but his gaze was caught by another dark shape beside the *Whelp* some yards away. Lanterns on the strange craft showed it had a lateen-rigged sail of the sort Thomas had seen in the Arabian Gulf. Turbaned men climbed ropes from it up the side of the *Whelp*.

A dhow! Not De Cartago's men, but Arab pirates! Thomas froze, his heart pounding.

Catching sight of the anchor rope, Thomas reached out and found it slimy to the touch. *Impossible to climb. And I might be seen whilst trying.*

Something bumped against the rowboat, dark lumps floating on the water. Thomas looked closer and saw it was a body. It turned and caught the light—it was Master Thatch. Sickened, Thomas wondered if he should pull the man onto the rowboat, perhaps try to resurrect him. As he reached out, nudging the body with his fingertips, air bubbled out from beneath Thatch's clothing and without its buoyancy, the body sank out of reach.

He heard voices on the dhow and the lantern light revealed a dark-bearded man gesticulating at turbaned sailors. Behind him was a glint of scarlet cloth with golden thread.

They've captured Lockheart! And the Lady Aditi!

Anger somewhat divorcing his mind from reason, Thomas released the anchor rope. He lowered himself to lie prone in the skiff, his chest over the bow so that his long arms could reach the water. Silent as a shark, Thomas paddled toward the dhow. No men appeared on its forward deck to notice him.

The last few feet Thomas glided, letting his hands and arms absorb the impact as he came up against the hull of the dhow. Clinging to the wood, he waited and listened.

He understood none of the melodious chatter, but it seemed the Arabs were all congregating in the center of the ship, perhaps to admire the prizes they had acquired. When Thomas could hear no voice or footfall near him, he dared to raise his head and shoulders to peer over the deck. The bulk of a low superstructure blocked his view of the rest of the dhow, but no man was in sight nearby. Willing strength into his already aching arms, Thomas hauled himself up onto the deck, kicking away the rowboat. He crawled forward to the wall of the forecabin and huddled there.

Laughter and exclamations came from mid-deck, and then soft footsteps approaching. Thomas scrabbled about, searching for a sail or rope to hide beneath; instead, his hands found a hatch cover. He pried it open and slithered down into it, letting the cover fall shut after him.

He dropped a couple of feet and landed in darkness, on what felt like coils of rope and mounds of fishnet. The footsteps overhead passed on at a slow, even pace. *Thanks be to God. I am undetected.*

The hold smelled like fish and wet hemp. He felt pinpricks of pain on his arms and belly—slivers from the worn wood of the hatchframe. *Now thou most brilliant idiot,* he chided himself. *Now what wilt thou do?*

Many footsteps approached, descending stairs somewhere ahead of him. Light glimmered, outlining a doorway scarcely two feet from his face. Arabic voices were close, laughing.

The dhow shuddered and rolled to one side. Thomas fell back against a mound of netting. The water beyond the bulkhead lapped louder and with a rhythm of low sea swells. *Damme, they have cast off! Now I am well and truly trapped.*

Someone fumbled at the latch of the door before him. *I must hide. But how, when I can see naught around me?* Thomas crab-walked away from the door until he was pressed against the bulkhead.

The door opened inward, and to his good fortune he was behind it, shielded from view. Lamplight streamed in, revealing that he was in a storage hold that filled most of the prow.

A couple of men leaned in the doorway. Something fell

or was thrown into the hold with a loud *whump* and the door shut again.

Thomas sighed with relief in the regained darkness. There came a moan from the center of the hold.

"Sir?" Thomas whispered. "Master Lockheart, is that you? Are you well?" He reached out and felt sodden velvet between his fingers.

"So. You. The young Christian who fears for his soul," said a soft voice in Latin. "Have you turned Judas also?"

"Senhor De Cartago?"

"Or are you a victim of their game as well as I?"

Thomas swallowed. "I do not understand, *Magister.* I came aboard in hopes of rescuing my friend and your Lady Aditi."

"Did you? Then you are a fool, although a charitable one. Your friend is a scoundrel, albeit a practical one. As for my Lady . . . she serves a power in ways unknowable to me."

"What are you saying, *Magister?* That Lockheart is in league with the pirates?"

"He said he would help us escape. That your ships could not sail, nor your men defend us. He said the coastal traders he had been dealing with offered him passage to Goa. But they must be paid, no? It is known there is a bounty on my head. 'Play the prisoner,' your friend said. 'You can escape when the time is right.' But he has allowed them to beat and drug me. And I think it is no role I play. My head shall pay for their passage."

"Why would your Lady deceive you so?"

"She serves a greater cause. I cannot blame her. There is much at stake if the wrong ones capture her."

Thomas heard more laughter outside; one hearty laugh he recognized. A coldness filled him. *Lockheart wanted me off the ship, knowing this would happen. With no able man aboard, this*

*plot was simple. And I have doomed myself by entering this viper's
nest. Well, they will discover me here eventually. The least I may do
is surprise Lockheart and let him know his foul deed has not gone
unwitnessed.*

Thomas kicked the door open and stumbled, blinking,
into a cramped cabin filled with swarthy men. Lockheart's
broad back was before him. "What have you done, man?"
Thomas cried.

Lockheart turned and his face went pale. "Thomas?"

"Aye, and what name have you now? Is't not Judas?"
Three of the Arab pirates grabbed him, pinning his arms behind his back. Thomas struggled only briefly, finding himself no match for them.

The Lady Aditi appeared from the far end of the cabin
and came up to him, eyes concerned. "You ignored my words,
Tamas," she said in Greek. "You have not been wise." She
patted his doublet, then removed the little wooden box with
its precious bottle.

"My journey is ended, Despoina, either way."

"Not necessarily," she said, handing the box to Lockheart. "But your journey will be longer now. And more difficult."

Lockheart glared at him, pained. "Dame Fortuna will
not release me from my charted fate, 'twould seem," he muttered. "I had hoped to spare you, boy. To spare us both."

"So. Will you kill me as you did Master Thatch?"

Lockheart shook his head. "That was the Lady's doing.
'Tis not yet your time to die."

His meaty fist came at Thomas's face and Thomas felt
the blow hard on his temple. The room spun as he fell back
against the men who held him. Unnatural bursts of light
sparkled before his sight, then dimmed to darkness absolute.

IX

APPLE: This well-loved fruit is said to have first come from the East. It is thought a cure for many ailments. In ancient stories, divine apples were sought as a means to immortality. They were used as magical charms, or tests of fidelity. Apples are also said to make one long for things forbidden. The apple may have been the Fruit of Knowledge in Eden, and because of Eve's fall, the apple is thought a fruit of temptation, disobedience, and the loss of innocence....

Brother Timóteo rushed down the hallway, clutching the record book to his chest. The pounding of his heart was more loud in his ears than the pounding of his feet. *I have sinned. I have sinned for the Padre, the Archbishop, and the Pope. It is wrong, wrong, forgive me, Great Lord, make it right, but I have sinned and it is wrong and I will surely burn in Hell forever.*

At matins that morning, Domine Pinto had whispered in Timóteo's ear that the records of Governador Coutinho's trial were to be found under a pile of papers in a storeroom near the kitchens. Little searching was necessary for Timóteo to find the leather-bound tome among the scrap paper, rags, and wood set by for kindling, as though some higher or lower power had intended Timóteo to take it. But he had had to speak falsehood to the cook, claiming Domine Sadrinho had sent him. The cook, of course, believed him for everyone in the Santa Casa knew that Brother Timóteo was good and God-fearing and never, ever lied.

The tiled hallway leading to the dormitories stretched before him, impossibly long. The bulky, heavy book made running awkward. Timóteo did not notice the side table whose stout leg protruded into his path. His foot caught on the table leg and he pitched forward. His arms flung open wide, sending the record book flying out like a captured bird released, the binding opening into wings.

With a great thump and clatter, Timóteo fell to the floor on his bony knees and elbows. The book landed soon after, sliding ahead of him down the hall, loose pages spreading like a lady's fan.

"Please no, Lord, please no. Let no one have heard," Timóteo whispered. He scuttled forward on hands and knees to gather the fallen papers. His hands trembled so that as he picked up each page, it rattled like a palm leaf in the wind.

The pages were out of order as he gathered them, and Timóteo tried to discipline his mind enough to put them back in proper sequence. They were not numbered and each page was filled with writing top to bottom, front to back. Timóteo had to scan the beginnings and endings of each to know which came after which.

At first, all he read were dry accounts of repetitious questions concerning relatives, church attendance, and the daily tasks of governing. Then he found the record of Coutinho's confession . . . and he stopped. Here were written names Timóteo had seen in his grandfather's books and *Os Lusiados*, people and creatures from a golden past, shrouded behind mists from Mount Olympus. The Governor had seen proof, he confessed, that the pagan tales of ancient times were true. A certain tale in particular.

Entranced, Timóteo reached out for the next page . . . and saw it lay beneath a soft leather boot and the hem of a black robe. Slowly, he looked up into the face of Inquisitor Sadrinho. *Ai, I will tell no more lies, Lord. Smite me now.*

His face impassive, Sadrinho said, "This is poor light for reading in, my son. And a poor place." He knelt down and gently took the pages from Timóteo's hands. He glanced at the paper a moment, then gathered up the others on the floor, replacing them within the leather binding. Without another word, Sadrinho stood, tucked the book under his arm, and turned to walk away.

"Forgive me, Domine," said Timóteo, still prone on the floor.

"Speak no more of it," the Inquisitor said mildly. "Pray tell Brother Pedro in the kitchens that I will have the saffron rice for my breakfast."

Timóteo watched him leave, waiting for the explosion of temper that must surely come. But there was none. This calm he found more terrifying than any lash of the bamboo switch. Timóteo gazed down at the arabesques on the tiles, not daring to rise, too shaken to cry.

Padre Gonsção stepped out of the Cathedral of Santa Catarina, his spirit refreshed by the morning services. The sunlight was bright, the air clear and brittle as glass. The day would be hot again, and the night as well. The plaza was already full of richly dressed men, shaded by parasols carried by slaves, as though a garden of gaily colored, mobile mushrooms had sprouted in the damp overnight.

In the distance, trumpets and shawms brashly announced a wedding or christening or other family upheaval. The breezes brought scents of pepper and cinnamon, fish and rancid meat.

Archbishop de Menezes came up beside Gonsção. The Padre noted that the Archbishop wore only a plain Benedictine robe, and had only one attendant who silently stood behind him. "A pleasant morning, is it not?" said de Menezes.

"Pleasant, Your Excellency?" said Gonsção, ruffling his white wool robe. "We will roast again like pigs today."

The Archbishop shook an avuncular finger. "You have not seen Goa in the blast of the monsoon, my son. The storms blow in great waves from the sea. The gales rip the fronds from the palms and tiles from the roofs. The rain pelts down like a shower of nails. Here in Goa, God is at his most dramatic."

A purple silk palanquin, carried by eight slaves, stopped alongside the steps of the cathedral. The cloth curtain was pulled aside and a lovely *mestiço* woman, chewing on a betel cake, eyed Gonsção suggestively. Gonsção scowled at her and turned away. The woman laughed and ordered her bearers to move on.

"Perhaps in Goa," muttered Gonsção, "God has greater need of dramatics."

"You may have a point," said the Archbishop. "This is no haven of saints. That is why I often dress as I am, in simple habit, so as not to attract undue attention. And I do not advise strolling about alone after dark. Yet, Goa has its beauty and its wonders. Would you like me to show you some of the city? As you may have heard, the miraculously preserved corpus of Francis Xavier may be viewed in the Church of Saint Paul. Pilgrims from all of Asia, Cathay, and even the Isles of Nippon may be seen paying homage there."

"You honor me, Excellency," said Gonsção, stepping down into the plaza. "But I am sure you have more important things to attend to. As do I."

"As you wish." Following, his voice low, de Menezes said, "Concerning your request for assistance, my son, I fear

there is little aid I can give you. I have approached Governador da Gama, but he and his ministers wish no contention
with the Santa Casa and will not speak against it. You must
understand, Sadrinho has *familiares* everywhere."

"I understand, Excellency."

"Meanwhile, I have heard that the English ships that so
bedeviled Captain Ortiz have been seen—they are harbor-
ing to the south, repairing damage as you surmised."

"Then we may have another piece of the puzzle after all.
I am expecting to see the record of Coutinho's confession
soon."

The Archbishop raised his brows. "Under the nose of
Sadrinho? The Grand Inquisitor chose wisely, indeed. You
are clearly a resourceful man, Padre."

"I am unworthy of your flattery, Excellency. My methods were not the most honorable." Gonsção noticed a group
of laughing soldiers clustered around the fountain at the center of the plaza. They were passing back and forth a small
earthenware pot which had many spouts, attempting to drink
from it. "What are those men doing?"

"Mm? Oh, it is a game, a sort of initiation among the *soldados.* The pot is called a *gorgoleta*, and one must be able to
drink wine from it without spilling any. A difficult task, as you
can see."

"How odd. I never saw such a thing in Lisboa."

The Archbishop shrugged. "Who can say where these
new customs come from? You are certain you will not see
more of our fair colony? We could visit the old castle in
Bardes, or take a ride in the countryside. I am told the ores
are so rich in Goa's hills, they have drawn alchemists from
the world over, determined to wrest gold and copper from
them."

"Not today, Excellency. But I thank you." *This mixing of
races, nationalities, languages, customs,* thought Gonsção, *it is a*

cacophony to the spirit. Goa is to civilization what the shrieks and babble of children are to music.

"Should you reconsider, feel free to seek me out. It is always a pleasure to speak with someone so recently from home. May God guide you in your work, my son."

"God give you good day, Excellency."

The Archbishop and his attendant strolled away, soon disappearing amid the bright-colored garments, parasols, and palanquins that filled the Praça do Catedral.

Gonsção sighed and turned toward the Santa Casa, hoping that Brother Timóteo would bring him something less trying to his eyes and less troubling to his spirit.

X

DATURA: This plant grows in the East and is also called
Thorn Apple or Devil's Apple. It bears leaves of an egg
shape which smell foul, and summer blossoms of a pale blue.
The juice of this plant will cause stupor and visions. It must
be used with great care, for too much is poisonous. In India,
it is used by thieves on those they would rob, by wives on
husbands they would cuckold, and princes on one another,
for it makes one act a very fool....

Thomas was rocked as if in a cradle, a cradle that smelled
of fish and old wood and the sea. An angel in the back of
his mind told him that he was hurt and had been drugged, and
that he should be afraid. But his thoughts would not cohere
enough to wonder where he was or what drug it might be.

He'd been this way before. Long ago, in childhood,
Thomas dreamily recalled a table covered with white cloth.
In a similar woozy, uncaring state, he had been carried in his
father's arms and placed upon a table. There had been the
taste of sweet wine and the smell of burning barleycorn.
There had been a pretty lady standing nearby, wearing only
a draped sheet. Two tall, slender hunting dogs had stood beside her.

The angel in Thomas's mind was upset. "This was not just," it said. "This should not have been done to you."

Thomas rolled his head and shut his eyes. He heard a distant rumbling, like thunder. Moments passed and the rumbling became the hoofbeats of horses. Three, he knew. It was always three.

Suddenly he was running through the forest, sunlight knifing through the trees, stabbing his eyes. His small, cloven hoofs barely touched the earth between each bound. He dared a glance behind at his pursuing tormentors; three women on horseback, their cloaks fanned out behind like wings. He could not see their faces. They shrieked at him with the shrill cries of falcons: "Murderer! Murderer!"

He faced ahead again and ran straight into the low branches of a yew tree. His antlers were caught in the boughs and he could not shake them free. The howling hunters at his back came closer and closer. He heard a whistling, and something smote him between the shoulderblades.

He gasped and opened his eyes. *Another nightmare!* Disoriented, Thomas turned his head. The shaking bamboo lattice walls around him were not what he expected to see. Wherever he was, it was no longer the Arab dhow.

Bamboo slats interwoven with palm fronds formed a roof not far overhead. He lay on hard wood planks. The floor rumbled and bumped and wobbled, jarring him against the wood. *I am in a moving cart of some nature.*

Carefully, he lifted his head and shoulders and tried to twist into a sitting position. He could not feel his arms and hands for some moments, then sucked in his breath. Intense tingling told him his hands had been tied behind his back and only now was his blood rushing to regain the territory that his weight had denied it.

"So, young lion, you are awake." The sorcerer De Cartago lay beside him, curled up on his side, his arms also bound.

His pale face wore several large purple bruises.

Dear God. Do I look as bad as he? What have they done to us?

"From the sounds you were making," De Cartago went on, "I would wager you were having unpleasant dreams."

"I am often beset by nightmares," said Thomas, surprised at the raspiness of his throat, as if it had been unused for a long time. "I have been since childhood."

"I am sure the datura did not help matters."

"Datura?" Thomas felt a growing itch on his buttocks and thighs. To his shame, he realized he had soiled himself—but not recently. He remembered nothing after being struck by Lockheart. "How long have we been sleeping?"

"I have been no more aware of the passage of time than you. Days, I would think."

"Days! We are fortunate to have survived."

"Perhaps. I expect they have fed us now and then, though I have no memory of it."

"Nor I. What is this datura?"

"Ever the seeker of knowledge, eh, *apothekos?* It is a common drug in Goa, used for deadening pain, or making one oblivious to the world around one. Perhaps you should seek it out and add it to your stores."

Thomas turned his head and peered through the bamboo wall beside him. He could see nothing but bright light and emerald shadow. "I wish I knew where we were."

"Their plan was to take us to Goa, herbalist. We must be near, from the stink of it. Near Goa, the Mandovi River is very wide and has a particular smell."

Thomas took a deep breath. It was hard to make out scents beyond his own sweat and offal, but he discerned dust, animal manure, rotting fruit, and the sea. Men walking ahead and behind the cart spoke in a language he could not identify, though some of it might have been Arabic.

"Who are these men who have us captive?"

"Pirates and thieves from Oman. We will not be in their gentle care much longer. Only until our ransom is paid."

"Is Lockheart still among them? Is he truly so low a man as to sell me to the Portuguese?"

"Who can judge a man's heart? I am sure mine was the only ransom he and Aditi wanted. You were an unexpected addition."

"But why—" Thomas suddenly shut his mouth, fearing what he was going to say was unkind, as if De Cartago deserved to be a prisoner and he did not.

"Why has he not freed you? I have no answer."

"Do you know who will ransom us?"

"You are probably only of interest to the *governador*, and he will likely send you to labor on one of King Philip's galleys. Perhaps the very one that you fired upon at my rescue. That would be justice, no? As for me, I will be sent to the place that demons guard in the guise of saints."

"Will the Lady Aditi not help you?"

De Cartago coughed. "She has given me a means of escape. Apothecary Chinnery, I have no right to demand a favor of you, and yet there is something I would ask."

"I am in little position to give aid, *Magister*."

"More than you know. My hands are bound and useless and I should like to borrow yours."

"My hands are bound also, *Magister*."

"But they may reach where mine cannot. Around my neck is an amulet bag filled with the same powder you used to revive your crewmate."

Thomas felt cold. "Indeed?"

"I have been injured and I would have ease. In Goa, the injury I face will be far worse. If you please, administer the powder to me, that I may rest."

"*Magister*, I would prefer not to use that substance again."

"Whatever damage you imagine it would do to your soul, it has already done. And you used it on one who was dead, while I am still living."

So much of my life has been devoted to the ease of suffering. What right have I to deny aid to this man? Let judgment belong to God. "Very well, *Magister*. With a condition . . . that you tell me the source of the powder."

The sorcerer raised his brows. "Ha. You are persistent, young lion. Remember, I have taken a vow not to name the source and no threat you can make will cause me to break it. However, I will give you clues on how to find it, if that will content you. If you have the courage, and Fortune is with you, you may seek out the truth for yourself."

"Very well. That is acceptable." *And if the source is not a danger to the soul, perhaps a profit may be gained from this unfortunate voyage after all. Assuming I survive.*

"Search the piping of my doublet, there on the bottom left hem. You will find a place more solid than the rest. There is a piece of paper rolled up within. Hurry, while we still have time."

Thomas turned and, looking over his shoulder, ran his bound hands along the edge of the sorcerer's black velvet doublet. He found the place described and teased out, through a cut in the piping, a small roll of parchment.

"It is a map," said De Cartago. "Do not look at it now. The dot at the leftmost edge is Goa, the one to the right and above it is Bijapur. The rightmost and lowermost dot is the hidden city where the source is. The Hindus call the powder *Rasa Mahadevi*. That is all I may tell you."

"Goa. Bijapur. *Rasa Mahadevi*. Thank you, *Magister*," said Thomas. Leaning forward, he pushed the roll into the top of his boot. He then walked back on his knees until his hands were near the sorcerer's neck. Clumsily, he felt around the collar, glad De Cartago was no longer wearing a ruff. At last, he found the thong for the amulet bag and tugged it out. He carefully worked the closing strings open.

Thomas paused to rest his aching hands and glanced over his shoulder at De Cartago. "Are you ready?"

"May your God bless and keep you, my friend," said the sorcerer. "I am." He leaned his head forward and opened his mouth, as though a worshiper waiting to receive the Eucharist.

Thomas shuffled back a little more until his hands could touch De Cartago's bearded face. His fingers found the sorcerer's open mouth and Thomas tilted the amulet bag into it, feeling the powder slide past his fingers. *I am the Resurrection and the Life. . . .*

De Cartago's mouth closed and Thomas let go of the bag. He moved around to face the sorcerer and watch the effect the powder would have.

De Cartago had closed his eyes and let his head fall back. In moments, his face relaxed, a slight smile on his lips. His breathing slowed and became even. All tension seemed to flow out of the man's limbs.

A potent medicine indeed. I must remember the amount the bag contained so that the same effect might be achieved again with a similar dosage. If its use be not a sin, what wealth this powder might bring to Master Coulter's shop. Mayhap more than we might have gained in Cathay.

Suddenly, the cart lurched to a halt and men walked up to it, shouting at one another. The back swung open and bright sunlight flooded in. Two swarthy men reached in, grabbing Thomas's arms. He allowed them to pull him out of the cart without resistance. He tried to stand as his feet hit the road, but his legs gave out beneath him.

His captors picked him up and let him lean against the cart. As they reached into the cart again for De Cartago, there came more shouting, and a woman's scream from the carts farther up the road. Men were leaping from the backs of the oxen and running forward, swords and knives drawn. Men on muleback galloped forward, kicking up clouds of dust. Thomas's captors also drew their weapons, and shouting an incomprehensible warning to Thomas, they left him to join their fellows up the road.

There was no one watching from the cart behind. It took a moment for Thomas to comprehend his luck.

"*Magister*, we have a chance to escape!" he whispered loud into the cart. "*Senhor!*" But the sorcerer lay unmoving. Thomas bumped the cart hard with his hip, but De Cartago did not awaken.

Knowing he had but moments, Thomas regretfully left De Cartago to his fate, and stumbled off the road into the underbrush of the palm forest. He fell against tree trunks and tripped over roots, his balance upset by his bound hands. The ground was in spots marsh-muddy and sucked at his boots. Palmetto fronds slashed at his clothing and skin. Yet he got up again and again and pressed on.

At last, he stumbled and was too out of breath to rise. He lay in a muddy ravine, overgrown by plants with large leaves of a dark green. He rolled onto his back and gasped in the moist, heavy air. He heard the cries of unknown birds, but no shouts of men. *It would seem I have made good my escape. But what shall I do now?*

Thomas sat up, and moaned, his whole body aching. He pulled at his bonds and found his hands nearly slid out of the rope. *The mud!* Thomas lay back and rolled his wrists in the mud some more and sat up again. This time, with effort and a little pain, he worked his hands free. With a great sigh of relief, he swung his arms back and forth. They felt light with their freedom.

He looked at his earth-stained hands. Thomas thought a

moment, then removed his doublet and shirt. He smeared the mud everywhere he could reach, and rolled in the ravine for the rest. He ran mud through his fair hair. For good measure, he rolled up his shirt and tied it into a sort of turban for his head.

There was nothing he could do for his blue eyes, but if Lady Aditi were any example, he thought he could not be that unusual. His slops were not unlike those worn by Arab sailors. But his boots . . . ah, the boots.

They were of russet leather, a gift from Master Coulter. Not so tall as the most fashionable in London, but still the finest that Thomas had ever owned. But they marked him as a European. With a heavy sigh, Thomas pulled them off, noting the rolled-up parchment that fell out.

De Cartago's map. May as well keep it. God willing, it may prove of use. Thomas slipped it into the drawstring hem of his slops.

A faint, metallic jingling caught his ears and he froze. *Do they search for me?* But the noise was not of men stalking through the jungle. It had a feminine sound. Thomas peered through the leaves at the edge of the ravine, and caught a glimpse of scarlet and gold, striding past him some yards away.

The Lady Aditi! Has she abandoned the caravan? She seems not to be searching, but aims for a known destination.

Again aware of a momentary opportunity to be seized, Thomas dropped the boots and followed her.

XI

ALMOND: This small tree bears edible nuts and blooms early in the year. It has long been thought a tree of hope, for it reminds one of the coming of spring. To the Greeks, it was an emblem of loyalty and constancy. It is thought sacred to the Virgin, and in the Bible appears as a sign of God's approval and forgiveness. In Tuscany, almond boughs are used for divining. Paste made from fruit of the almond will sustain one where there is no food or water to be found....

Padre Gonsção strolled through the walled gardens of the residence wing. It reminded him of the patios of the fine villas and monasteries in Portugal. But there were banyan trees among the cypress, cardamom bushes amongst the carnations, coconut palms amidst the orange trees, lotus amongst the lilies. Gonsção found a sprig of rosemary and crushed it between his fingers, inhaling its fragrance. He missed Lisboa very much.

There was a stone bench beneath a huge, hideous banyan tree, and Gonsção sat there, appreciating the shade, if not the shade giver. He heard rustling from a nearby stand of bamboo. Someone was peeking out at him.

"Timóteo?" Gonsção beckoned to the boy.

"Padre." Timóteo shyly came to the bench.

"I have not seen you for days, my son. No one I asked knew where you were."

"I have been at chapel, Padre. Praying. And fasting."

"But why?"

"I have wronged someone, Padre. But I am confused, and I do not know whom I have wronged."

"Sit, Timóteo. Tell me. Perhaps I can help you."

The boy sat and began to speak softly and rapidly. "The day after we talked, Padre, Domine Pinto told me where to find the records of Governador Coutinho's trial. It was in the kitchens. It was going to be burned."

Breathless with hope, Gonsção said, "Did you rescue it?"

"I did, Padre. But, as I was trying to bring it to you, I tripped in the hall. So stupid, I tripped. And the book fell all over. I was picking it up again and . . . and Domine Sadrinho saw me."

Gonsção's hope died instantly. "What misfortune! What did the Domine say to you? Was it he who punished you with prayers and fasting?"

"No. That is the strange thing, Padre. He said nothing. He picked up the book and walked away. I have been so afraid, I have hid myself, and prayed for my sin to be forgiven. But I still do not know which is my sin. I failed in helping you and the Archbishop and the Pope, but I feel I have also wronged Domine Sadrinho."

Gonsção sighed and patted the boy's shoulder. "I believe you are without blame, Timóteo. You did what you thought was best. Do not punish yourself."

"It is my fault you did not get the book, Padre. If I had not stopped to read the pages, I would have cleaned it up before the Domine saw me."

"You . . . *read* the ledger?"

Timóteo nodded. "I could not help it. Forgive me, Padre."

"Praise be to God," Gonsção whispered and he grasped both the boy's shoulders. "Listen, my son. This is very important. You are forgiven, believe me. But do you *remember* any of what you saw?"

The boy nodded again. "I cannot forget it, Padre."

"Please. Tell me. Did you see a list of *familiares?*"

"No, Padre."

"Did you see the governor's confession?"

"Yes. He said he was tricked by sorcerers who showed him proof that the pagans of Greece were right!"

"Greece?"

"Yes, Padre, the Olympians. He said so."

Gonsção wondered if the boy's childhood interests were infecting his mind. "What proof was this?"

"A powder, Padre. Powdered blood that he said brings the dead back to life! He said it was the blood of a goddess, but I saw the name and he was wrong."

"Of course he was wrong."

"She is not a goddess, Padre, she is a monster!" Suddenly, Timóteo looked past Gonsção's shoulder. "The Domine. Forgive me. I must go." The boy jumped to his feet and dashed back through the stand of bamboo.

With a frustrated sigh, Gonsção turned. Indeed, Domine Sadrinho was approaching down the main path. The Inquisitor did not seem to see him. As Sadrinho was about to pass by, Gonsção called out, "Good morning, Domine. God be with you."

The Inquisitor looked up startled, then smiled. "And with your spirit, Padre. Good morning. I was told I might find you in our gardens. You have even chosen an auspicious place to sit."

"I have?" He turned and looked at the ugly tree beside him.

"That is a form of fig tree. I am told one like it was the tree under which the philosopher Siddhartha gained wisdom."

Gonsção frowned. "Is that a Hindu philosopher? What have you to do with such knowledge?"

"You are close, Padre. He was the founder of Buddhism. In this land, one finds oneself learning all manner of things. A foreigner like you would not be expected to know. But enough of esoteric rambling. I have what may be good news."

"Indeed?"

"Yes. The sorcerer Bernardo De Cartago has been captured and is now in Goa. It is rumored the mysterious Aditi may be with him."

"Excellent news, indeed, Domine. How was this done?"

"A group of *muçulmano* pirates found the bounty we offered attractive and knew where to find the English ships. As God willed it, one of the Englishmen was mercenary enough to deliver the sorcerer and the witch himself."

"Truly, Our Lord aids us in unforeseen ways. I trust we will be able to question them soon, then?"

"I expect so. I have sent a brother with some *soldados* to intercept the caravan. They should be returning shortly."

"Good. There will be a tribunal this afternoon—" Gonsção stopped as a flushed young Dominican, his white robe dusty, hurried toward them.

"Ah, the deputation returns," said Sadrinho. "Greetings, Brother Marco. I was just telling Padre Antonio our good news. We have the captives safely, I trust?"

The young man was agitated and would not meet their gaze. "Padre. Domine, there has been . . . an unfortunate occurrence." Sadrinho's face lost all expression. "Unfortunate occurrence?"

"I, that is, the man we were to . . . to bring—"

"Breathe calmly, Brother," said Gonsção. "Tell us as simply as you can what has happened."

"And I do not wish to hear," said Sadrinho, "that this sorcerer has conjured up an English fleet out of the dust to spirit him away."

"No, Domine. I went with the *soldados* out to the Panaji road, as you instructed. We found there the *muçulmano* caravan. But when we went to claim the sorcerer, we were told he was dead, and that another Englishman and the witch had vanished."

"Dead," said Sadrinho. "Did you confirm this?"

"Yes, Domine. We examined the body. It was the man you described."

Sadrinho struck his hand with his fist and uttered some indiscreet blasphemies.

"It would seem," Gonsção said with a sigh, "that our sorcerer has spirited himself away in a most final manner."

"I do not think," Sadrinho said slowly, "that we should jest about a soul now lost to Hell."

I do not think, Gonsção thought, *that is why you are angry.* "Forgive me, Domine. A thoughtless remark. Tell me, Brother, was it discernible how the sorcerer died?"

"No, Padre. We found no fatal wound on him, though he was somewhat bruised. There was some blood around the mouth. He had soiled himself, but the *muçulmanos* said he had been drugged with datura and that is a natural consequence."

"Is it possible he died of disease?" said Gonsção.

"I suppose so," said the young Dominican. "Though we saw no obvious signs of pox or cholera upon him."

"A most convenient disease," growled Sadrinho. "He chooses the moment before we claim him to die."

"We cannot know at what moment he died," said Gonsção.

"But the Domine may be right," said Brother Marco. "The *muçulmanos* said they heard him talking to the other man in his cart nearly until they opened it."

"Other man?" said Sadrinho.

"Yes. An Englishman was in the cart with De Cartago."

"The same Englishman who arranged his delivery?"

"I think not, Domine."

"And is this Englishman dead also?"

"No, Domine, but he has escaped. Apparently there was an altercation. The traders who were bringing the captives believed they were being set upon by a rival group of sea raiders, just outside the city. There was much confusion. The Englishman and the witch chose that moment to flee."

Sadrinho growled, "It is what I deserve for trusting heretics. This was your idea, as I recall, Padre."

"I apologize," said Gonsção, "if my plan had flaws, but still all is not yet lost. Do we know what the Englishman looked like?"

"The *muçulmanos* said he was young, tall, and light-haired."

"If he is not skilled in local ways and tongues, it will not be easy for him to find refuge in Goa. If he is still in the area, we may yet uncover him."

The young Dominican nodded. "I know a few places where he might seek sanctuary. The *soldados* are already searching the city."

"Very well," said Sadrinho. "Go and assist them. And do not return until you have better news."

"Yes, Domine." The young Dominican bowed and ran back out of the garden.

"Padre, forgive my slow wit, but why should we bother searching for the man who was captive with De Cartago? Foreigners in Goa are a civil matter and usually not our concern. What good is he to us?"

"Consider, Domine . . . an Englishman is held prisoner to be ransomed by another of his country. What possible ransom could be gained unless the young man knew something? Perhaps this fair-haired one is also in De Cartago's cabal, perhaps a recent convert. Perhaps the sorcerer confessed something to him on his deathbed. It is a poor hope, I grant you, but it is our best chance to recover something out of this misfortune."

Sadrinho gave him an appraising stare. "You may be right, Padre. I see Grand Inquisitor Albrecht had his reasons for sending you to us. You are like a good hunting hound: once you have your teeth on a matter, you are hard to shake loose. I shall keep you informed if I hear of anything." With a slight bow, he turned to go.

"One more thing, Domine. Concerning Brother Timóteo . . ."

Sadrinho became very still. "Yes?"

"You were right to trust him with the task of advocate. I find him to be a boy of excellent qualities. You may be assured that I will speak well of him, and your training of him, to the Grand Inquisitor on my return to Lisboa."

"I . . . am gratified, Padre."

"Yet, I saw him briefly this morning, and he seemed most agitated about something. He would not tell me what it was. I did my best to reassure the boy, for I am sure whatever was preying on his mind, he was not at fault."

Sadrinho gazed back over his shoulder, his expression unreadable. "Of course not. He excels at obedience, and always does what he is told to do. By anyone. How could I blame him for anything? Good day, Padre."

XII

🌿 BELLADONNA: This plant brings forth bell-shaped flow ers of a russet or purple hue in summer, and black berries thereafter. It is also called nightshade, or the Devil's Cherries. Its fruit and pale root hath many medicinal uses to soothe the rheumatics, colics, and fevers. Yet in too great an amount, it is a deadly poison. To the ancients, the berries were said to be used by the goddesses of Fate to cut off the lives of mortals. In the language of the Italies, its name means "beautiful lady." It is not known whether it is named thus for its use to pretty the eye among young women, or because it hath been used in poisoning them....

The gold and scarlet figure swayed, glimmered, disappeared and reappeared amidst the foliage ahead of Thomas. *'Tis though she is a woman-shaped will-o'-the-wisp of the Hindu marshes.* He hoped his thought was but an idle comparison. There were those who said marsh lights were lost souls, leading men to their doom. But the Lady Aditi seemed to know where the dry pathways lay, and Thomas's now-bare feet were grateful.

In time, they came to an ancient ruin of a city wall, covered with vines and perhaps fifteen feet in height. There was a breach through which the Lady Aditi easily passed. Thomas followed with little difficulty. *'Tis a wonder she has not seen or heard me. Surely I have been crashing through the brush like a wild boar to keep up with her.*

On the other side of the wall was an open-air bazaar. Constant distraction threatened Thomas as he passed great brass bowls full of cinnamon, pepper, ginger, cardamom; spices that would make a man's fortune in Europe. He passed blankets covered with fruits he had never seen before, and his stomach reminded him he had not eaten in quite a while. The Lady Aditi led him past a trader of elegant, slender-necked horses, a merchant selling incense, aromatic gum and wood, a woman displaying flowers of crimson, fuchsia, and white, a rack of jewelry of gold, silver, and copper. Every sense threatened to be overwhelmed, seduced, yet Thomas had to keep his attention focused on the Lady Aditi's moving form.

The crowd in the bazaar seemed to cooperate in his endeavor. No one gave him much regard, yet they instinctively parted out of his way, never jostling or hindering him. *My disguise must serve me well—I am hardly given a second glance.*

At the far end of the bazaar, the Lady Aditi approached a low, windowless thatched house. Two wiry men in *dhotis* sat on a bench just beside the house's cloth-covered doorway. Aditi bowed to them and the men leapt up, clearly surprised and pleased to see her. After some animated conversation, Aditi bowed again and entered the doorway.

So. What now, fool? Thomas had no reason to expect active assistance from the woman who had betrayed De Cartago. *Yet he said that she did so in service to a higher cause. A cause that has naught to do with me. That I know of.* He looked out over the bazaar, listening to the unintelligible foreign tongues. The colors of the canopies wavered and he felt a wave of hunger and weariness. *If I seek out shelter on my own, I may collapse on the street, prey to any stranger. Better I try the stranger I have some acquaintance with.*

Thomas went up to the doorway. The two men who had greeted Aditi were again chatting on the bench, and did not notice him. Thomas cleared his throat, but it did not seem to distract them from their conversation. He went right up to them and bowed as the lady had, palms together before his face, as if praying. "*Rasa Mahadevi,*" he said, as they were the only Hindu words he knew. "Aditi." He pointed at the doorway. "*Rasa Mahadevi.*"

The guardsmen frowned and glanced at him sidelong, as if not wishing to see him. One stood and pulled the curtain aside and called into the house, "Sri Aditi!" He then spoke words Thomas did not understand.

The curtain was sharply pulled open and the Lady Aditi reappeared in the doorway. "You," she said in Greek. "The false alchemist. Why do you continue to follow me?"

"Forgive me, Despoina, but I am a stranger here. I have nowhere to go. I need your help."

"My help! It is not enough I have shown you the way into the city? Why should I help you further?"

Thomas hadn't considered how he would garner her aid, hoping that feminine pity would suffice. But now a ruse sprang to mind as a slender thread to salvation. "Because we are seekers on the same path, Despoina."

"Ha. You know nothing of my path."

"I shared the kidnappers' cart with Despos De Cartago. We were awake more than was intended and we spoke a great deal. I learned much from him."

Aditi's gaze burned like blue fire. "Bernardo would never have broken his vow."

"He broke no vows, Despoina. But he felt I was worthy to begin the philosopher's journey. If I proved myself, I would find the source of the *Rasa Mahadevi*. What he told me was an inspiration to seek the path of truth. On that path, only you can lead me."

"Tcha." She tossed her head, yet gave him a look he recognized from visitors to Coulter's shop; someone who wants to buy, but needs convincing.

"With what I learn, I could return home to England and spread word of your goddess, whose name is strength, in my own land. Please, Despoina. Let me come inside and rest, and talk with you further."

"You cannot come in." She spoke harshly to the men at the door and stalked back into the house, flinging the door curtain closed behind her.

Well. 'Twas worth the try. The men at the door pulled curved knives from their *dhotis* and gestured contemptuously at him, waving him aside. With a sigh, he stepped away, wondering what he would do now. Their shouts brought him out of his impending gloom, and their gestures indicated he was to enter a gate in the low wall beside the house.

One of the men held the gate open for Thomas and shut it after he entered. Thomas found himself in what might have been a very miskept garden, except the smell informed him it was more likely a slop yard.

A wooden door at the side of the house opened, and a small girl in a brown sari emerged, carrying a wooden tray. On the tray were a plain wooden cup containing a white liquid, and a bowl with some rice mixed with chunks of yellow fruit. She placed this on the ground a few feet from Thomas and returned into the house, never looking at him.

Hunger overtook his sense of propriety and Thomas sat on the ground, scooping the rice and fruit into his mouth as fast as he could. He sipped from the cup and found it to be fermented coconut milk. In his parched, ravenous state, it tasted marvelous. "Pure nectar," he murmured.

"It is called *feni,*" Aditi said from the doorway.

"My Lady," Thomas sputtered. "I thank you. I thought

you had turned me away." He raised the cup to her before drinking again.

"I would, if I were more wise. You are a bad omen, Tamas. Why didn't you follow your friend? You are his *dharma*, not mine."

"You mean Lockheart? I did not see him. I only saw you, and therefore followed."

She shook her head and clicked her tongue. "You are filthy."

"Ah. The mud. I wished to disguise myself. It would seem to have worked, for no one took much notice of me."

"That is because you look like a *Mala*—one of the lowest castes of people, suitable only for carrying away filth and dead things. No one would touch you. But there is one aspect that gives you away."

"My eyes?"

"A true *Mala* has more dignity."

"You are unkind. Where is that tenderness of heart that is the glory of your sex?"

She smiled darkly. "You know little of women."

A cloud passed over Thomas's heart. The only woman he had had much chance to observe was Anna Coulter and she was nothing like this Hindu witch. Anna was sweet, demure, obedient, and kind; she had none of the arrogance of this creature. And, truth be told, had not the grace of movement nor handsomeness of face of the Lady Aditi either.

"You are ignorant of how to tie a turban as well," she went on. "A man's turban shows his family and his caste. Here—" She came close to Thomas and bent over him. Without touching him, she deftly snatched the shirt from his head.

With her so near, Thomas could smell her sweat mixed with the scent of patchouli. He could see her form through the diaphanous sari, the swell of her breasts. His blood pounded loud in his ears. Head swimming from the *feni*, it was all he could do not to reach out and take hold of her.

She set the rewrapped shirt on his head and stepped back. "There. Now you are only half an imbecile."

"Thank you," Thomas said with a heavy sigh. *Lord, why are we poor mortals tempted so?* He tried to think of Anna, but found her face was hard to recall.

"So. What did Bernardo reveal to you?" said the Lady Aditi.

"Enough. He told me how your goddess was wise and powerful." *God forgive me, but I must assure her.* "He told me the name of the powder was *Rasa Mahadevi*. He told me its source was in a place east and south of Bijapur."

She paused, biting her lip. "That is a long and dangerous pilgrimage."

"I have already come a long way, Despoina."

"Yes, but seeking wealth. The reward you receive at the end of this path may be less pleasant. How was Bernardo when you last saw him? Did he escape as well?"

"No. He was resting peacefully when our chance came, and I could not wake him. I had administered the *Rasa Mahadevi* to him from a bag he had carried round his neck. It eased his pain most marvelously. It is indeed a most powerful medicine, Despoina. I wonder that you admonished me not to use it so."

Her gaze was unreadable. "I do not doubt my judgment. But at least Bernardo rests peacefully."

"I suppose, if the caravan has fallen apart, and Lockheart fled, he need not fear meeting his ransomers now."

"No. He need not fear."

"Do you know where I might find Lockheart? Where he may have gone?"

"No. I would not trust him, were I you. He is a strange man; demons pull his spirit many ways. He fears his *dharma* and tries to run from it."

Thomas's feelings regarding the Scotsman were pulled many ways as well. *He tried to spare me by sending me ashore, yet he would have ransomed me to the Portuguese. He could have killed me, yet he did not. He befriended me upon the voyage, for no discerned reason.* "Yes, he is a strange man, Despoina." Thomas finished the last of his rice.

Softly, Aditi said, "The path you seek is treacherous and deadly. In Goa, we are hounded by the priests of the Orlem Gor, the Holy House of the Portuguese. It would be no kindness to let you stay with me, for I would only bring you into danger. And you would be a danger to me. You must undertake your journey on your own. But I will do this much for you; there is a man in Goa, a monk, who helps those of your land. He is known as Padre Stevens. After you have rested a while, I will guide you to him. That is all I can do."

Thomas bowed in Hindu fashion. "That will be great help indeed, Despoina. I thank you."

Aditi turned and called in through the doorway. The girl in the brown sari reappeared, carrying some rolled-up calico. She spread this on the ground before the door and went back inside.

"Here is your bed," said Aditi. "Though I will be thought profligate for they must destroy the cloth after you lie on it. Normally, *Mala* sleep on the dirt." She bowed to Thomas and reentered the house, closing the door behind her.

Groaning, Thomas crawled toward the cloth and lay down. It was pleasant just to be on a surface that was not moving, his arms free. He closed his eyes.

And opened them what seemed only moments later. The girl in the brown sari was poking him with a stick. As soon as he looked at her, she dropped the stick and ran inside. The palm fronds overhead were gilded with the light of a late-afternoon sun.

Hours must have passed. Have I slept so long?

The Lady Aditi came out, idly brushing her long, dark hair. She wore a blue sari, now, and several gold bracelets on her wrists. On one upper arm, she wore a silver bracelet in the shape of a serpent biting its tail. "How do you feel, herbalist?"

Thomas stood, still aching but rested. "Better, Despoina."

"Good. Then let us go swiftly. I have learned where Father Stevens may be found at this time of day. I have arranged for some men to carry me by there in a *dholi*. I will drop something as we pass the monk, so you will know."

"Very well. Again, I thank you."

"May your journey be successful, Tamas. May the Goddess receive you kindly." She left, closing the door behind her. Thomas heard noise outside the gate and it swung open. One of the men waved his long knife at Thomas. *"Choli, choli, choli!"* he cried.

Passing through the gate, he saw the Lady Aditi seat herself in a covered litter. Two men picked up the poles, one in front, one behind. They began to run and Thomas found himself hard-pressed to keep up.

Again, the streets of Goa provided constant distraction: a jumble of East and West, inhabited by all manner of men from Europe, Africa, Arabia, and Asia. The houses became two-story and roofed with colorful tiles. Rotund men of wealth sat on the balconies, fanning themselves. Slaves and servants hurried past, carrying waterpots, or baskets, or leading laden donkeys. Women dressed in European gowns of fine damask or velvet walked freely, accompanied by maids-in-waiting. Muslim women passed like ghosts in long, cream-colored gowns that showed nothing but hands and feet. Hindu girls with bare midriffs and diaphanous skirts, and large gold hoops through their noses, passed him laughing and singing. All was a concatenation of colors, costume, scent, and sound. But it seemed the mixing produced a greater intensity, just as grinding garlic and ginger together created a more powerful medicine than either would be alone.

Just barely could Thomas keep his attention on the bouncing litter ahead of him, waiting for the Lady Aditi's signal.

At last, her slender arm appeared outside the litter and a dark object fell from her hand. Puffing, Thomas stopped where it lay, watching the litter disappear into the crowd. He felt a pang of regret that he might never see the Lady Aditi again, nor truly learn who she was.

Thomas found he was on a quiet side street, with a small park to his left. Under an enormous fig tree, a grey-haired Jesuit sat, talking with a richly dressed Hindu. *How strange the manner in which events in the world sort out . . . that now my life should depend upon a papist monk. I trust Parson Hoopes back home would forgive me.*

As Thomas approached, the Hindu took subtle notice of him and averted his gaze.

Thomas stopped some feet away and called out in a loud whisper, "Father Stevens?"

The monk looked up with some surprise and excused himself to the Hindu. He stood and came over to Thomas.

"Father Stevens, I am English, and a stranger here. I am told you might help me."

The monk softly shushed him and said, "Kneel as though I were giving you blessing, my son."

Thomas knelt and the monk laid a hand on his shoulder. "Father, I am dressed as a low-caste. Perhaps you should not be touching me."

Father Stevens smiled. "I am dressed as a Jesuit, my son, and we touch anyone. Tell me, have you but late come from two ships that were stranded to the south?"

Astonished, Thomas said, "Yes, Father, I have."

"And did you come to Goa as a prisoner of Arab pirates?"

"Truly, Father, you are blessed with prescience."

The old monk sighed and shook his head. "The local *soldados* have come round and spoken to me. I fear they keep watch on me e'en now. You are sought, my son, as a suspect of a murder."

"Murder? But I have killed no one!"

"There was no Goan *fidalgo* in the cart with you as you were brought into the city?"

"There was, but—" Thomas went cold. De Cartago had not moved when Thomas called to him. *But the powder should have healed! Did he substitute poison and not tell me?* "A serpent's bite to him who breathes," the note with the bottle had said. "A serpent's skin to him who does not." *Resurrection for one who is dead, but poison to one alive. And both Aditi and De Cartago knew it!*

"Alas, Father, I fear I have been tricked. I am an apothecary by trade, and I was giving what I thought to be medicine to the man, not poison."

Father Stevens patted his shoulder. "I am heartened by your distress, my son—it leads me to believe your profession of innocence. I understand that some medicines become poison to one too weak to withstand it, and the East produces potent medicines indeed. You may very well be blameless."

"Can you help me, Father?"

"If 'twill not offend you to wear the habit, I will see if I can hide you among my brethren for a time. We are a wandering order, and it will cause no suspicion if you board a ship so attired. Come, we must depart from the streets quickly before you are seen." The old monk set off down the cobbled road and Thomas trotted beside him, trying to look humble.

"May I ask where in England you are from, Father?"

"Wiltshire, my son. Bushton. I studied at Winchester and Oxford, though not very long."

"How is it you have come to this far place?"

"Oh, through Rome and Lisbon. 'Tis a long story. At Saint Andrew's College, I read of the work of Saint Francis Xavier and that inspired me to become a missionary in the East. So here I am. I expect you have more worldly reasons for being here."

"I never intended to be here at all. My expedition had been bound for Cathay."

"Mmm, I've no doubt there's a purpose in your coming to Goa. The Lord works in ways mysterious . . . hush now, we've come to a more populous area."

The street fed into a corner of a large plaza, with a fountain in the middle. Father Stevens began to turn toward a side alley when five men, wearing loose shirts, dark trousers, and swords at their sides, stepped away from beneath a colonnade and approached them.

With casual enmity, they blocked Thomas and Father Stevens's way. *"Dominus vobiscum, senhores,"* said the old monk.

Thomas crouched behind the monk, uncertain how to behave.

"Padre Estevão," said one of the armed men with a nod. *"Boa noite. Quem é seu amigo?"*

Father Stevens prattled a while in Portuguese. Thomas got the impression he was being described as a new convert for the Church. The armed men did not seem convinced, however. One of them walked up to Thomas and snatched the turban off his head. *"Louro,"* the man said with a sneer. He grabbed Thomas under the arm and pulled him up. *"Levante-se, já!"*

"E alto," said one of the others, noting Thomas's height. An argument ensued between the old monk and the *soldados.* But after a minute of shouting, it was clear Father Stevens was not succeeding. The old monk crossed himself.

"Forgive me, my son, but I cannot stop them. I will do what I can to provide defense and surety for you. Do not give up. God—"

"Nay, forgive *me*, Father," Thomas said, as he roughly shoved the old monk into the midst of the soldiers. Thomas turned and ran as fast as he could the way they had come. His feet pounded the hard bricks in the street but he ignored the pain, searching for an alley mouth, doorway, anyplace he might hide. The swordsmen were shouting and following close behind. Thomas ducked under a camel bearing rolled-up rugs, knocked over a loinclothed boy carrying a parasol, slapped a startled donkey out of his way, and into the path of his pursuers. People on the street yelled after him, but he could not tell if they shouted encouragement or informed the soldiers of his passing. His legs were burning, starting to give, wearied by the trek through the marshes and the run after Aditi. A dark alleyway opened to his left and he dashed into it.

Cats and chickens and children scattered. Women covered their faces and scolded him. It was as though his nightmares of being hunted prey had come to life. He smelled cardamom and cooked lentils. He pushed his way through damp and drying lengths of cloth. His face and chest slammed into a stucco wall and he fell backward to the dirt.

Gasping, exhausted, stunned, Thomas could only sit, waiting, as blood trickled from his nose. Voices came closer, surrounded him. Again he was roughly pulled to his feet and his arms wrenched painfully behind his back. Too weak to fight, he allowed his wrists to be tied, and the armed men to lead him to whatever doom awaited.

XIII

BAMBOO: This tall grass grows in the East. It has a hollow stem, which is put to a multitude of uses, and leaves shaped like dagger blades. The stem may be eaten, but must be cooked first, otherwise it is poisonous. In India, the bamboo is symbolic of friendship and fires of divine origin. It is said to have sprung from the ashes of a girl who was tricked into marrying beneath her caste. It is believed in the East that if the bamboo blossoms, famine and other calamity lie ahead....

Sri Aditi sat with her arms wrapped around her knees as her *dholi* bounced and jostled. Her men knew where to take her: But she did not know if she would be welcomed there. She did not dare look to see if the foreigner still followed.

At last her bearers' pace slowed, and sounds quieted around her. The *dholi* settled to the ground and the cloth cover was raised. With as much grace as she could manage, Aditi unfolded herself and stood up.

They were in the side garden of a large, regal stone house that had stood before the Portuguese, or even the mughul shahs had come to Goa. The garden was shaded by *asoka* trees, bright with scarlet blossoms. Iridescent peacocks pecked their way through luxuriant ferns and champak bushes.

Sri Aditi removed two gold bracelets from her wrists and handed one to each bearer. "I thank you. Go, but take only side streets. Do not return to this place unless you are sent for."

The men bowed and silently departed.

A servant in a long cream-colored *jama* tunic and turban appeared at the door, and his eyes opened wide with alarm. "Sri Aditi. We had heard you were gone."

Aditi bowed. "So I was, Dwarpal. But the breath of Indra has blown me back. I must once again beg assistance from your masters."

The servant glanced toward the garden gate. "No one saw you come here?"

"I believe no one knows where I am."

He seemed dubious. "You had best come inside and wait. But I do not know what my master and lady will say."

"I understand. I am as distressed as they will surely be. I can only hope they have some kindness yet to spare for me."

"Lakshmi has worked greater wonders. Come inside, quickly."

Aditi followed Dwarpal through richly appointed side corridors, feeling more like a thief who has been discovered than a guest.

Dwarpal stopped and indicated a doorway that led onto a central garden. "Here is a place you may wait in comfort. I will have clove tea brought to you, if you wish."

"That would be most pleasant. You reflect the grace of your masters, as always, Dwarpal." Aditi bowed and walked out into the colonnaded garden. It was largely filled with a rectangular pool upon which floated pale lotus blossoms. A single spout of water fountained from the middle of the pool. Jasmine and narcissus grew beside it, scenting the air. Twilight was falling and the evening star could be seen in the indigo sky.

She heard a series of tentative notes from a familiar *raga* and looked to the far corner of the garden. A blind musician sat on a step, playing a *vina;* one gourd set over his shoulder, the other on his lap.

"Gandharva!" Aditi walked over and sat at his side. "I never expected to see you here."

The blind man tilted his head. "Could that be . . . Aditi? I had heard you had escaped and sailed away on the great sea."

"I did, Gandharva. Or, I tried to. Bernardo's ship was caught, by foreigners even the Portuguese do not like."

"Misfortune indeed. Is your friend Bernardo—"

"He has tasted of Her Gift and passed on. It is better so, given what would have happened to him in the Orlem Gor, what he might have divulged."

"Ah."

"It has all gone so wrong, Gandharva. Everything. We have failed. Now I am a fugitive in a place that was once home."

"Aditi, Aditi, you must be weary. Never have I heard you speak with such despair."

"Never have I felt so hopeless."

"Despair is an illusion, my Lady. A blindness no less crippling than my own. The Mahadevi has great trust in your wits and your strength, as do I. All will turn around."

Aditi sighed and rested her chin on her knees. "Unfounded hope can be illusion also, Gandharva."

A serving girl wearing a green *kurti* overblouse walked up and placed a silver tray at Aditi's feet. On the tray were a porcelain cup of clove tea, and beside it a small round of betel cake. Aditi normally did not chew betel, but this evening her spirits badly needed soothing.

With a deep bow, the serving girl departed.

"Mmmm." Gandharva sniffed the air. "The lord's servants get more beautiful each time I visit."

"How can you tell? She brought us some *pan-supari*. Would you like some?"

"No, though I thank you. With one sense gone, I need to trust all the rest. With them I can hear the grace of a girl's step or scent her well-chosen perfume. Beauty may be beheld in darkness as well as light."

"Is that so?" Aditi took a bite of the betel cake, thoughtfully chewing the confection of palm nut, lime paste, vine leaf, opium, and spices. "Darkness and light. I was sent an omen of darkness today. What will happen, do you think, when the Mahadevi learns of my failure?"

The blind musician shrugged. "You know She has a different perspective on these things. To Her, our sorrows are but contrary breezes, disturbing Her thoughts only as wind disturbs grass."

"What if She is disturbed more than that?"

"It will depend upon Her mood, I suppose. What is the worst? You will become a beautiful adornment to Her garden."

"You do not reassure me, Gandharva."

"I say it only because I think it unlikely. Tell me what terrible things have happened."

"Zalambur is dead. Serafina is now in the Orlem Gor, enduring their torments. Bernardo is dead. In order to save my own life, I returned to Goa in the company of pirates. I had to give one of the foreigners the vial of Her Gift. Bernardo trusted a young man with some knowledge of Her, though I do not know what. This young foreigner followed me to Goa, when I escaped from the pirates. I aided him too, directing him to one of his countrymen. I am not sure why."

"It is surely in keeping with one's *dharma* to help strangers in need, is it not?"

"So they say. This young man was strange. Do you know, he rolled in mud, thinking it would disguise him?"

"Animals roll in the dirt to cover their scent, I am told. Perhaps the young foreigner thinks like an animal. Surely any Westerner would do well to cover his stink, no?"

"They do not seem to bathe much, it is true. But the mud did not cover him enough. It was obvious his hair and skin are a peculiar color. Bernardo called him a young lion because the foreigner's hair was tawny-yellow, like a lion's fur. This young man is truly darkness and light, Gandharva; he calls himself *Tamas.*"

"You have been thinking a lot about this fellow. Were you attracted to him?"

Aditi took another bite of the betel cake and chewed some moments before answering. "I do not know. Gandharva, you have traveled more than I, and seen more of the world even though you do not see. Have you ever felt, upon meeting someone, that there is a thread that binds you to him? That he is important, somehow. Have you?"

"Not I, but I hear it happens to others. There are those who say it means you have known this person in a former life."

"I do not believe in other lives. But Bernardo must have thought there was some reason to trust or encourage this Tamas. Perhaps because he is an herbalist; they share some knowledge with alchemists."

The blind musician nodded. "Men of like mind can be inclined to share secrets. You and the Mahadevi have shared secrets and, in some ways, I think you are very like her."

"No one can be like the Mahadevi."

"That is not so. I have heard Her say Herself She had two sisters, back in the ancient times."

"Ah. What an age of miracles that must have been."

"So the stories say, my lady. But I think some wonders

grow more wondrous over time and telling, like exuberant weeds."

"Every now and then, Gandharva, I think you doubt our Mahadevi's godliness."

He held up his hands. "Do not doubt me, my Lady. Ever since the Mahadevi brought me back to the Land of the Living, I am Hers utterly. But I am a storyteller and I know stories."

"Hm. Is that why you are in Goa? Telling stories to the Marathas?"

He shrugged again. "I come. I go. I leave tomorrow for Bijapur."

"I should go with you."

"Why?"

"Why should I stay? They hunt me here, and I will fare no better than poor Serafina if I am caught." Aditi rubbed her forehead with her fists. "Why does the Mahadevi expect so much of us? It would be much simpler if She would just come here and show Herself, prove Her power."

"There would not be much left of Goa if She did. Besides, it would ruin the game for us lowly mortals."

"You think of all this as a game?"

"She surely does."

"When people die to spread word of Her?"

"I understand the most exciting games are those in which the most is gambled. What more precious wager is there than life? It is all well for gods to be great and powerful, but if they did everything, what would be left for us mortals to do?"

Aditi shook her head. "Stand aside and laugh, grateful it is not us who work and suffer? But you still have not given me a reason why I should stay in Goa."

"Because there is nothing to be gained by your departure. If you leave now, you are fleeing your *dharma*, decrying the unfairness of it all, and, worst of all, bringing nothing of interest to the Mahadevi. You know how She despises whiners. If you wait, the Wheel may turn more in your favor. You may learn something of note, and thereby be able to distract Her from disapproval. If you return to the Mahadevi empty-handed . . ."

"You are right. That would enrage Her more. I have met a man fleeing from his *dharma*—a most pitiable character. I should not want to be like him. I almost was."

"There, you see? Await your chance, my lady. That is my advice to you. I say again, you are intelligent and clever. You will know the moment when you see it. Does Agni not renew himself out of his own consuming fire? Surely something worthwhile is to be gained out of this misfortune. You will see."

XIV

ASAFETIDA: This resin is of a russet color, and comes from fennel grown in Persia. It is most notable for its foul smell and bitter taste. Some call it Devil's Dung. Yet it hath been used in the East as a spice, and there is called food of the gods. Powdered asafetida will cure fits and ailments of the stomach. Worn in an amulet about the neck, it is said to ward off disease and witchcraft....

Thomas paid little attention to where he was led until they approached a large outcropping of rock at the edge of the city. An iron gate blocked an opening within it. Three more *soldados* stood guard at the gate. As his captors bantered with the gatekeepers, Thomas noticed a noisome odor drifting out of the narrow, cavernlike entrance. *Does some unwashed oracle await within, to riddle me my future?*

At last, a *soldado* unlocked the gate and Thomas was shoved inside. He stumbled down a dark, sloping tunnel, trying to hold his breath as the odor became stronger. His captors held kerchiefs over their noses, but did not offer one to Thomas.

He turned a corner and fell against another barred gate

of iron. The chamber beyond was dim, filled with man-shaped shadows. The stench was overpowering: a fetid mixture of excrement, urine, sweat, every effluvium of mankind, rotting plants, and decaying flesh. Thomas coughed, fighting nausea.

The bars swung away from him and Thomas fell forward, toppling over a ledge. He landed on his side on a stone floor that was slimy and reeking. He rolled to his knees and retched unrelentingly. All that came up was sour liquid. Yet his stomach heaved so violently, he feared he might disgorge the very organs from his body. *What an ignoble manner it would be in which to die.*

He thought of all the stomach-ease medicines on Master Coulter's shelves: mint and narcissus, hawflower tea, peach twig syrup. All far away and useless. But the thought seemed to lessen the spasms and Thomas became aware of people close around him, fingers poking at his hair, his breeches, his feet. He heard soft laughter, and men talking in different tongues. Someone beside him said, *"Bem-vindo, estranho. Bem-vindo a Aljouvar."*

I need not wait for death to enter Hell, thought Thomas. *I am already there.*

Someone shouted the others aside and grasped Thomas's shoulders, helping him to stand. In broken Latin the samaritan said, "Breathe fast, friend. Like a dog in summer. It will help. Come."

Thomas panted as he was led to a wall and leaned against it. Faint light streamed in from unseen cracks in the rock overhead, and he began to see a little of his surroundings. Thomas turned to thank his benefactor and started. Beside him was a face dark as the ebony masks of Africa, a Hindu face with broad nose and brown eyes.

"Good," the Hindu said. "You feel better now?"

"I do," Thomas managed to say. "Thank you, stranger."

Working at Thomas's bonds, the Hindu said, "Your hands are free now."

"Thanks be to blessed God," Thomas sighed in English, rubbing his wrists. As his eyes adjusted to the gloom, he saw he was in a deep grotto, whose stone floor had been worn smooth by the constant treading of feet. Rats chittered and clambered everywhere. In the center was a raised circular cistern, where men went to relieve themselves. There were some dozens of ragged, bearded men in the chamber: some pacing back and forth like animals in a cage, some rocking silently where they sat. Some lay on the floor and cried out to Santa Maria, or Allah, or some multisyllabic pagan deity. Some lay still, sleeping, ill, or dead. The rest, whether turbaned Arab, well-dressed Goan, near-naked African, long-jacketed Hindu, or indeterminate race and nation, sat calmly talking, praying, or gambling with stones. Not a few watched Thomas with idle curiosity.

"By Jesu," said someone seated near him, in accented Latin. "I believe you have found us a Brittanian, Sabda."

Thomas looked down and saw a man in stained and threadbare silk doublet and breeches. His fair, untrimmed beard and hair had been combed. The man's eyes were blue. "Are you also from England, sir?"

After a moment's pause, the man held up a broad hand. "Pieter Van der Groot, of Rotterdam."

Thomas grasped the hand carefully, his wrist still aching.

"Sabdajnana, I am called," said the Hindu, with a bow. "And may we know your name, good sir?"

"Chinnery. Thomas. Of Londinium."

"Chinritamas."

"Um, no. Just Thomas."

"*Tamas?* Hmmm . . ." The Hindu muttered something.

The Dutchman laughed. "Sabda says that your name has surely led you to this place. *Tamas*, in his tongue, means 'darkness.' "

"Does it? Then truly I am in my element, for my prospects have never seemed darker. Is this man Sabda your servant?"

Frowning, Van der Groot said, "He is my friend. He is a learned doctor and a Brahmin, the noblest caste in this land. The Mohammedans call him a *hakim*."

"I see. Forgive me, I meant no insult." Thomas bowed Hindu fashion to Sabdajnana. "And you have shown me un-expected kindness in this place . . . wherever we are."

The Brahmin bowed in return, with a smile.

"This is the Aljouvar," said Van der Groot, "the Governor's keep, where any Goan or foreigner with blood in his veins and ill luck in his life spends time. But let me tell you, I have seen more charity and nobility of spirit in this hell-pit than I have seen in the world outside. Brought so low, we become brothers in adversity."

A thin, wiry man with a sparse black beard and mustache strolled over and flopped with supple ease to the floor beside Van der Groot.

"Except for Joaquim, here," the Dutchman went on in a louder voice, "who is brother to no man. Is that not so, Joaquim?"

"You do me dishonor," said the small man in Portuguese-accented Latin. "You do not even bow to greet me, as a proper gentleman should. Do not tempt me to challenge you for your rudeness. That would not be gracious in front of your new friend, Pedro."

"That is unfair of you, Joaquim. You know my legs are still not healed and I can in no way bow as well as you."

"Ah, I forget. We must forgive the crippled. So, who is this golden-haired angel who visits us in Hell?"

"Allow me to do the honor of presenting Thomas Chinnery of Londinium. He is an *inglês*, Joaquim."

The small man gasped comically. "An *inglês! Madre de Deus*, save me from this child-eating heretic, Pedro!"

"I beg your pardon," said Thomas coolly.

"This obnoxious personage," said Van der Groot, "is Joaquim Alvalanca, the most entertaining son of a dog I have ever had the pleasure of sharing a prison with."

"Ah, that is twice you insult me, Pedro. Truly, you become too familiar."

"Forgive me, Joaquim, I am but a rough merchant and I know nothing of the tenderness of a gentleman's pride."

"The quality of a gentleman," sniffed Joaquim, "is shown by the tenderness of his pride."

"In that case," said Thomas, "I am honored to make the acquaintance of someone who is so unmistakably a gentleman." He attempted a grand bow, such as those he'd seen on the streets of Goa. But as he dipped his head, it began to swim with dizziness and he fell forward.

The Brahmin Sabdajnana caught one of his arms. Joaquim leapt up and took his other arm. Together, they eased Thomas to the floor.

"Sit, senhor, please," said Joaquim. "You do me too much honor. Do not fear to sully yourself. From the smell of you, that has already been done."

"I fear I am in need of food," said Thomas.

Sabdajnana placed a cool palm against Thomas's forehead and neck. "Signs of fever. You must take care, good sir."

"Alas, senhor, we are not fed for a while yet," said Joaquim. "I hope you do not starve before then. Even if you are a devil-fornicating heretic."

"Thank you," said Thomas dryly. "Even if you are an idol-kissing papist."

"Ah! He pierces me to the heart, Pedro! Shall I challenge him?"

"Patience, Joaquim. He suffers enough, being here and in your company. You are not such a gentleman that your pride cannot withstand a little piercing. Besides, he might win the duel, and you know I would go mad without you here to pester me."

A light appeared, bobbing near the iron gate. Men rose from the grotto floor, came forward from the walls, arms outstretched, imploring in many tongues. A *soldado* outside the gate held up a lantern, illuminating two monks in brown robes, their faces hidden deep in their cowls. Thomas felt a glimmer of hope.

"Paulistas," said Joaquim, eyeing them curiously.

"Jesuits," said Van der Groot to Thomas. "They sometimes come on behalf of someone's family or to give charity. They aid the unfortunate and have no great love of the Santa Casa."

The *soldado* pointed in their direction and the monks looked at Thomas, gesturing to each other.

"Ah, perhaps they bring you food, senhor."

But after a minute, the monks silently departed. The lantern-bearer followed, leaving the grotto in a darkness even deeper than before. The prisoners returned, resigned, to their former places and pastimes.

"I had hoped," sighed Thomas, "that it would be Padre Stevens. I spoke to him before my arrest. He offered to help."

"I have heard of him," said Van der Groot. "I had once hoped for his aid, myself. But I learned that Padre Stevens had angered the governor some years ago, by helping three of your countrymen escape Goa. He is not trusted by the authorities, and I think there is little he can do."

"Yes. He was taking me to his fellow Jesuits when we were stopped by soldiers. They did not believe his excuses for me, and so I was dragged here. Senhor Alvalanca, you spoke of a Santa Casa. Is that—"

"The Inquisition, senhor," said Joaquim. "And pray that holy house takes no interest in you, heretic *inglês.*"

Thomas had heard many tales told in hushed whispers concerning the Inquisition's torments, presented as more damning evidence against papists. The stories were oftimes so lurid, he had wondered how many were true.

"So what terrible crime brings our Senhor Chinnery to the Aljouvar?"

"You forget, Joaquim," said Van der Groot, "in this city, merely being a foreigner can be crime enough. There was a rumor spread even here that not long ago, a mighty fleet of English warships chased down the greatest of Goa's carracks, nearly capturing her. You would not happen to have come from such a fleet?"

"No," said Thomas, nearly smiling. "My fleet was but two ships, and although we did attack a carrack, we did not take her. We were badly damaged and had to harbor near Calicut for repair, but while there, we were set upon by Arab pirates. I was trying to rescue a friend I believed they had captured, and in the effort found myself made captive and drugged. When I awoke, I was in a cart on the road to Goa."

"Strange," Van der Groot said, rubbing his beard. "I did not think the Oman raiders sailed that part of the Indian sea."

"But surely," said Joaquim, "though to be an *inglês* is a crime indeed, there must be something more. Else the *paulistas* would be allowed to post surety for you. Is there no other charge, senhor?"

Thomas sighed. "It is believed that I have murdered a Goan gentleman."

Van der Groot sucked in his breath. "Then God help you, friend."

"But of course!" said Joaquim. "A duel, no? This pretty boy found himself a lady with a jealous husband."

"No, nothing so adventurous," said Thomas. "I am an apothecary, by trade. I was administering a medicine to a man. But it would seem, instead of a healing substance, it turned out to be poisonous."

"What medicine," said Sabdajnana, "was this you gave him?"

Thomas was startled a moment, then remembered the Brahmin was a doctor and had an interest in such things. "It was a brown powder. I understand your people call it *Rasa Mahadevi.*"

"*Rasa Mahadevi!*" Sabdajnana gasped.

"Do you know of it?"

"Only in rumors, Tamas. Its name means 'blood of the goddess,' and it is thought to be a most sacred and powerful medicine."

"And so it is, for once I used it to bring a man back from the dead, but for the Goan it was his doom."

"You have used this amazing substance?"

"Only twice."

"How marvelous! Where did you get it? Do you have any of it with you?"

"No. What I had was taken from me on the pirate ship. I had gotten it from the very man who died from it—a Portuguese alchemist. What goddess is it supposed to be from? Do you know its source?"

Sabdajnana raised his brows. "The Mahadevi, of course, which is 'Great Goddess.' But no one knows where the powder comes from. Some say it is found deep in the Deccan desert, or the Bengali jungles. Some say it is the blood of a *naga.*"

"*Naga?* What is that?"

"The *naga* are a fabled race of people, half man, half snake. I do not know if they truly exist."

Mayhap thence comes the mention of serpents with the bottle. What a wonder, if this be true.

"So," said Joaquim, "you are a sorcerer, as well as a heretic."

Thomas glared at the small man. "The proper use of medicaments, drugs, and herbs has nothing to do with sorcery." It was hard enough to suffer innuendos from the Royal College of Physicians, let alone from an ignorant, sharp-tongued Iberian. Thomas felt his face grow flushed and he felt too warm and too cold at the same time. He buried his face in his hands.

Sabdajnana grasped his shoulder. "How do you feel?"

"Not well."

The Brahmin and Joaquim helped Thomas turn and lean back against the wall. "I meant no insult, senhor, forgive me," babbled Joaquim. "Here, I will tell you my story. That will bring a smile to your face, yes? I am a guest of the Aljouvar because I am a thief. An incompetent thief, no less. What did I steal? A loaf of bread, senhor."

"Were you so poor?" said Thomas. "You seem too well educated. Or are you a student?"

Joaquim laughed. "In Goa, senhor, the only subjects I have studied are how to drink, how to fight, how to fuck, and how to kill a man a hundred ways. In Lisboa, I was a proper student, at a seminary, which is why my Latin is so exceptional. But my family fell into disfavor; I had no fortune left in Lisboa. So I sailed to the Golden India, where they said rubies and emeralds hang from the trees and the dark-skinned girls grant every wish.

"In Goa, I became a *soldado*, as must any man without wife or title. We fight to defend our precious colony. I am put in barracks with ten others and we are told that if we serve well and find wives, we will become *fidalgos* and no longer work but own fine estates and walk the *avenidas* with slaves to hold parasols over our heads."

Joaquim leaned closer and lowered his voice. "But, senhor, they did not tell us that we earn only two *reis* a day. That ten men must share one good shirt. That all we are given to eat is rice and salt fish, and only water to drink. The *gobernador* would rather spend on his wife and *amigas* than on his *soldados*."

"Careful, Joaquim," said Van der Groot.

"I no longer care, Pedro. So, senhor, we steal. Some have ladies bring them food in trade for loving. Me, I have no *amiga solteira*, so I stole a loaf of bread. But I was caught, and our *sargento* needs an example, so here I am. A thrilling tale, no?"

"How long have you been here?" said Thomas.

"Two, maybe three months."

"So long? Has no magistrate spoken to you?"

"No, and if I am lucky, they will forget I am here at all."

Thomas sighed. It was both consoling and distressing to hear the woes of others. "What of you, sir?" Thomas said to Van der Groot. "May I hear your story?"

The Dutchman scratched his beard. "Mine seems hardly worth the telling. But in the view of the *governador*, I am a thief as well. The ships of my countrymen are no more welcome than yours in these waters. We Dutch are known for our skill in trade and Portugal holds her conquests jealously. I was caught trying to set up mercantile contacts with some traders among the Marathas. The authorities were not pleased."

"And you have spoken to no one either?"

"As with Joaquim, I hope it will be a long time before I do. I fear it will not go well for me when judgment is finally passed." The Dutchman shifted his sitting position and Thomas noted the unnatural stiffness of his legs.

"What happened to you?"

"I tried to escape and was beaten by guards. It is nothing."

"I see." Thomas could tell it was more than nothing but decided not to press the Dutchman on the matter. "Can you tell me what might happen to me? Have you any advice to offer?"

"If they are convinced you are a murderer, or want to blame you anyway, you have little hope but to escape. The guard can sometimes be lax or be bribed. You might hide, for a time, among the Mohammedans or Jews in Goa; there are some unfriendly to the Portuguese who would not betray you. Your best chance is to flee overland. Go east, into Bijapur territory. The sultan there, Ibrahim 'Adilshah, dislikes the Portuguese but welcomes all other foreigners."

Bijapur. I have heard of that place—Ah! 'Tis the second dot on De Cartago's map; the way to the source of the Rasa Mahadevi.

"And you, *Magister*," Thomas said to Sabdajnana. "What brings a learned man like you to this place?"

The Brahmin sadly shook his head. "Men of knowledge, if not Christian, are suspect in Goa in these times."

"Men of knowledge, if they are rich, you mean," said Van der Groot. "They were probably jealous of your wealth, Sabda. See if you have any left when you return home."

The Brahmin sighed and looked away.

"I thank—" Thomas coughed and the world spun around him. He grew hotter, as though internal flames threatened to consume him. He wanted to melt, or expand like bread in an oven. His arms and legs felt heavy as stone.

"The fever," he heard Sabdajnana say over him. "It is getting bad."

Of course it was the fever, he had treated it so often.

Why, some pennyroyal and lavender should do the trick, should it not, Dame Smythe? And there was Dame Coulter gazing down at him and shaking her plump cheeks, saying, "God should not give such a father a child." But who was she speaking of? His father, of course, just before she insisted Master Coulter send him on this voyage far, far away from the women on horseback who haunted and hunted him in this burning, night-dark forest. He could hear their shrieks and horrible cries, and he ran through the fire, but he could bring no breath into his lungs and the branches kept slapping his face as he ran—

A mighty slap and Thomas saw the face of a demon hovering over him.

No, it was Sabdajnana, very concerned. "Tamas?"

"Senhor!" Joaquim said in his ear. "Senhor, you must awaken. They come for you."

Aching all over, Thomas let them pull him up.

There was a monk at the gate, a kerchief over his mouth. A key rattled in the iron lock.

"Padre Stevens?" Thomas whispered. He looked around, expecting another chorus of wails and pleas from the prisoners. Instead, there was silence. No man called out or even acknowledged the monk at the gate. If anything, the prisoners shuffled deeper into the shadows, turning their faces away.

The monk entered the pit alone, carrying a lantern. His robes were not brown, but white with the black cape of a blackfriar. The monk walked straight toward Thomas.

"Alas, senhor," whispered Joaquim. "I fear you are for the Santa Casa after all."

The blackfriar stopped before them and pointed at Thomas. He said to Joaquim, "*É ele inglês?*"

Joaquim nodded, gazing down at the floor.

"Courage, Thomas," said Van der Groot.

The monk motioned to the guards at the gate. As the men

stepped down into the grotto, bringing chains, Joaquim whispered again in Thomas's ear. "Remember us, senhor. For once you come to know the hospitality of the Santa Casa, you will remember the Aljouvar as Paradise."

Padre Gonsção lingered in the deepening shadows of the Cathedral of Santa Catarina. The mass was long over, but he was loath to leave the comforting Iberian arches, altar, and pews. The high windows were paned with mother-of-pearl, allowing in diffuse, milky light, as though one were under water. *How apt, this sanctuary. For I fear I haven't the skill to swim amidst the turbulent, murky waters of life in Goa. Lord preserve me, that I do not drown in it.*

The huge wooden doors behind him opened and a solitary figure, a monk, walked in. He genuflected at the aisle and sidled over to the pew where Gonsção knelt. It was not until the monk was beside him that Gonsção recognized Brother Marco.

"God grant you good evening, Padre."

Gonsção sighed and crossed himself as if finishing prayers. "And to you, Brother Marco."

"He has, Padre, to all of us. At last I bring good news."

"I am pleased to hear it. But give me these tidings outside. These walls echo so, the doves in the rafters might hear our whispers."

"Certainly, Padre."

Gonsção allowed Brother Marco to lead him out to the cathedral steps. The sun was disappearing behind the tall houses, spreading long shadows over the still-crowded central plaza. "Do these people never go home, Brother Marco?"

The young monk laughed. "They are more fond of going to each other's homes, Padre. Goa is a festive city."

Gonsção clicked his tongue. "I am surprised any work of serious consequence gets done here."

"Precious little does," said Brother Marco. "But, to my news. The *inglês* whom we thought we had lost has been found. He was taken to the Aljouvar, but one of our brothers has retrieved him and brought him to the Santa Casa."

"Well, that is some progress. It would have been better to find De Cartago alive, but we must content ourselves with second-best. I trust, then, there will be an audience this evening?"

"Not so soon, Padre. The *inglês* was ill and feverish, and Domine Sadrinho wished him to have some time to recover before he is interviewed."

"I see." After so much delay and misdirection, Gonsção found himself wondering if this was just another trick. "You know, Brother Marco, it occurs to me that given the importance of this *inglês* to our investigation, we should give him the best of advocates. I think Brother Timóteo would do very well for him, no?"

Brother Marco smiled. "Truly the mouths of the wise drink from the same fountain, Padre. Inquisitor Sadrinho has already assigned Brother Timóteo to that duty."

"Has he? This is encouraging news indeed."

Something across the plaza caught Brother Marco's attention for a moment. "I . . . must return to attend to preparations for our new guest. Please pardon me, Padre." He turned and swiftly departed in a direction opposite whatever he had seen.

Gonsção raised his brows, surprised. *But so much is strange here, it is doubtless not worth asking about.* With a sigh, he continued down the cathedral steps, ambling after Brother Marco.

Out of the corner of his eye, he saw two brown-robed figures step away from the plaza fountain in his direction. He sent a small prayer heavenward, for Gonsção found the Jesuit passion for poverty, charity, and evangelism somewhat trying. His prayer was, evidently, too late, for the *paulistas* walked directly up to him. Gonsção nodded to them, choosing to make the best of things.

"God grant you good evening, Brothers."

"And to your spirit, Padre, may God grant peace." The Jesuit who spoke was a white-haired man of perhaps sixty, and his Portuguese was oddly accented. The brother beside him was stocky and had curly black hair. From the way the man shrugged and twitched in his wool robe, Gonsção gathered he was new to the cloth.

"I have not seen you near the Santa Casa before," said the old monk knowingly. "Are you recently arrived in Goa, Padre?"

"I have been here but these two weeks, Brother."

"Then may I welcome you to the liveliest parish on God's earth. I am Padre Tomás Estevão."

"Ah. I believe I have heard of you. You are an *inglês*, are you not?" *And I have a guess as to why you have approached me.*

"Alas, that is my homeland, but I am exiled until His Holiness retracts his bull, or Her Sovereign Majesty Elizabeth returns to the Mother Church. I do not think either to be likely. This is Brother Andrew, of Scotland, a country more temperate in faith, if not in weather."

Gonsção nodded politely to the hirsute monk, and received in turn a cool smile. *There is something cunning behind his eyes. All is not what it seems.* "I am told, Padre Estevão, that you are a student of the local heathen languages."

"Why, yes," Father Stevens said proudly. "I have put together a Canarese grammar and I am currently working on a long devotional poem in the style and tongue of the Marathas. I call it my Christian Purana."

Gonsção tried to keep his dismay from showing. "If I

may ask, Padre, whatever would possess you to try such a thing?"

"Oh, it is a great challenge, I know. But I felt it worth the attempt, in order to reveal the Christian faith in a manner familiar to the Hindu. And also to demonstrate to the faithful the beauty of the language and poetic forms used by the native people. But I will not be tedious, as so many writers can be, with tales of my work in progress. I have learned that one of my countrymen is now a guest within the Santa Casa. A young, fair-haired man, named as I am, Thomas. I believe him to be innocent of the charges laid against him, and I wish to testify on his behalf and offer him counsel."

As I thought. Gonsção put on the most gracious smile he could manage. "Naturally, Padre, you are concerned for your unfortunate countryman. But I must regretfully inform you that I am only an observer here. I have no direct authority in his case. I do not know what charges you are referring to. I do know that the Santa Casa has made no mistake in making him our guest; Inquisitor Sadrinho is very interested in his testimony. He will be well treated, I assure you. Now I have already told you more than my position permits. If you like, I will send a message to the Inquisitor Major that you wish audience with him. You understand, he may not respond for some time. Inquisitor Sadrinho is a very busy man."

The old Jesuit smiled as well. "I have dealt with Domine Sadrinho before, Padre. I know how busy he can be when he thinks it necessary."

"I am glad you are patient and understanding, Padre Estevão. Now, if you will excuse me, I have matters to attend to."

"One moment, Padre," said Brother Andrew. His harsh Portuguese seemed more that of a soldier than a scholar. "There is a thing Padre Estevão did not mention. I believe the young *inglês* is not wanted so much for himself, but for what he may have learned from the man he accompanied to Goa. A certain Senhor Bernardo De Cartago."

"I have spoken all I can on this," Gonsção said. "It will not—"

"But the mistake, you see," Brother Andrew went on, "is that this De Cartago is thought to be dead."

"—do you any good to . . . what did you say, Brother?"

"That this same Senhor De Cartago, who is said to be a sorcerer, is not dead."

Gonsção found himself at a loss for words. *It is as though they heard my thoughts from across the plaza. Can this be true, or another ruse? I must not show that this is important to me.* Yet he somehow could not keep his mouth from dropping open and his eyes from staring at the Scots monk.

"Is this not a matter of interest for the Santa Casa?" said Brother Andrew, blinking, all innocence.

"How . . . how do you come by this knowledge?"

"If you will but give us a little of your time, Padre," said Padre Estevão, "we will gladly explain."

I do not know enough to judge this. I do not know where De Cartago's body lies, or if it even exists. I cannot fully trust these men, yet I do not trust Sadrinho either. If this is something he does not know, or is hiding from me, it is the greater interest of my mission that I learn more. "Very well. I am listening."

XV

POPPY: This plant has silver-green leaves. It brings forth
white, red, or purple flowers in midsummer and round seed
pods in late summer. Syrup of the poppy is an excellent medicine, for it removes all care, all recognition of pain or danger or difficult circumstances, and brings blissful sleep. Yet
great care must be taken in its use, for too strong a tincture
will bring too deep a slumber, and one must use garlic or another strong substance to revive the sleeper. To the ancients, the poppy was sacred to Ceres and Diana and 'twas
thought a plant of death. Some say the red flowers first
grew from the blood of a dragon slain by Saint Margaret.
Others say it grew from Christ's blood as it dripped from the
Cross. 'Tis known everywhere that the poppy grows well
in battlefields....

Thomas awoke with a cool, dry breeze caressing his face,
the sort of morning zephyr that betides a noontime
scorching. He could hear the chatter and screech of tropical
birds beyond the wall beside him. From a distance came
cries of street merchants and the clamor of church bells.
There was a faint scent of lime wash amidst the odors of sea
and fruit orchards. For a moment he believed himself back
in London on a summer's morning. But his other senses and
memories told him it could not be so.

Above him was a white vaulted ceiling. The wall at his
right was whitewashed as well, with a small barred window
set high in it. Thomas watched the dust motes drift down on
the shafts of light. He struggled to sit up, but had to lie back

again from dizziness. His body ached all over and he moaned. *I remember now. I have been ill with a fever. I wonder where I am?*

He looked down at himself. He was now wearing clean garments that were not his own; cotton trousers and a loose cotton shirt, but no shoes. He had been bathed. Thomas reached up to scratch his head and found that his hair had been cut, very short. *Truly, I am not the man I was in my last memory.*

With slow care, Thomas at last managed to sit up. He had been lying on a counterpane of red and white checkerboard weave. Beneath that was a straw mat on a pallet. *Not a luxurious bed, but far better than many I have seen in a good while.*

He was in a cell perhaps ten feet square. Against an adjacent wall stood a plain wooden table, on which sat two earthenware pots. Beside the table was a straw broom and a covered stool pan. Across the room from him was the door, which had a grated window in the upper portion.

Can this be the fearsome Santa Casa? I am in a cell, certainly, but 'tis furnished more like a frugal, well-kept inn.

A round, swarthy face appeared at the window in the door. It uttered a grunt of surprise and turned to speak to someone Thomas could not see. There came the rattle of a key in the iron lock and the door swung silently open.

The owner of the broad, scarred face was a stocky man who wore a truncheon on his belt. He strode in, smiling.

"Morning," Thomas murmured, with a nod.

The man said nothing, but stood aside from the door. A boy of about twelve to thirteen years, wearing a brown robe, entered. His bowl-cut hair was black and he had large brown eyes and light cinnamon skin. He carried a wooden plate that he set on the cot beside Thomas. The plate held rice, a fillet of fish, and a sausage.

His stomach growling with hunger, Thomas eagerly took up the plate. "Bless you and thank you, little Brother," he said between mouthfuls of rice.

"Deus lhe dê bom dia, senhor," said the boy, his face solemn but hopeful.

Thomas swallowed and said, *"Utorisne lingua latina?"*

"I do," said the boy in that language. "It is fortunate that you do also. I am Brother Timóteo."

The tall man, clearly a guard of some sort, cleared his throat and gave the boy a warning glance, still smiling.

"I am called Thomas Chinnery. Could you do me the favor of telling me where I am?"

The boy blinked. "You are in the Sacred House, senhor. Ah, but you would not have known. You have been ill."

The guard clicked his tongue. The boy sighed and he pressed his lips together in annoyance. Thomas wondered what might be going on. *Perhaps the boy breaks some monkish rule. So, this is, indeed, the dreaded Inquisition. It is fair enough in appearance, so far. Might it be fair in its dealings also? What would cause De Cartago to prefer death over imprisonment here, or bring Joaquim to say the Aljouvar is Paradise in comparison?*

Thomas ate more bites of fish, sausage, and rice while his visitors waited with patience. At last, he asked, "When may I speak with someone in authority?"

"Soon," said Brother Timóteo. "I am to be your advocate."

Thomas nearly choked on his rice. "You?" *A child is to be my spiritual solicitor? What manner of court is this?*

"Do you feel well, senhor?" the boy asked with genuine concern.

"Pardon me. I am well. I merely breathed in some rice."

"And your fever, it is gone?"

"It would seem so. Have I been treated with any medicines?"

The boy tilted his head. "Why do you ask?"

"Um, curiosity. That is all." Thomas had learned that, in certain places, there were dangers in admitting his profession.

"I treated you myself," said the boy proudly. "I learned herbal medicines from my grandfather, Garcia de Orta."

"De Orta?" said Thomas. "Truly? I have read his book, *The Colloquy of Indian Simples and Drugs.*"

Brother Timóteo's eyes widened. "You have heard of my grandfather? And read his book? From so far away?"

"Indeed so. That book was part of the reason my master sent me to the East."

The guard coughed loudly and scowled at the boy. Brother Timóteo cast his gaze downward and turned away.

How strange. The boy is not permitted to speak freely to me. "As you are my advocate," said Thomas, watching the guard, "can you say what will be done with me?"

Staring at the floor, the young brother said, "You must set your thoughts on what sins have led you to this place, senhor. My masters, the Inquisitors, will show you all mercy if you open your heart to them and to God."

These words, which should have been reassuring, sent a chill through Thomas. "Thank you. I will." He hoped it was the expected response. "I look forward to having that chance."

"When you are well, senhor."

"I feel well enough." Thomas stood and felt his knees buckle. The boy rushed to his side and grabbed his arm, easing him down to the floor.

"You must rest, senhor. Let your body and soul gather strength."

The guard rolled his eyes and grumbled in Portuguese. Another voice was heard outside the door. *"Irmão Timóteo!"*

Brother Timóteo released Thomas's arm. "Excuse me, senhor." The boy walked apprehensively out the door. The guard nodded to himself, as if a suspicion had been confirmed.

Thomas waited, chagrined at his weakness. He wondered

if it were a remnant of the fever, or not enough food. *Beef tea would be a good remedy, or a sachet of cumin and thyme. Perhaps an infusion of elderleaf. No such remedies here. Mayhap I could persuade the boy to bring me some garlic. I wonder to whom he is speaking. He does not sound happy.*

Brother Timóteo reappeared, frowning. He came to Thomas's side. "Senhor," he said, "you are to see my masters now."

"Good," said Thomas. He slowly stood, commanding his knees to hold fast. To his surprise, they obeyed.

The guard came toward them, snapping a piece of black cloth out of his belt.

"This is for your eyes," said Brother Timóteo. "You are to see only what is permitted. And we must bind your hands. And you are not to speak unless it is asked of you. Guests of the Santa Casa must be silent. It is the Rule."

Thomas felt a growing dread as they bound his wrists and blindfolded him. *Not to see. Not to speak. This fair gaol may be the stuff of nightmare yet.*

After a brief, awkward walk down corridors silent except for the echoes of their footsteps, the black cloth was taken again from his eyes. The room before him was a stark contrast to his light and airy cell.

The Audience Hall was a long room filled by a long, heavy table, around which sat long-faced men in black robes. The enormous crucifix that filled the far wall evoked thoughts more of punishment than of salvation.

At the far end of the great table, a secretarial monk sat hunched over a huge ledgerbook, quill poised like a throwing dagger in his hand. To his right sat a man whose bearded face was pocked and rutted like London's cobbled lanes. To the left of the scribe sat a smaller man, who seemed bored but watched Thomas with hooded eyes.

Brother Timóteo walked up to the tall, scarred man and said, with a deferential bow, "He speaks Latin, Domine."

"Good. Then we shall not need an interpreter. Be seated."

The guard prodded Thomas toward a wooden stool at the near end of the table. Despite his bound hands, Thomas managed to sit without falling. *Well. At least they allow me this small comfort.*

The tall Inquisitor nodded at a leather-bound prayer book on the table in front of Thomas. "Place your right hand upon the missal."

"Your pardon, Domine," said Thomas, "but my hands are bound."

The Inquisitor rapped on the table. "You are not to speak until it is asked of you." He nodded at the guard and Thomas felt the bindings removed. Thomas rubbed his wrists, then laid his right hand on the book.

"You must swear that all you will say before us shall be the truth, and that you shall observe the Rule of Silence and repeat nothing of what occurs here."

"I swear to speak entirely the truth."

Brother Timóteo stepped toward Thomas. "You must swear to the Rule of Silence also, senhor, or you will be returned to your cell."

How strongly will this oath bind me? Thomas wondered. *Could I steel myself to not speak of this place, should I ever leave it? How much more is my soul damned if I do not? How long will they let me languish in my cell if I do not?* "I so swear," he said, at last.

"Your name?"

"Thomas Chinnery. May I ask the names of those I am addressing?"

The Inquisitors frowned.

"You must not ask questions!" Brother Timóteo hissed, almost pleading. "Only the Domines Sadrinho and Pinto may ask them."

The tall Inquisitor glared at the boy. "That is all our guest needs to know," he said darkly.

At least the boy dares give me answer, though it does me little good, thought Thomas.

"What is your city and land of origin?"

"London, England."

The Inquisitors shared a knowing look. "Your occupation?"

"I am apprenticed to an apothecary."

"An apothecary. That is one who deals in herbs, drugs, poisons, and alchemical substances, is it not?"

Thomas began to sense the traps being laid for him. "Other than the alchemical substances, that is correct."

The Inquisitor did not acknowledge Thomas's qualification. "What was your business in Goa?"

Thomas managed not to say *I have no business in Goa.* "I was captured by Arab sea rovers and brought here. For what purpose, I do not know."

"It is a long way for pirates to bring an *inglês*. Do you know why you are a guest of the Santa Casa?"

"No, Domine."

"You have no idea whatever?"

Thomas paused in surprise. *Does he seriously believe I ought to know?* "I think, Domine, that is for you to tell me."

Brother Timóteo looked scandalized. The taller Inquisitor sighed, tapping his index finger on the table.

Thomas raised his brows innocently and waited. *As well hung for a sheep, as they say.*

"Senhor, you must tell them why you are here," said Brother Timóteo.

What sort of advocate are you? thought Thomas. He finally

said, "I presume I am here because I am a foreigner."

The Inquisitor Major stared blandly at Thomas. "Of what interest should nationality be to the Church Catholic?"

What mad game is this? "Because of my nationality, it may be thought that I am in Goa illegally."

"That is a secular matter and not our concern. What transgressions of the spirit have brought you to our attention?"

Gritting his teeth, Thomas said, "Because of my land of birth, it may be thought that I am a heretic."

"Let it be noted, he admits to the sin of heresy."

"That I may be *thought* a heretic!"

"Are you an eight-day Christian, senhor?"

"I beg your pardon?"

The Inquisitor sighed. "When did you become a Christian?"

"Since birth, Domine."

"Were you baptized in the Mother Church?"

"I was baptized in . . . the Church of England."

"And does this Church of the English follow all the precepts of the Holy Mother Church of Rome?"

Thomas fell silent, wishing he had Lockheart's quicksilver tongue.

"We have learned," said the Inquisitor, "from others of your country, that it does not." The ghost of a smile played about the Inquisitor's lips. "And that people of true faith in the Mother Church are persecuted in your country."

"That is a political matter."

"We think not. You were in the company of a man whom we know to be a notorious sorcerer. This Santa Casa had been seeking him for some time."

Ah. Now we come to't. Carefully, Thomas said, "I was brought to Goa in the same cart as a man whom some said was a sorcerer. I escaped from the cart, but he did not. I later heard that he was dead."

The Inquisitors waited, saying nothing.

"Am I accused of his murder?"

"Murder," said the Inquisitor Major, "while a grievous sin, is nonetheless a matter for secular authorities, and not our concern. I repeat, what has brought you here?"

Thomas stared, scarcely comprehending what he heard. "Do you . . . do you believe that I might have practiced sorcery with the man?"

"Did you?" asked the Inquisitor, eyes lidded.

"No! What manner of trial is this? I will be damned if I will play guessing games with you!"

The eyes of the black-robed men widened and Thomas realized he should have held tighter rein on his tongue. He stared down at the table, face hot.

Brother Timóteo gently touched his shoulder. "Please calm yourself, senhor," he pleaded. "Believe that God watches, and behave yourself decorously, for this is His sacred house."

The Inquisitor Major glared again at the boy. Brother Timóteo gazed at the floor, murmuring apologetically in Portuguese.

"It would seem you are being more a distraction than a good advocate, Timóteo. You are dismissed from this hearing."

In silence, the boy turned and walked out of the chamber. Although the little Brother had been of little help, Thomas felt a loss at his leaving.

With icy calm, the Inquisitor regarded Thomas again. "It is not our purpose here, senhor, to play 'guessing games.' And we do, indeed, fear you are damned. We found this in your clothing." He held up the small roll of parchment De Cartago had given Thomas.

I have not even looked at what was writ thereon, Thomas thought, beginning to panic. *De Cartago said it was a map.*

"Do you still deny that you have practiced sorcery?"

Thomas shut his eyes. "I do not know what is writ on that parchment. De Cartago had me take it for safekeeping. I am not a sorcerer."

"Let it be noted that Senhor Chinnery is, as yet, unrepentant."

"How can you . . . you have no proof, no witnesses! How dare you accuse me of anything?"

"We can produce witnesses, senhor, who heard you murmuring spells with the sorcerer. They believe you used sorcery to create chaos in their ranks so that you could escape." The Inquisitor shrugged. "But that is of little importance. It is the sacred charge of the Santa Casa to let each guest seek for himself the sin in his soul. Only when he, himself, has recognized his sin, can he freely confess, purge his soul of evil, and be forgiven by God. It would, in fact, be wrong of us to make accusations and tell you your error, for it would deny you self-knowledge. You might simply parrot what we say, and thereby avoid humbling yourself before Heaven."

Dear God. Not only does his face resemble the lanes of London, his mind is as mazelike. Am I in the presence of madmen?

"Perhaps the fault lies with us," the Inquisitor went on. "Our kindness may have spared you the hard delving of the soul that leads to revelation. Perhaps your errors will become more clear to you through privation. Perhaps even harsher treatment may be needed to bring the truth to your eyes. To do the blessed work of saving your soul, we are prepared to do whatever is necessary. And we are, senhor, very patient."

XVI

LILY: This plant hath a long stem, bulbous root, and flowers that are bell- or horn-shaped. It is sacred to Saint Catherine, and it is said to have first grown from the fallen tears of Eve as she was driven from Eden. Juice of the lily heals poisonous bites, and the ground root will soothe burns. To some, the lily is the flower of the degenerate and the cowardly. Others say it represents the soul and is a flower of death, and will grow upon the grave of an innocent man who has been executed. In the Church, the lily hath long been symbolic of purity, and the Resurrection. . . .

P adre Gonsção stood in the last of the morning shade at the back gate of the Santa Casa. He leaned back against the stucco wall, waiting. He had spent the night ascertaining that the Santa Casa did, indeed, have the body of the sorcerer De Cartago, in a box in a cool, damp cellar. No one had come to claim him. Perhaps understandable; anyone who did would immediately be under suspicion of colluding with the sorcerer's cabal.

Gonsção had spoken with the monk who had examined the body. The monk had been quite certain: De Cartago was dead beyond a doubt.

Have these Jesuits sunk so low that they will resort to tricks and lies in order to help their countrymen? Have they forgotten that duty to God comes before duty to nation?

Down the street, amidst the jostle of people, the old Padre Estevão and the burly Brother Andrew were approaching at a brisk walk.

Well. They have much to prove, these paulistas. *And if they cannot, they will learn that we of the Santa Casa do not take such foolishness lightly.*

The gate beside him opened and Brother Timóteo ran out, all flailing arms and legs. "There you are, Padre!" He rushed up and grasped Gonsção's sleeve. "The *inglês!* Domine Sadrinho has started his tribunal, when he is not even well enough yet. You must come!"

"*Madre Maria!*" Gonsção breathed, then chided himself for the outburst. *Of course Sadrinho did not inform me.* He looked back toward the approaching Jesuits. *Were they part of his plan to distract me or are they a separate problem?*

"Padre, please!"

"Yes, Timóteo. Thank you, I will go at once. But I must ask something of you. Those two *paulistas* are coming to speak with me. What they have to say is very important, so I want you to invite them to the tribunal. Do not fear the Domine; he will want to hear what they say. I shall take full responsibility."

Bewildered but obedient, the boy said, "As you wish, Padre," and ran out into the street to intercept the Jesuits.

Gonsção went inside the gate and strode as fast as he could to the Audience Hall. *If the* paulistas *were Sadrinho's ploy, I may, at least, embarrass him. If they are not, they may prove an annoyance and may gain me time to learn more. If they can do as they claim . . . well, it is not every day one witnesses a miracle.*

The guards at the door to the Audience Hall were startled, but did not bar Gonsção's entry. Gonsção threw open the doors of the hall, gratified to see the surprise on Sadrinho's face.

The tribunal had been clearly under way for some time, but it was poorly attended. Inquisitors Sadrinho and Pinto were present, along with the secretary, who looked back and forth between the Inquisitors and Gonsção in perplexity. But the required seven witnesses were not to be seen, nor was the Archbishop. *Even more curious.*

At the near end of the table, facing away from Gonsção, was the fair-haired young *inglês*, attended by his heavily muscled cell guard. The *inglês* seemed pale and weary.

"Forgive my tardy arrival, Domines," said Gonsção, with a hasty bow. "But I have only just learned that this tribunal was taking place."

Sadrinho produced a sickly smile. "Forgive us, Padre, but we were unable to locate you in order to inform you."

"Of course. I have been out collecting information pertinent to this case. In fact, by amazing coincidence, I have been approached by two men who can bring valuable evidence. They will be here shortly."

Gonsção walked around the table and stood behind the secretary. "If you will permit me to review what has already been said?" Gonsção turned back the pages of the ledger and scanned the notes.

Sadrinho's smile melted into a frown. "You have asked others to come to this tribunal without my permission? That is impermissible, Padre."

"I understand. Ordinarily, I would never think of doing such a thing. But what these men have told me is so . . . extraordinary, Domine, that once you have heard them, I am sure you will agree with my judgment. Ah, here they are."

The Jesuits stood in the doorway, peering inside anxiously.

Inquisitor Sadrinho stared at them a moment, then rose

from his chair. "Padre Estevão. Somehow I am not surprised. Padre Gonsção, I regret to inform you that you have made an error. Padre Estevão begs mercy for any of his former countrymen. I am sure he has nothing to offer concerning this particular case."

Gonsção could tell nothing from the Inquisitor's expressionless face. "If you will but hear them, Domine, you may believe otherwise."

He gestured for the two monks to enter. The old Jesuit immediately went to the side of the young *inglês* and whispered urgently to him in their guttural, hissing tongue. The young man was surprised and apparently pleased to see him.

The Scots monk approached with more caution. Not without reason, it appeared, for when the young *inglês* saw the burly monk, he stood and growled a word even Gonsção understood. *It would seem the word for "illegitimate child" is similar in all languages. So, they are acquainted. This becomes more interesting still.*

"Your visitors are upsetting our guest," said Sadrinho. "With all respect, Padre Gonsção, I must insist that these men depart before we continue this tribunal."

"I beg but a moment of your patience, Domine. For I surely believe Cardinal Albrecht will find their testimony of interest, and therefore you should be made aware of it."

The name of the Grand Inquisitor seemed to give Sadrinho pause. "Very well. A moment, then. Speak."

"This is Brother Andrew of Scotland. Pray tell this court, Brother, what you have told me."

The burly monk smiled at the Inquisitor. "Rejoice, for I bring you glad tidings, Domine. The man you have truly sought, Bernardo De Cartago, is not dead."

Gonsção coughed. *This monk dares jest with Scripture? Sadrinho, of course, will not recognize it.*

"Not dead?" said Sadrinho, raising a brow. His mouth

twisted into an amused smile and he glanced at Inquisitor Pinto. The smaller man shook his head. "How very odd," Sadrinho went on. "Is it not his body, then, that lies in a coffin in our cellars?"

"It may be his *corpus*, indeed," said Brother Andrew, "but in a state of deep slumber, not death. As I have explained to the good Padre, the heathen fakirs and yogis of this land are capable of feigning death for long periods of time. I submit to you that De Cartago has learned this trick in order to escape your scrutiny. For the sake of poor, innocent Senhor Chinnery here, I offer to awaken the sorcerer for you."

"Awaken him?" said Sadrinho. "By what means?"

"Prayer, and a relic."

"What relic might this be?"

"A powdered mixture of blessed herbs and the dried blood of Santa Margarita. From my homeland. I carry it with me always."

"Powdered blood." Sadrinho became very still, like a cat that has sensed movement in the grass.

"Yes, Domine."

Could this be the same powder Timóteo said he had read about in the ledgers? thought Gonsção. *The powder that brought good men to doubt their faith? No wonder Sadrinho is fascinated.*

"You should teach more caution to your tongue, Brother Andrew," said Gonsção. "Or one might assume you are a sorcerer yourself."

"Me? May the Good Lord strike me dead at this moment if that is so. I have learned what I know about sorcery from the *Maleus Maleficarum*, a text for defeating witches, not emulating them. Will you allow me, Domine, the chance to prove my claim?" Brother Andrew clasped his hands over his belly and waited.

It would seem, thought Gonsção, *the surprise I brought to Sadrinho is better than I'd planned.*

"Of course," Brother Andrew went on, "this is with the understanding that, if I am successful in awakening the sorcerer, you will release the young *inglês* into our care."

It was Gonsção's turn to be surprised. "I never made such an agreement with you! The Inquisition does not bargain for souls like a moneychanger in the marketplace!"

"That has not always been true," said Padre Estevão, "in my experience. The value of a soul is not always beyond price. Even ancient Abraham bargained with God for the souls of his people."

"Domine, I apologize—"

But Sadrinho held up his hand. "No, no apology is needed, Padre. You were correct to bring these men here. I think there is much to be learned from this Brother Andrew."

"And, of course, if I fail," the Scots monk said, "you have me at your mercy, to do with what you will."

"You speak as though the Santa Casa actively seeks souls on whom to render judgment."

"The enthusiasm of the Inquisition in her duties is legendary," said Brother Andrew.

"Only because our purpose is misunderstood," said Sadrinho. "But we will accept your bargain, Brother, on the condition that, should you fail, Padre Estevão also suffers whatever consequence befalls you."

Padre Estevão cast a worried glance at the Scots monk. With a sigh, he crossed himself and said, "I so agree. God help me."

Sadrinho nodded. "Excellent. This tribunal is suspended while we test Brother Andrew's claim." He picked up the silver bell from the table and rang it twice. The two door guards stepped in, hands on their truncheons. "Go to the mortuary and get the body of Senhor Bernardo De Cartago."

"Bring it *here,* Domine?"

"That is what I said, did I not?"

The guards bowed and departed in an instant.

For the next uncomfortable quarter of an hour, Padre Estevão prayed with the young *inglês*, who seemed not to comprehend what was occurring. Inquisitor Pinto shifted in his chair and plucked at his sleeve. Inquisitor Sadrinho watched Brother Andrew with a predatory gaze. *What madness have I set in motion?* thought Gonsção.

The guards returned, carrying on their shoulders a plain wood coffin. Their faces wrinkled with disgust as they set the box onto the long table, shoving the missal and silver bell out of the way. Carved into the coffin lid were the letters *M.N.*, standing for *Morto Negatio*, indicating that the remains it contained were of one who had died unrepentant.

The smell issuing from the coffin was eloquent of what lay within.

"It would seem," Gonsção said as he came around the table to stand beside the Jesuits, "that you have much to prove, Brother Andrew."

Sadrinho watched with calm curiosity. Inquisitor Pinto stood and backed away from the table, crossing himself. The young *inglês* also backed away until he bumped into his cell guard, who firmly grabbed his shoulders. The secretary turned pale and wrote a few hesitating notes in his ledgerbook. The guards who had brought the coffin looked as though they would rather be elsewhere.

"Open it," Sadrinho said.

They winced, but the guards pulled their truncheons from their belts. They struck at the coffin lid until it fell off and clattered onto the table. Fetid air spilled out and the guards staggered back, hands over their faces, coughing.

Gonsção held his sleeve across his nose and mouth and peered into the coffin. The bearded corpse was naked, except for a stained cotton cloth draped over his loins. His skin was grey and the abdomen slightly distended from bloating. The initials *M.N.* had also been carved into the skin of the sorcerer's chest, probably by the monk who did the final examination. The flesh on one wrist had been chewed upon by some opportunistic rat. "*Feigned death*, you say, Brother?"

"Yes," said Brother Andrew. "Remarkable, is it not?"

Gonsção stepped aside and gestured at the corpse. "In that case, by all means, awaken him. Or show us the magnitude of your folly."

Brother Andrew pulled out of his sleeve a piece of folded parchment and opened it carefully. "If you will begin the prayers, Padre Estevão," he said, bending over the edge of the coffin. The old monk rolled his eyes to Heaven and crossed himself. Softly, he began to intone the Ave Maria.

From a pouch hanging at his belt, Brother Andrew removed a small opalescent bottle and tugged at its cork stopper.

"No!" cried the young *inglês*. He lunged toward the Scots monk but was restrained by his cell guard.

Brother Andrew muttered something at him.

Sadrinho raised his brows and walked over to the young man. "You recognize the bottle, do you?" he said in Latin.

The fair *inglês* stared at the floor and did not speak.

"Please continue, Brother Andrew," said Sadrinho.

Padre Stevens was now on the Lord's Prayer, as the Scots monk unstoppered the bottle and poured a fine brown powder from it onto De Cartago's mouth. The powder bubbled and liquefied, turning a deep crimson as it seeped between the grey lips.

I have heard the blood of martyred saints will sometimes turn to liquid on feast days or occasions of great import, thought Gonsção. *Is this such a miracle? Or is it the blood of a mythical beast, as Timóteo says, and we are committing a heinous sin?*

Brother Andrew restoppered the bottle and placed it back in his belt-pouch. A long minute passed as they all stared at the man in the coffin.

"Well?" said Sadrinho.

"Perhaps, because he has been in the stupor so long, the powder is slow to take effect."

Gonsção sighed, disgusted, and turned away.

He heard a loud thud behind him.

What now? Despite himself, he turned again to look. The coffin jumped violently on the table, with no man touching it. *Merciful Heaven. Might it be . . .*

The coffin rocked once more.

Brother Andrew said, "You see? At last he wakes from his peaceful slumber."

"God help us," breathed Padre Stevens, aghast, and he crossed himself again.

The young *inglês* hid his face in his hands. The pale secretary appeared ready to crawl beneath the table. The guards who had brought the coffin stepped back, their truncheons at the ready. Heart pounding, Gonsção stepped up to the coffin and looked in.

The grey body shuddered. The eyes opened.

"Rise, you stinking Lazarus!" declared Brother Andrew. "In the name of the Almighty, rise and face the world with the rest of us suffering souls."

His arms trembled like a man with palsy, but the sorcerer reached up and grasped the sides of the coffin. The chewed-upon wrist leaked dark blood, but skin was growing back over the wound. Gonsção again covered his face with his sleeve. *Powdered blood that brings the dead to life, just as Timóteo said. The blood of a monster. What have we done? Have we dredged up a tormented soul from the depths of Hell?*

Slowly, the once-dead man rose up to a seated position. His head lolled about on his neck and his facial muscles spasmed, uncontrolled. His terrible gaze took in the room, and all standing in it, blood-red eyes blazing with horror and accusation. He fixed his stare upon Sadrinho and opened his mouth, revealing a black mass of rotted flesh. His jaw worked to speak, but instead he emitted a loud, strangled roar.

"So," murmured the Inquisitor, "it is true." And he smiled.

This proved too much for the thin secretary, who bolted from the chamber, whimpering prayers.

De Cartago rolled his head to face Brother Andrew and growled something dark and incomprehensible.

If he speaks curses, I would be well afraid, thought Gonsção.

Brother Andrew paled, but said, "Are these the thanks I deserve, senhor, for rousing you from harmful slumber?"

De Cartago did not speak but his baleful stare was cloquent.

"Do you know where you are, Senhor De Cartago?" Gonsção asked as forcefully as he could. "This is the Santa Casa. Blasphemy and sorcery will not be tolerated here. Whatever nightmare you may have come from, in this Holy House you will behave in the correct manner."

De Cartago swiveled his gaze to Gonsção. He nodded once, knowingly, and Gonsção felt chilled to the heart. His hand shaking, Gonsção reached for the rosary at his belt and raised the crucifix before him.

The risen sorcerer grinned ghoulishly and emitted thick, grunting laughter.

"I would not be so reckless, Senhor De Cartago," said Sadrinho. "For your traveling companion"—he indicated the young *inglês*—"has yielded *this* up to us." He held up the small roll of parchment.

De Cartago turned his head to glare down at the young *inglês*.

In Latin, the young man said, "No, *Magister*, I did not give it to him. They searched my clothes and found it. I told them nothing—" Perhaps realizing the indiscretion of his words, Senhor Chinnery shut his mouth and eyes and turned his face away.

Brother Andrew sucked in his breath and clicked his tongue.

Sadrinho ignored the outburst from the *inglês* and held out his hand toward Brother Andrew. "Give me the bottle."

Brother Andrew hesitated and the guards edged closer to him. With a sigh, he pulled the bottle again from his pouch and gave it to the Inquisitor. "There is not much left."

Another roar came from the coffin, and De Cartago swung a spindly grey arm toward the Inquisitor. Sadrinho deftly stepped out of the sorcerer's reach. But De Cartago had leaned too far, and he and the coffin toppled off the table and onto the floor.

"Poor man," said Sadrinho. "He must not yet be . . . fully awake. One of you—take him to an empty cell where he can rest before we question him."

The guards' faces turned ashen. "Please, no, Domine."

"If you need rest as well, there are plenty of cells empty and available."

Gonsção knew he should interfere—it was not proper to threaten servants of the Santa Casa in such a way. But he, too, was eager to have the ghastly, resurrected sorcerer removed from his sight.

Through gestures, the guards determined which one would take the grisly duty. The unfortunate one lifted the coffin back onto the table and picked the sorcerer up in his arms, grimacing in disgust. De Cartago waved his arms and legs and tried to beat at the guard with his fists. But his muscles still seemed not to obey his will, and his strength was clearly failing. His blows were weak and most missed their mark.

"Treat him gently," said Sadrinho. "His soul is precious to us, being so dearly recovered. We do not want him to sleep so soundly again so soon."

"Yes, Domine," growled the unlucky guard, and he swiftly departed with his gruesome charge.

Everyone in the chamber sighed as soon as the sorcerer was gone. Gonsção lowered his crucifix. *Dear God, forgive us.*

"The air already smells sweeter," murmured Sadrinho.

The young *inglês* coughed and began to retch.

"Return Senhor Chinnery to his cell, if you please," said Sadrinho to the cell guard, who seemed only too happy to comply.

"Wait!" said Brother Andrew. "You agreed he was to be released to us if I awakened your sorcerer."

Gonsção marveled at the mask of compassion that appeared on the Inquisitor's face. "But, clearly," said Sadrinho, "you must see that the young man is too ill to travel. He must recover first. And the proper forms must be written and signed." Sadrinho nodded at the cell guard, who took the *inglês* from the chamber.

"I had hoped you would be a man of your word, Domine," said Padre Stevens.

"Have I yet broken it?" said Sadrinho. "I have every expectation that Senhor Chinnery will be leaving the Santa Casa soon. I assure you that you will be informed when he does. Now I must ask that you leave, Padre Estevão. We have already broken several strictures by permitting you to visit, but given the extraordinary circumstances, I will not hold it against you."

"Very well," grumbled Padre Stevens. "We shall be waiting. Come, Brother," he said to the Scots monk.

"No," said Gonsção. "I must ask that Brother Andrew remain with us a while longer. After all, it may be that we have just witnessed a miracle, and we should learn as much about it as we can. Grand Inquisitor Albrecht in Lisboa would, no doubt, wish to hear of it. On the other hand, if it was sorcery, Brother Andrew should be concerned for the state of his soul. For his own sake, surely, he should stay and discuss this amazing occurrence further with us."

Sadrinho nodded to Gonsçao, a touch of admiration in his eyes. "My thoughts exactly, Padre. There is much in this mystery to be explored. Please stay, Brother Andrew. I am eager to hear all about this wondrous relic you have brought to us."

"But I tell you, there was no miracle or sorcery at work here," protested Brother Andrew. "Only a Hindu trick that I was able to foil with prayers and a pinch of powder!"

"Oh, I enjoy hearing about Hindu tricks," said Sadrinho. "Perhaps you may teach us how not to be fooled again. Good day, Padre Estevão."

The old Jesuit sighed and gave the Inquisitor a curt nod. To the Scots monk, he said, "May the Good Lord keep you and protect you . . . Brother." He departed, weariness in his step.

As soon as Padre Stevens was beyond the door, Gonsção turned to the Scots monk. "Please sit with us, Brother Andrew. Tell us exactly where you got this relic. The blood of Santa Margarita, you say? She must have been a martyr of rare accomplishment."

Brother Andrew neither moved nor spoke.

Sadrinho shook his head. "Padre, you are too impatient. You have forgotten how men are led to speak the truth."

"Surely you are not going to put *me* to the question?" said Brother Andrew.

"The state of your soul is the concern of your Order, Brother. We have the duty to inform it of any transgressions we observe. It is for your Father Superior to give whatever penance may be required. But I am sure that will not be necessary, and that your answers to a few simple questions should satisfy us. I noticed, for example, that Senhor De Cartago seemed to recognize you. Do you know him?"

"I . . . was a passenger on the English ship that captured him."

"English heretics permitted a Jesuit to sail with them?"

"Not all Englishmen are judgmental, and my money for passage was deemed as good as any man's."

"I see," said Gonsção. "And Senhor Chinnery seemed to recognize you as well. Was he also on this ship?"

"He was, Padre. The young *inglês* is an herbalist and a healer. Naturally, our work overlapped at times."

"Ah. But his greeting to you just now was not what I would call friendly."

"No. We . . . quarreled before we parted company."

"Hm. There is overlap between the work of herbalists and that of witches. Did you ever see any such sorcery performed by Senhor Chinnery?"

"No. Never."

"I noticed Senhor De Cartago recognized the bottle of miraculous powder. He must have seen it before, yes?"

"Yes, I had shown it to him."

"And Senhor Chinnery as well?"

"Yes, of course."

"Of course. And it would seem Senhor Chinnery knew the importance of its contents, given his reaction when you produced it here. Did you ever lend the powder to him, for . . . awakening fakirs?"

"He used it once, to bring a cabin boy out of a stupor."

"Am I to understand," said Gonsção, "that an English heretic trusted a papist relic? I have heard that some would rather die than do such a thing."

The Scots monk shrugged. "He knew its efficacy, and healing, to him, was of primary importance."

"More important than his soul?"

"Surely," said Brother Andrew with an anxious smile, "the prayers said with the application of the powder would shield his soul from harm."

"Do you know," said Gonsção, "there are certain persons who call themselves white wizards, who claim prayer to be an important part of their sorcery. I find this even more heinous than the Black Art, for these persons would harness angels as slaves to do their bidding. I do not believe, Brother, that prayer is enough to save a man's soul, if he accompanies it with foul deeds. Did you allow Senhor De Cartago to use the powder?"

"No!"

"But he knew what it was."

"We had learned he was an alchemist, and Senhor Chinnery was short of medicines. So we discussed with him what we had and whether he had knowledge or stores to help us."

"You trusted a sorcerer's knowledge?"

"I had no proof that he was a sorcerer, nor did he ever claim to be. And even evil men may give useful information."

Gonsção sighed and took a few steps toward the giant cross hanging on the wall. "We would like to believe you, Brother, truly. But we have heard that one person aboard your ship betrayed De Cartago and Senhor Chinnery to the pirates who brought them here to Goa. For all I know, that Judas may have been you. In which case, none of what you say can be credited."

"If I had wished to be so rid of him," growled Brother Andrew, "why would I have come here to his aid?"

"That is an interesting question. No, no." Gonsção held up his hand. "Speak no more now. Mistakes are made when a man speaks in haste. But, you see, too many pieces are missing from this puzzle. It worries me."

"Yes," said Sadrinho. "Perhaps you should stay with us until the young *inglês* is well. While here, you can give him counsel. Perhaps you can impress upon him the peril his soul may be in. Of course, you will both be permitted to leave, as soon as we have a more complete and sensible explanation. Of particular interest to me is the origin of this wonderful relic. No Santa Margarita I have heard of is described as having shed healing blood. It must be that your memory has temporarily failed you. We will give you time to think and pray, Brother, until you can give a more reasonable answer."

"I will not be harmed?"

"Surely a brother in Christ will give us no cause for harm?" Sadrinho nodded at the remaining guard.

"This way, if you please, Brother," said the guard. "We have a pleasant room available for you in the residential wing."

His fists clenched and unclenched, but the Scots monk at last relented. "Until later, then, Domine. Padre." He allowed himself to be led from the chamber.

"And God go with you too, Brother," said Gonsção, even though Brother Andrew was beyond hearing.

Sadrinho gazed down at the opalescent bottle in his hand and stroked it almost lovingly. "I must thank you, Padre. You have done more for our investigation than I ever hoped."

"Will you, then, do me the kindness of trusting me with what you know, so that I may better understand what it is I have brought you?" said Gonsção.

"Indeed. You have earned it. You know, when you first arrived, I was uncertain about you, Padre. I was not sure we were . . . pursuing the same goals. Now, it would seem whatever our original intentions, our arrows fly to the same target.

Come to my offices after vespers tomorrow. All knowledge I have shall be yours as well."

"Why so long a wait? Can you not tell me now?"

"There are some thoughts I must put in order, so that I may present it to you as a coherent whole. But you will hear all of it, I promise you." Smiling like a child with a long-desired new toy, Sadrinho held the bottle to his chest and walked out of the chamber.

"What have you done?" came a loud whisper behind Gonsção. He started and turned around. Inquisitor Pinto, who had stood so silently in a far corner of the chamber that Gonsção had forgotten his presence, approached, the hems of his black robe sweeping the floor. He came right up to Gonsção, a frown on his small, handsome face.

"That is what I hope to learn, myself, Domine."

"Don't you see? I thought you had come to Goa to return this Santa Casa to its proper duties and concerns. That is why I helped you. This . . . *pulvis mirabile* has been an obsession with Sadrinho, ever since he learned of it. He has thought of little else. Now you bring the very thing I prayed he would abandon within our very walls. There will be no end of it now. We are undone. God have mercy on us."

"Forgive me," Gonsção began to say, but found he was speaking to Inquisitor Pinto's departing back.

Gonsção felt his shoulders droop, whether with the weight of responsibility or from weariness he was not sure. Last to leave the great Audience Chamber, Gonsção shut the doors behind him and lingered in the hallway.

He found himself staring at a wall hanging on which was embroidered the emblem of the Dominican Order. It depicted Saint Dominic, holding an olive branch in one hand and a sword in the other. Below the saint were a dog with a burning brand in its mouth, and an orb surmounted by a cross. On a banner above the saint's head were the words "Justitia at Misercordia."

It had been Saint Dominic who, when a soldier, had said, "Kill them all. God will know his own." *Dear Lord*, thought Gonsção, *would you could grant us that same power; to know who is your own and who is not, while they yet live.*

XVII

HOLLY: This bush is evergreen and bears thorny leaves. In early summer, it brings forth white flowers which, in autumn, are followed by red berries. Care must be taken in its use, for the berries are poison to children. 'Tis said the Cross of Christ was hewn from holly wood and, as penance, the holly no longer grows tall. Also it is thought the Crown of Thorns was made from the holly, and that the berries, which once were yellow, became red from Our Lord's blood. The Welsh believe that to take holly into the house ere Christmas Eve invites quarrels. To bring it into the house of a friend is to bring death. In like wise, it is dangerous to pick holly that is blossoming, and treading upon the berries brings ill fortune....

Thomas sat rocking on his cell pallet, chin to his knees, thoughts as chaotic as a cloud of gnats. *Wherefore did I speak when De Cartago looked at me? Surely I have doomed myself. Wherefore did Lockheart reappear in monk's guise, to brave the Santa Casa and bring the alchemist to life again? Did he truly believe 'twould free me? I am surrounded by madmen, judge and rescuer alike. Lord let me retain some semblance of my own wits. I shall need all I have to endure and escape this place.*

The cell doors rattled and his now-familiar guard came in. Behind him came Timóteo, holding a large roll of parchment tied with a red ribbon.

"Good evening, little Brother," said Thomas. "I thank you for the help you tried to give at my tribunal. A pity you had to leave so soon. You missed a most amazing sight."

Brother Timóteo did not meet his eyes and his face was very grave. "So I have been told, senhor." He put the rolled-up parchment on the cot beside Thomas.

"What is this you bring me?"

"I bring the only advice permissible to one in your place, senhor. You must look into your soul, examine your sins, and beg the Lord for forgiveness. This document is a declaration of confession, senhor. Domine Sadrinho says that if you sign this, he will clear the way for your release. He believes you have been misled by others and knows that you can be forgiven."

Thomas shrank away from the parchment as if it were fire. "I thought arrangements were being made to release me to the care of Padre Stevens."

Timóteo sighed. "You will be released, senhor. But it is the duty of the Santa Casa to look after your soul. If we were to let you go without giving you the chance to confess, it would be as though we were sending you to Hell."

Ah. I am yet a heretic to them, and must not be permitted to depart as such. "Which sins does that document . . . allow me to confess?"

The boy stole a glance at the guard, who was idly examining his fingernails. "Heresy, senhor. And sorcery. I do not know what else."

And I had thought my soul in peril ere now. To confess to heresy would be to renounce the faith he had been born into and baptized in. *To renounce it!* In Fox's *Book of Martyrs,* Thomas had read of many who died in torment during the bloody reign of Mary rather than turn apostate. *Have I as much courage as they? When I am so close to escaping this madness?* "Surely," he said to Timóteo, "you do not know what you ask."

His eyes sad, the boy said, "It is not I who ask, but if it

were my place, I would ask it. I do not want your soul to be claimed by the Evil One."

The boy truly believes in what the Inquisition teaches. "This is difficult to explain, little Brother, but according to my faith, by giving me this to sign, that is precisely what may happen."

Timóteo shook his head. "That cannot be true. Your heretic church has lied to you."

Or yours to you. Holding his anger in check, Thomas said, "I think not."

"God sees the truth," said Timóteo, "and Domine Sadrinho and all Inquisitors are inspired by God."

If so, Heaven help us, thought Thomas. He had no more arguments to offer in the face of the boy's unshakable faith. "What will the Domine Inquisitor do if I sign?"

The boy tightened his lips. "I do not know exactly, senhor. Those who confess and are absolved usually remain a guest of the Santa Casa until the next auto-da-fé. At that time, sentence is passed and they are released into the world, to await the justice of the *governador.*"

"I see. When is the next auto-da-fé?"

"I cannot say, senhor."

"When was the last one?"

"Before Christmas last year."

"And the one before that?"

"I do not remember, senhor."

"So. I could be here for years. How merciful."

Brother Timóteo seemed near tears. "Please, senhor. Others have found peace here and joy in the forgiveness of God. What are years in this sinful world compared to eternity in Heaven?"

This boy will make an excellent priest someday. Unfortunately. "Before I sign, can you tell me what may have become of the other Jesuit who was at my tribunal, Brother Andrew?"

The guard at the door turned and loudly cleared his throat.

"You must not concern yourself with others, senhor. Not while your own soul is in such peril."

"I see. And . . . if I do not sign the confession?"

Brother Timóteo gazed down at the floor. "Then may God have mercy on your soul."

"Are you implying I will be killed?"

The boy looked up, shocked. "The Santa Casa does not kill!"

"There is no torture? None of your guests ever die at the Inquisitors' hands?"

Timóteo averted his gaze again. "The Domines do all they can to compel guests of the Santa Casa to see the truth."

"And if the guests cannot withstand that compulsion?"

Timóteo picked up the roll of parchment and thrust it at Thomas's chest. "Please, for the love of God, sign, senhor!"

Thomas felt his heart twist within him. He could sign just to ease the tender pain he saw on the boy's face. *Whatever demon inspires you, little Brother, it has a power more terrifying than Satan himself.* "I . . . will think on it. Please, I must have time."

Timóteo sighed and twisted the rolled document awkwardly in his hands before laying it back down on the pallet. "As you wish, senhor. I will leave this with you, should God bless you with a change of heart." He turned and walked back to the guard. The cell guard grunted a question and Timóteo shook his head. The guard glanced at Thomas and also shook his head, clicking his tongue, as if Thomas had been a naughty child.

The guard and Timóteo both departed, and the closing of the door rang unnaturally loud in the silence that followed.

Thomas looked at the parchment and wondered if he

dared untie the ribbon and read it. Or if he should simply tear it up. He noticed something dark and pointed sticking out from between the parchment and the counterpane. With superstitious care not to touch the document itself, Thomas tugged at this new object. It was a yellow-green leaf, long and tapering, like that of a capsicum plant. He sniffed at it.

Is this what is called the betel? He had heard it was used by the Arabs to prevent scurvy. It was also said to be mildly narcotic, and an ease to pain. *Wherefore should the little Brother gift me with this? Is it a hint of what is to come?*

Voices and footsteps again approached his cell. Thomas stuffed the leaf into his cheek, tasting a sharp burst of bitterness.

The doors of his cell opened again and Inquisitor Sadrinho walked in. "God grant you good evening, senhor," he said with a pleasant smile.

"I hope He shall," said Thomas. "Have you come to release me?"

The Inquisitor's smile fell only a little. "Not yet, senhor. I understand you are not quite ready. We had hoped you would open your soul to truth and receive the joy of God's forgiveness. Well, these things can take time. I thought, perhaps, a walk would help to clear your mind. We find that exercise is often helpful to our guests. Will you allow me the pleasure of your company?"

Thomas paused, startled. "Am I given a choice?"

Sadrinho shrugged. "You may remain here in solitary contemplation, if you prefer."

Is this more madness? Does he plan to cajole me into signing the "confession"? The gift of the betel suggests a more dread possibility. But if I turn him away, he will only come again later. "Very well. I will go."

"Good." Sadrinho motioned to the guard.

Thomas stood and the guard came up and untied his wrists. For a moment, Thomas hoped he would, at last, have his hands free. But the guard spun him around and retied his wrists behind his back.

"A mere precaution," said Sadrinho. "And you will have to be blindfolded again."

"Is that necessary? You have me bound. Why should you blind me as well?"

"You forget, senhor, our aim is the cleansing of your soul. There is much you might see that would distract you from that goal. I have no wish to see our work undone so soon. Therefore, the blindfold."

As he said the very word, the dark cloth was dropped before Thomas's eyes and tied behind his head. The guard prodded him in the back and Thomas stepped forward, out of the cell.

"May I ask," he said, "if Brother Andrew is still here, and a prisoner, as I am?"

Thomas felt a light, stinging blow on his shoulder. "Shhh," hissed the guard.

The Inquisitor said, "You are not to speak, outside of your chamber, unless I request it. We must not distract others in the contemplation of their sins."

More madness, thought Thomas.

It took some concentration to walk bound and blind, even guided by the heavy hand of the guard. Still, from the echoes of their footsteps, Thomas guessed that they walked along a corridor that had open space to the right, perhaps a courtyard. They were above ground level, for there were sounds echoing from below.

To his left, a man screamed out, pleading in Portuguese, *"Jesu pau! Jesu pau!"* The guard moved away from Thomas, and he heard the scraping of metal on metal as a cell door was unlocked. There came the sound of a series of sickening blows, accompanied by shouts of *"Silêncio!"* followed by moans of pain.

Thomas could only stand and wait during the beating, powerless. He bit down on the betel leaf in his cheek and sucked hard on the astringent juice, hoping its effects would divert his mind.

"This is the men's wing," said the Inquisitor calmly, as if nothing untoward was occurring. "The women's wing is below."

And what indignities do your women guests suffer, I wonder? thought Thomas, though he said nothing. Soon the cell door slammed shut again and Thomas felt another prodding in his back. *Am I now stained with that poor man's blood?*

As they walked on, Thomas was unable to keep track of the turns they made from one corridor to another, and he soon felt lost. At times, the Inquisitor would give some useless tidbit of information, such as, "Here is where we receive petitions from families of our guests," or "This was once the palace of the Sultan of Goa; here was the zenana where he kept his hareem."

They passed by a room that smelled of baking bread, onions, and spices, and Thomas heard the clatter of pans and kettles. Some paces farther, Sadrinho said, "There are descending stairs here. Go on, but mind your feet."

Thomas felt forward with his right foot and stepped down clumsily. He felt with his left to get the measure of the next step before trying it. The stairs had a worn depression in the center, implying that many feet had passed this way. The steps seemed to be of roughly equal height, so Thomas continued down with more confidence.

When he reached the bottom of the steps, the Inquisitor said, "Stop," and swept past him. "We will now honor you, senhor, with a sight few of our guests have the opportunity to see."

Keys rattled in a lock ahead of him and a door opened. A gust of damp, cool air brought with it odors reminiscent of the Aljouvar. For a moment, Thomas found himself wishing he were back again in the noisome grotto of the Governor's Keep, in the fellowship of comprehendable men. *Joaquim had the right of it. Was he once a guest here, I wonder?*

"Have care," said the Inquisitor. "Here are more stairs."

These steps were narrower and uneven, and Thomas was forced to feel his way with caution, one shoulder against a wall of damp, cold stone. Faint voices and sounds at the edge of his hearing set his flesh to creeping and his hair to rise. They were the moans of men and women who had lost all wit and hope, wailing despair at hard, unhearing walls.

The moans became more apparent, and the odors more thick, as Thomas descended. He began to wonder if the Santa Casa had its own, private entranceway to Hell. *But no Beatrice or Eurydice awaits to guide me out. Only the Inquisitor. Did he not claim to be a man of God, I would think this nether realm to be his true abode.*

The steps ended at an uneven stone floor. Thomas was turned to his right, and guided into a room that smelled of a recent lime wash. A door was shut behind him and the blindfold was at last taken from his eyes.

Inquisitor Sadrinho stood before him, composed and welcoming as any generous host. "This is our questioning room. Our guests, we find, are often curious about those tools we employ to bring a lost soul back to God. I thought you, as a foreigner, might also be interested in seeing them."

Ah, here is his cajolement. Thomas had heard of the ritual showing of the instruments. For some prisoners, that alone had been enough to turn them apostate and bring confessions of heresy. The narcotic effect of the betel leaf gave Thomas some feeling of distance and calm. *These dramatics I should have the courage to withstand.*

The white room was lit only by thin tapers in sconces near the corners. Formless shadows wavered behind the tables and unrecognizable engines of metal and wood. "These," said Sadrinho with a grand sweep of one arm, "truly help to bring the earthly mind to attention. Here, for example, is the table upon which we administer the *poltro*." He proudly held up a jar containing a linen strip and explained its use. "Over here is the Throne of the Blessed Virgin." He pointed to a chair with a lead cowling whose inside bristled with blunt iron bars that would bear down on the tender portions of the body of whoever sat in it. Against another wall was the infamous rack, upon which one's limbs could be stretched beyond endurance. In one corner were "Spanish Boots" in which a man's leg could be crushed; in another stood a stack of thumb screws and pots to hold boiling oil.

Sadrinho expounded on each like a priest enumerating the sacred treasures of his cathedral. Meanwhile, the guard was meddling with the ropes binding Thomas's wrists. *Now, I wager, they will retie my hands afore for no good reason. Were my hands to be freed, I could leap forward and strangle the Inquisitor. Would I dare it? I would be slain for it, no doubt, and damned besides, but the thought hath its charms.* Thomas almost smiled.

"And this," Sadrinho exclaimed as something new was hooked around Thomas's wrists, "is the *polé*, called by some the strappado!"

Thomas was hoisted into the air, an agony of pain ripping from his wrists to his shoulders. His breath whooshed from his lungs and he found it tremendously difficult to breathe in again. He opened his mouth, but could not find the air to scream. His tongue lolled uselessly and the wad of chewed betel leaf fell to the floor.

Sadrinho bent down and picked it up. He waved it beneath his nose, then glared up at Thomas. "Where did you get this?"

Thomas was incapable of answering. He kicked his legs and wriggled his shoulders, which felt as though they would burst out from their sockets and through his skin. Movement only increased his pain.

"No matter," said the Inquisitor. "The effect of the betel will dissipate soon, and the strappado will make its full benefit felt. I will leave you until then. I suggest, in the meanwhile, that you meditate upon your sins and pray for guidance."

"For the love of God, Domine!" Thomas gasped out. "How . . . how can you—"

"As you have said, senhor. For the love of God." Sadrinho turned away and blew out each of the tapers but one. With a nod to the guard, they both departed.

Thomas fought back the panic that threatened to flood his mind. *Men have survived this. Men have survived worse. I must be calm.* Through effort of will, he managed to still his movements.

Dear God, the pain. Once the effect of the betel fades, how can I possibly endure it? He had seen many clients come into Master Coulter's shop, each with a differing experience of pain. Some bore what must have been constant agony with a sad, wincing smile. Others would scream at the barest touch of a bleeding lance. For some, pains-ease medicaments would be an instant benison. For others, nothing worked at all. *Which sort of man am I?*

He remembered suffering the birch rod as a child at his father's hands, and pummelings received as a schoolboy. But such pain was brief, and there had been much time to heal afterward. Thomas could not hope that this torment was the worst he would undergo at the hands of the Inquisition. *Unless I sign their damnable confession!*

The rope creaked above him like a ship's anchor line. *God, even to be back in the stinking hold of the* Whelp. *Lord, if my soul means aught to thee, let this rope break and release me.* But the rope remained secure as he swung slightly back and forth, a pendulum running down in time.

He tried to distract himself with thoughts of pleasanter moments. He brought visions of Anne Coulter to mind, her sweet, round face and gentle hands, hazel eyes and shy smile. But these features were quickly replaced by those of the Lady Aditi, and a memory of her form and scent as she bent over him to remake his turban. *'Tis though I were bewitched. Oh, Anne, forgive me.*

He tried to empty his mind entirely, as Eastern mystics were said to do, to let the pain become merely another feature of the room, distant from him. He focused on sounds: the dripping of water, the faint cries of others in torment, the scratching of what might be a rat by the door.

"Thomas?" someone whispered.

He involuntarily twitched his head toward the sound, sending sharp new pain into his shoulders. "Ah . . . who?"

"Shhh . . . Struggle not, lad. 'Twill make it worse. Becalm yourself."

"Andrew!" Thomas breathed, trying to keep still. "For the love of God, man, cut me down!"

"That I cannot do. We'd not escape from here. They let me see you, thinking I might minister to your soul and encourage you to confess."

"If you have any shred of Christian charity left in you, then at least ease the weight on my arms!"

"Ach, very well." Lockheart came out of the shadows and wrapped his arms around Thomas's legs, raising him a few inches. "But it will hurt the worse when I let you down again."

"My thanks," Thomas breathed, gulping in air as he slumped against the Scotsman's head and shoulders.

"I've not been given much time to speak to you, lad. But take heart, there is hope."

"Is there?" The sweetness of air in his lungs distracted Thomas and thought did not come clearly. "Have you taken the cloth and vows so earnestly that your prayers shall save me?"

"This garb is but a guise lent me by Father Stevens, to gain me entrance to this earthly circle of Hades. In some manner, it is fit for me, but that is a tale for another time. We must conceive a plan for your escape. I had thought that a risen De Cartago would be all the Santa Casa sought, but I hit only near their true desire."

"What might that be?"

"The bloody powder, lad! 'Tis not the sorcerer they wanted, but his knowledge of the source of the blood."

How bizarre, that my interests and the Inquisitors' should be so meet. "But they have De Cartago now. He can tell them."

"D'ye think you'd be in this position, lad, if he would or could? I hear the powder is slow in healing him. His tongue is yet full of rot and he cannot speak. He has no sense in his limbs—they can stick him and twist him and it frets him not. I hear he's put their best torturer off his dinner."

"A petty vengeance, that."

"Petty, indeed, and the reason the Inquisitor now aims at you. Methinks he has a whiff of the truth for he easily scented my lies. But to the matter—De Cartago befriended you, did he not?"

"Not as such."

"Well, then, thought you a fellow traveler, perhaps. Did he tell you aught of where the powder might be found? If you know anything, therein lies the path to our freedom."

The map! Sadrinho has it now. But De Cartago had to tell me what its symbols meant. So. I have a card to play. But can I trust

Lockheart? He might well take the answer from me and leave me here to rot. With so fine a thread to hang my hopes on, I must be canny.

"Did he tell you, lad, where the source of the powder lies?" Lockheart shook Thomas's legs for emphasis. "Did he?"

"Ah! Be still, I beg you. He . . . he may have. I must think on it. The pain . . . makes it hard to remember."

Lockheart sighed. "Think well, then. Have they given you a confession to sign?"

"Aye, they have."

"Sign it, then. These men free no one until a confession has been obtained. It keeps their record unblemished."

"Their record?" Thomas said. "What of the blemishment of my soul? Shall I say that I bugger goats in the graveyard or drink the blood of baptized babies? Would you have me damn myself?"

"As our good Captain Wood might have said, better to sin and live and have more time for penance, than to die for naught. Have courage, lad. Many a danger have I faced o'er the years, yet death shall not have me until I choose the time."

"Will it not? Tell me, Andrew. Is that why you betrayed the Captain and us all?"

Lockheart paused. "Mayhap. Mayhap 'twas death I feared. But I meant harm to no man, even you. 'Tis why I sent all ashore that night, as I tried to send you. 'Twas a heavy blow to my heart to see you on that dhow. But I tried to make amends. I set an altercation with a rival band of brigands as we came near Goa, at a time when I knew they'd let you from the cart. You escaped as I hoped, as did I and the Lady. I had thought 'twould be the end of it. Then I met Father Stevens to request his aid and he said you'd been arrested.

"We spoke at length. He entreated me to help him free you. My shame o'erwhelmed me and I took it as another sign that our fates are truly enjoined."

"An omen," Thomas said softly.

"If you would have it so. So I am here, captive to my duty, and thereby the Santa Casa. Only you can set us free."

"Could you not have left well enough alone? Because of your theatrics, I am now thought a sorcerer and condemned to torment unless I damn myself. Was it truly mercy brought you here? Or are you as besotted by the wondrous powder as the Inquisitor? Did you resurrect De Cartago for your own benefit, and now turn your hopes on me? Mayhap you want me to reveal what I know for your own gain, and once you have it, you will leave me here to die."

Lockheart released Thomas's legs, letting him drop. White-hot pain seared Thomas's arms, his shoulders snapped, and his lungs lost their air.

"How dare you, boy!" Lockheart cried, voice harsher than Thomas had ever heard. His shadows were monstrous against the pale wall. "You've no damn idea what it is I want! 'Twas you who came after me on that dhow, dragging the whole tapestry of the Fates with you as if you were bound to their warp threads and Hecate was your puppetmaster! As for taking your secrets and leaving you here, I say to you: Neither I nor he who sent me on our damned-to-the-devil voyage believe that this should be your time and place to die." Lockheart turned and walked to the chamber door.

"Sent you?" gasped Thomas through his agony. "Who . . . sent you? Andrew?"

But the door slammed shut, leaving only an echo for answer.

XVIII

BIRCH: This tree has white, papery bark and arrow shaped leaves. In summer, it brings forth green catkins. Its name may be from the Latin "to strike," for birch wands have oft been used for punishment. It is said that Our Lord Christ was beaten with birch staves. A bundle of birch rods was the symbol of Roman power, and their right to punish by flogging. Birch branches have, as well, been used to beat evil spirits off one's land or to beat demons out of lunatics. Some say witches make their broomsticks from birch, yet others say such brooms can sweep witches away....

The goat at her side bleated in annoyance as Aditi led it toward the temple. "Peace, foolish one," she said. "You will see Paradise soon, and perhaps a better life." She had once been told by the Mahadevi that a goat was Her favorite animal to receive in sacrifice. Tugging at the smelly beast, Aditi could not imagine why. She was only grateful that the family of Marathas who supported her generously gave her one, in exchange for prayers to the Goddess.

The temple to Mahadevi was small, and on the outskirts of Goa, beside the Mandovi River. So far, it had been overlooked by zealous Jesuits or Mughuls. The dome was simple and whitewashed, not gilded. The carvings of women on the pillars and architrave were modest.

Few other people were there that afternoon for *puja*. Still, Aditi kept her *orhni* pulled low over her face. She handed the goat's rope tether to a Brahmin at the temple's side gate. As one of the *Komti* caste, Aditi could have performed the sacrifice herself, but such a show of wealth and devotion might bring undue attention to her. She also disliked harming animals. She sighed as the goat was taken, bleating mournfully, behind the gate.

My regrets, foolish one. It must be. Ahimsa was all well and good, but the Mahadevi hungered and needed to be fed so that She could bring forth Her gift of Life.

Aditi had also given the priest a strip of palm leaf on which she had inscribed a message to the Mahadevi. With the aid of one of the temple doves, she had a better chance than many petitioners to have her message received. She had also given the priest some coins for a prophesy. Normally, fortune-telling was beneath the dignity of a Brahmin, but there was one at the temple who had a large family to support and would do so. It was beneath Aditi's dignity, as well, to ever seek augury. But having been closeted for days in the home of her supporters, she felt as though lost in a treacherous desert without night stars to guide her.

Before entering the temple, Aditi walked down the steps to the Mandovi River and walked into the water up to her knees. She was thankful the river was slow and warm at this time of year. She ritually washed her hands, arms, and face, taking care that her features were exposed to no one. She took from the cloth sling at her hip a lotus blossom and set it upon the water, letting it float away on the current. She bowed to the god of the river and walked back up the steps.

Aditi dried her feet and entered the temple archway, fearing what she might see. The idol of the Mahadevi was, in fact, two statues standing back-to-back. One of the four-armed figures was a beautiful, sweetly smiling woman, holding in her four hands stalks of rice, a cooking pot, a flower, and a water jar. The other, however, was a fierce, snarling female demon, who held in her hands a sword, a drum, a wine pot, and a severed head. Both represented the Mahadevi, in her aspects as life giver and death dealer.

The priests would turn the statues as they gauged which aspect of the Goddess was ascendant. Aditi was relieved to see that the beneficent side of the idol faced her as she entered. The idol wore a bright garland of scarlet *asoka* blossoms, although they had begun to wilt.

Aditi knelt at the base of the idol and took from the sling at her hip a small covered bowl of rice, a tiny flask of scented oil, and some strands of saffron wrapped in a palm leaf. She left these at the Mahadevi's feet and lay down, prostrate, on the cool stone of the temple floor.

Her prayers were simple. *Bring increase to those who have aided me. Forgive me for my failures. Guide me in what I must do now. Help me return to you safely.*

Aditi was not of Brahminic family, and therefore she did not concern herself with the finer points of theology. She did not question the divinity of the Mahadevi, or to what extent the goat sacrifice would appease Her, or whether the Goddess could see and hear through Her image in the temple. What mattered was *dharma*, doing the right thing. All else followed. Besides, the Mahadevi was quite real to Aditi, in a way few other worshipers ever experienced.

Aditi's family had been caravaneers. Their home had been Rajasthan, but they traveled far and wide across India. By the time Aditi was five, she could ride a camel. By the time she was six, she spoke four languages fluently: her native Sindhi, Kashmiri, Persian, and Urdu. When she was seven, her family undertook a long journey south, with a large wealth of goods, bound for Calicut. To avoid harassment from the Portuguese, they had not taken the coastal route, instead risking travel across the barren and largely un-charted Deccan plateau.

Two nights out of Bijapur, they were set upon by brig-ands. Their camels were stolen or scattered. Aditi's family was slain as she hid in a hollow among the rocks. She had been too shocked and terrified to cry, and was abandoned, unseen by the thieves.

The following morning, she saw one of the camels, head-ing west, away from her. Her father had instructed her, when lost in a wilderness, to follow a camel—it will find water. So, without a look back at the bodies of her parents and broth-ers, she numbly walked after the camel. She walked all day, sucking stones to prevent thirst, chewing on sticks to quiet the rumblings of her stomach. And the camel led her to a broad brown river, with a little village beside it.

The villagers were astonished to find the girl-child walk-ing out of the wilderness alone, amazed at her blue eyes which were not uncommon in Rajasthan but unknown in the Deccan. They called her Aditi after the goddess of the sky, and at once took her to their holy mountain, Bhagavati.

There was a city in a hollow at the top of the mountain, cut from the living rock and hidden from view. A temple palace dominated the city, and therein lived the Mahadevi. Aditi was presented to the Goddess, as a gift fallen from the sky. And the Goddess accepted her, almost as if she were a daughter.

But Aditi never saw the physical person of the Mahadevi, only shadows behind screens, for all knew to look upon Her face was death. Instead Aditi was raised by two old women, one small and sweet but weak-willed, the other tall and stern but wise. They had been old forever, they told her, and Aditi believed them.

And Aditi learned another language, Ellenica, which the Mahadevi and the old women spoke. And she was taught how to read and write, and she learned history and geography and mathematics. When she was old enough, the Mahadevi sent her back out into the world, to be Her eyes and Her messenger.

Aditi owed the Mahadevi her life, just as Gandharva did, and therefore served Her with nearly unquestioning devotion.

Aditi heard a scraping sound ahead and she looked up from the floor. The idol was turning. It stopped halfway, so that one side of each aspect was visible. The flower garland had been removed and replaced with a garland of rat skulls.

The priest who did fortune-telling peeked out from behind the idols. He caught Aditi's gaze and shook his head sadly before disappearing again.

Ai. Her mood is changing for the worse. It will not go well for me. She sat up and bowed once to the idol. *Have mercy, Great Mother. I have done what I could.*

Brother Timóteo descended the stairs toward the dungeons, letting his feet slap heavily on the stone. He had no heart for the tasks that lay ahead. *Why did I give the* inglês *the betel leaf? The Domine was right to scold me; it will take longer for the* inglês *to search his soul and find the will to confess. It is just for the Domine to punish me. But why did it have to be this? Santa Maria, could you not have made him more merciful? No, forgive me. I am being tested. Let me prove myself worthy.*

He tugged on the iron latch of the door at the bottom of the stairs. As it opened, the wails of lost souls assailed his ears. *Lord, they cry out for Your forgiveness. Do You hear them?*

Timóteo took two long keys from a rack on the wall and plodded down the central passage. He whispered a benediction at every cell he passed, his heart torn by each tormented sinner who caught sight of him and begged to be released.

At the door of the seventh cell on his left, Timóteo stopped. "Learn what comes of alliance with sorcery," Domine Sadrinho had told him. Timóteo swallowed hard and put the key in the lock. He turned it and the door swung open, silently.

A foul smell washed over him and he coughed and wrinkled his nose. It was not an odor of the living. Hugging his prayer book tightly to his chest, Timóteo walked in. *Deus lhe dê bom dia, Senhor De Cartago.*

The thing in the chair rolled its head up to stare at him. Timóteo crossed himself, trying to remember that what sat before him was once a man and a creature of God. The sorcerer's arms and legs and fingers were bent unnaturally in many places, and it seemed the ropes that bound him to the chair were more to help the man stay upright than to restrain him.

"He has not, as yet," said De Cartago, his voice so thick that it took a moment to understand him. "Who are you?"

"I am Brother Timóteo, senhor. I am to be your advocate." Timóteo wished he did not sound so small and timid.

The sorcerer laughed, a horrible, liquid barking noise. "What have you done, child, that they send you to minister to the *dead?*" De Cartago thrust his head forward at this last word and Timóteo jumped back, startled.

Anger began to override his fear. "You are not dead, senhor. You should be grateful that the Santa Casa has given you another chance to recognize your sins and confess before God. By now you must know what peril your soul faces. You should welcome our help."

"Help? The Santa Casa seeks only to help itself. To whatever it can steal. Or destroy."

"That is a lie!" Timóteo instantly regretted the outburst and tried to calm himself. An advocate must be gentle, at all costs, to show the guest the benefit of mercy. What would Domine Sadrinho say? "You have been misinformed, senhor." He looked at the floor and saw that the sorcerer's rice bowl was still full. Flies and beetles crawled over it, feasting where the guest did not. "You have not eaten."

"I have no desire for food."

"If you do not eat, you will starve and die."

"Yes."

"But your soul will return to Hell, if you die without first confessing."

The sorcerer's lips parted in a twisted smile. "Is that where you think I have been?" He leaned forward as far as the ropes would let him. "I know a secret," he said in a sepulchral voice. "Would you like to hear it?"

Timóteo paused. "Perhaps."

"I know what lies beyond death."

"Of course. You know that you should fear for your soul."

De Cartago jerked his grinning head from side to side. "It is not what you think. All you have been told is false."

Timóteo's thoughts whirled in turmoil. *He lies to confuse and frighten me. But what has he seen? To know what happens after death—but he will not be truthful with me. The Devil has got his tongue and I must pay no attention.* For a moment, Timóteo wondered whether he faced the soul of De Cartago at all, or if the corpse had been possessed by a demon. "I will not listen to your lies, senhor. If you have a soul, we will work to save it, even if its fate does not concern you now. There is more of the powder left. The Domine will bring you back again if you die without confession."

"Oh, most skilled tormentor," sighed De Cartago. "But it does not matter. The *Rasa Mahadevi* will run out and what then? Try as you might, Death is one power the Santa Casa cannot bend to its will."

"I wish you could see us differently, senhor. See us for the merciful assistance that we offer. The Domine said I should tell you that even now he seeks the source of your sorcerous powder. It will go better for you if you could confess it to him yourself."

De Cartago laughed again, darkly. "Ah, for your Domine Sadrinho to meet Her—there would be a sight."

"Her? Do you still believe your powder comes from a pagan goddess?"

"Belief is not necessary, boy. I am certain of it."

Not for the first time since Padre Gonsção had come to the Santa Casa, Timóteo felt like two people in one mind. Part of him dearly desired to ask the sorcerer everything about the creature he called a goddess. To know if she was real, if she was just as the legends said. But his duty was to try to save De Cartago's soul, not to encourage his misplaced faith. *Is this how the old* governador *was drawn into sin? Santa Maria help me.* "But this creature you worship, she is not a goddess. She is a monster, no?"

The expression on De Cartago's sunken face was hard to read in the gloom. "A monster? Some men might see her so. But those who see her so do not live long."

"So. This creature is not so merciful as Our Lord."

The sorcerer's head began to droop. "I will not argue philosophy with you, child," he said softly. "You are too young and know nothing of life."

"I know what is Truth, senhor. And that is what you should fix your thoughts upon."

"Her name is strength," De Cartago whispered. He shut his eyes and his body slumped in the chair.

"Senhor?"

The sorcerer made no sound. Timóteo did not dare touch him to see if he still lived. Timóteo backed out of the cell, swiftly shutting the door behind him. He leaned against the cold corridor wall, shaking. *What will the Domine say? Have I failed? Was I too proud, thinking I could win against a demon? What if what the sorcerer said was true? No, I must not think it.*

He reminded himself there was one more chore ahead of him. One that might, in some ways, be even worse than what he had just experienced. With a heavy sigh, Timóteo locked De Cartago's cell and plodded again down the corridor of lost souls.

XIX

CLOVER: This tiny meadow plant is spoken of in many tales. It is said that clover leaves will rise and tremble when a storm approaches. The meaning of the clover changes with the number of their leaves. A clover stem with two leaves means one will see one's beloved soon. A three-leaved clover is the sign of the Trinity and will protect one from evil—although the ancients thought it a sign of the three goddesses of Fate. A clover with four leaves, the sign of the Cross, is rare and brings great powers to see through illusion, to heal the sick, and to escape harsh circumstances. A five-leaf clover brings ill luck and sickness, but if given away, good fortune returns....

At the door of the first questioning room, Timóteo prepared himself for his next duty. He murmured a prayer and put the iron key in the lock. This door also opened silently. The hinges in the Santa Casa's dungeons were kept well oiled, so as not to be distracting to those contemplating their souls. Timóteo shut the door behind him and looked up. *"Bom dia,* senhor."

The *inglês* was not doing well. He had suffered the strappado for many hours now, and his face was white, his limbs stiff and trembling. His eyes were closed.

"Senhor?"

"Ahh!" The *inglês* jerked awake and cried out with new-found pain.

"Forgive me, senhor," said Timóteo. "I come to give you refreshment." He took from the wall a long, sharpened staff. From his leather satchel he removed a sponge that had been soaked in wine, and stuck it on the point of the staff. This he held up to the *inglês*'s mouth. "Drink, senhor. Please."

The resemblance of this act to another was not lost on Timóteo. *Thus was our Lord aided as he hung on the cross. Thus were the sins of man redeemed. Will this man understand, and submit himself to the forgiveness of God?*

With some difficulty, the *inglês* managed to suck on the sponge and swallow. After a minute, Timóteo took the sponge away.

"More, if you please, little Brother," gasped the *inglês*.

"I am not permitted to stay long, senhor." Timóteo sadly put the staff back on the wall, and the sponge back in his satchel.

"Wait. Stay. Do you, by chance . . . interpret dreams, little Brother?"

Another Bible story came to mind. *Perhaps these are signs of hope.* "I do not know. What have you dreamed, senhor?"

He whispered rapidly, trying to use little breath. "It is often the same dream, only differing in its forms. I have just had it again. There are three women, sometimes on horseback, sometimes not. They hunt me and I am prey. They call me a murderer and other hateful things. I always wake as they are about to catch me. This time, however, I was already caught and bound. I hung above a stewpot as they danced, jeering at me. I struggled but could not escape. Then you woke me."

Timóteo thought a moment. "Perhaps these women are demons, senhor. They hunt your soul, hoping you would fall away from righteousness. Now that you have fallen, they have caught you and your soul will descend into the fire."

"But I have had these dreams since I was a child. Have demons hunted me for so long?"

"We are always in danger, senhor, from the forces of Hell. But there is hope in this dream."

"Hope?"

"You are not in the fire yet. You can save yourself. I must go now. Is there anything you wish me to tell the Domine?"

The *inglês* swallowed. "Yes," he whispered.

Timóteo stepped closer. "I am listening, senhor."

"I . . . will sign the confession."

Timóteo's heart leapt with joy. "You will? And seek God's forgiveness?"

"Yes," he gasped loudly.

"Then we are both blessed this day, senhor!"

"Tell the Domine . . . please say that I am ready to tell him what he most desires to hear."

"Most gladly, senhor! God bless and keep you. I will tell the Domine at once!" Timóteo flung open the door and dashed through it, not bothering to close it behind him. Bounding up the stairs, he ran as though his feet bore the wings of angels.

The guards came in short order to cut Thomas down. The sweet rush of air into his lungs made the pain of movement almost bearable. He was weak, and could not stand on his own. His arms hung at his sides, useless, his shoulders dislocated. He was blindfolded once more and a guard carried him to a room in which two monks bathed Thomas and rubbed his back and chest with warm, scented oils. Thomas nearly wept, so exquisite did this feel after his torment.

He was returned to his cell, where a repast awaited him: the table was laden with a roast chicken, rice, oranges, and wine. Brother Timóteo was also there, smiling as though it were Christmas. The boy gladly helped Thomas eat, holding up pieces of chicken for him to bite into, sectioning the oranges, holding the wine cup to his lips, and wiping away any spillage or crumbs.

"Blessed is this day!" Timóteo said. "I knew you would be one of the saved, senhor. Glory to God in the highest!"

Thomas's thoughts, however, were not so joyful. *God forgive me. I've not the strength to suffer for my faith. If I've not sinned yet, I surely will by night's end. Many a lie must be told this night if I am to have chance of escape. So have pity, Lord, and let us say it is not for the sake of my miserable life, but for the sake of work undone, that I owe to others.*

Thomas shook his head at the next cup of wine offered. "I have had enough, little Brother, I thank you." *I must keep my thoughts clear of the fog of drink.*

Brother Timóteo cleared an area on the table and placed there a plumed quill pen in an elegant silver inkpot. Then, like a merchant presenting his most prized rug for sale, the boy unrolled and held forth the confession.

"Sign, senhor, and be free."

Thomas stared at the parchment, deliberately not reading the words thereon. He tried to lift his right hand, but his arm was too weak and it dropped back to his side. He felt a touch of pride at his rebellious limb. "Forgive me. My arm—"

"I will help you, senhor." The boy wiped the nib of the quill on the lip of the inkpot and gently placed the pen in Thomas's right hand. Standing close by his side, Brother Timóteo lifted Thomas's arm over the document and positioned his hand at the bottom.

With a heavy sigh, Thomas scrawled the initials *T.C.*

"Well done, senhor!" The boy snatched up the document and gently blew on the ink to dry it. Thomas let his arm fall back into his lap, spattering ink drops from the pen on his trousers.

Brother Timóteo did not seem to notice; he removed the pen from Thomas's hand and placed the quill back in the inkpot.

Inquisitor Sadrinho appeared at the open door of the cell, silent and austere in his black robes.

"Domine!" said Brother Timóteo. "He has signed!"

The Inquisitor opened his arms to Heaven and uttered a *Deo gratias.* To Timóteo, he said, "You have done very well, my son, you have redeemed yourself. You know where to take that."

"Yes, Domine." The boy gently rolled up the parchment and dashed out the door.

The Inquisitor nodded at the cell guard, who bowed and also departed, shutting the door behind him.

Thomas was alone with Domine Sadrinho. It occurred to him that now would have been another excellent opportunity to do violence upon the Inquisitor's person. But, of course, weak and disarmed as he was, Thomas knew he would only do little damage to the Inquisitor, and perhaps great damage to himself. He tried to smile, but found he could not bring himself to it.

"I understand there is something you wish to tell me," the Inquisitor said.

Thomas took a deep breath. "You wish to know the source of the powder that brings the dead to life."

The Inquisitor glanced back over his shoulder, then stepped toward Thomas, eyes narrowed. "What substance do you speak of?"

Lord, let him not be mad, not now. "The powder which is called *Rasa Mahadevi,* or the Blood of the Goddess. The powder which the monk named Brother Andrew used to bring De Cartago back to life."

"Hmmm," said Sadrinho, feigning disinterest, but his eyes belied him. "What goddess is this you speak of?"

Thomas thought hard. He had never been told a name other than Mahadevi, except . . . "Her name is strength."

A sharp look from the Inquisitor told Thomas he had said something important. He could only hope it was the right thing.

"But surely," Sadrinho said, "you no longer harbor pagan beliefs? You have signed our confession, after all."

"No, Domine. That is why I am willing to speak to you."

"And why should the Santa Casa be interested in this substance?"

"I can think of many reasons. If the enemies of the Mother Church have control of it, think what harm they may do."

"Mmm. And you say you can tell us where the enemies of the Mother Church might find this powder?"

Now for it. "I can do better. I will show you."

The Inquisitor frowned. "What do you mean? On the map we found in your clothing?"

"No. I will guide you, or someone from the Santa Casa, to the place where it can be found."

Sadrinho chuckled. "I hope you do not intend to play me for a fool, senhor."

Lord, let me be convincing. "There are reasons I cannot simply tell you, Domine. The site is well hidden and protected. I can tell you this much: The source lies to the east and south of Bijapur."

The Inquisitor's gaze intensified. "We already know that. What more can you offer?"

Ah. He has decided to buy my goods. Thomas shook his head. "I have not been to this place, Domine. I have only that knowledge De Cartago gave me. He said there would be signs and riddles to be solved along the way. He did not say what these will be, or where they will be. But that I have the knowledge to recognize and solve them when they are encountered."

Sadrinho drew himself up and did not speak for long moments. "It occurs to me that you may simply be very clever and hoping for a chance at escape. Yet, if what you say is true, then your guidance would be a godsend indeed. I must consult others on this. For now, rest yourself, Senhor Chinnery. You have been through a terrible trial, although you cannot deny its salutary effect on your soul. For now we have your confession, and much becomes possible. God grant you good evening, senhor." Sadrinho knocked on the door and departed when it opened.

Was that last a threat or promise? But the greed fairly shone through every pocked pore of his face. Lord, let it rule him, that I might leave this house of madness.

XX

CORAL. This substance has the shape of a plant, and
the hardness of stone. It is said to grow in the sea, and can be
found in many colors. For medicinal use, coral must be
ground only in a marble basin, else it will cause harm. As a
powder or in tincture, it will cure many ailments of the body.
Worn in an amulet, it guards one from all manner of madness
and fascinations. Bound to a masthead, it will ward from all
tempests of nature. Coral of the purest red will keep at bay
demons and furies, but brown coral will attract them. Yellow coral is, in the East, a gem of everlasting life....

Padre Gonsção stood outside the massive oak doors of
Domine Sadrinho's study. The upper panels of the doors
had been carved in deep relief: Saint Catharine bound to the
stake on the left door, Saint Dominic and his sword on the
right. The lower panels both depicted souls burning in
the flames of Hell, arms held upward, imploring. Gonsção
touched the head of Saint Catharine and asked for her blessing. Then he knocked, and a native page bowed him in.

Domine Sadrinho sat behind an enormous ebony desk,
his steepled fingers resting against his lips. He was facing
away from the door, toward the window, whose shutters were
open. A scent of jasmine wafted into the room from one of
the courtyard gardens. The copper-gold light of the setting

sun lent an almost beatific glow to the Inquisitor's face.

Gonsção crossed an expanse of thick-piled Persian rug and sat in a rosewood chair cushioned with red velvet. Preferring not to be the first to speak, he waited to be noticed.

After a moment, Sadrinho tilted his head and regarded the Padre. "Have you taken a vow of silence, Antonio? That would be awkward."

"No, Domine. I did not speak because I did not wish to disturb your thoughts."

"You do me too much kindness, Antonio. I arranged this meeting with the very intention of sharing my thoughts with you. Shall I send for refreshment? I see that you have already made yourself comfortable."

"Thank you, no, Domine." In the stiff, high-backed chair, facing the secretive Sadrinho, Gonsção did not find it possible to be comfortable.

Sadrinho nodded at the native page, who bowed and departed.

"Well, I am eager to hear what you have to tell me," said Gonsção. "Has our visitor, Brother Andrew, been more forthcoming with a reasonable tale?"

"He has proved helpful, in his own way. You know, I do regret not having confided in you from the moment you arrived. With your forgiveness, I may ascribe it to the Santa Casa's need for caution with strangers, given our work."

"Of course," said Gonsção, fighting impatience.

"Had I exercised more dispatch in finding the records of Governador Coutinho's trial for you, you would have sooner realized the importance of what the Jesuits brought to us yesterday."

"True, that would have been useful." Gonsção did not think the Inquisitor noticed the irony.

"But no matter. It has gone well, in the end. You see, it was the very powder that Brother Andrew used that has been the key to the cabal we have been investigating. I believe it was through use of this powder that De Cartago and his collaborators, Zalambur, Senhora Resgate, and the mysterious Aditi corrupted the former governor and viceroy. They were told the powder was the blood of a pagan goddess, blood that brings the dead to life. And as you have seen, the substance indeed has that power. It is no wonder they were convinced, no?"

"I can see how it might be persuasive," said Gonsção, having heard nothing he had not already deduced. "I take it you have been able to question De Cartago then, and you have confirmed this with him."

Sadrinho sighed. "Alas, the sorcerer was so decayed, he felt none of our tender ministrations and thus told us nothing. He did not eat or drink and has died again. With what little of Brother Andrew's powder remained, I revived him."

"You . . . used the powder yourself?" Gonsção began to understand Domine Pinto's alarm. "We have no idea where it comes from. Have you no concern for the state of your own soul?"

"Nonsense, Antonio. God would not have put this substance into my hands if I'd not been intended to use it. And it was for His work, after all. Ah, watching breath return into that cold corpse, Antonio! An experience I shall not forget. But it was to no avail. De Cartago quickly succumbed once more. As we have no more of the powder, De Cartago is lost to us."

"A pity, of course. But his soul is lost to God, not to us."

Sadrinho opened his hands outward as if to suggest that it was much the same thing.

"I am concerned, Domine, that you may be sliding into the same pit that snared Coutinho and the others."

Sadrinho smiled. "Antonio, you cannot be serious. Do you fear I shall believe it was the dried blood of a pagan goddess?

Give me more credit, if you please. In my opinion, Coutinho and de Albuquerque were deceived."

"And what do you believe to be the truth of the matter?"

"Clearly there is a foreign power who is importing this substance in order to corrupt Goa's government. There are many who are displeased with Portugal's presence on this continent. The Sultanate of Bijapur still bristles from its loss of Goa."

Gonsção nodded. "This is reasonable. And disturbing. Do you know which foreign power may be doing this?"

"Not yet."

"And where might this foreign power have found such a powerful substance?"

Sadrinho leaned forward on the table. "India is a vast continent, Antonio. You have no idea of what wonders are to be found here. But I have lived here many years, heard many stories and seen many amazing things. There are animals, in the interior, that can be found nowhere else. Spices and minerals abound with unknown properties. Might it not be that this blood is from a rare animal? Snakes have been often mentioned by the conspirators, I will point out. The Hindus speak of a race of creature part man, part serpent, that lives in the wilderness."

"But this may be mere folklore, Domine. Our own people have stories of El Cuélebre, a serpent with wings that guards mountains of treasure and possesses powerful enchantments."

Sadrinho's eyes flashed. "Yes, interesting, is it not? Then, again, the powder might not be blood at all, but dried sap from a rare tree, or a form of iron ore whose appearance and scent mimics blood."

"Yes, I suppose such is possible," said Gonsção. "But the power of resurrection must belong to God alone. Therefore we must still regard this substance, whatever its source, as evil. Its use must be forbidden by the Santa Casa."

Sadrinho clicked his tongue. "You amaze me, Antonio, with such provincial thinking. Is a sword evil? Perhaps when a thief or murderer wields it, but not of itself. Surely your Saint Dominic did not carry an object of inherent evil. Were the swords held by those who drove the heretic Moors from our homeland evil? Do you think that the battle we of the Santa Casa wage against heresy should be a *mourisca*, to be danced with paper horses and wooden swords? Here, Antonio, delivered into our hands, is a *real* weapon for our holy armory."

Gonsção tightly gripped the arms of his chair. "What need does the Santa Casa have for such a . . . weapon?"

Sadrinho rapped the table with the palm of his hand. "I cannot believe you are so blind, Antonio. By the very use we have already made of this powder! With its help, we can, with certainty, obey one of our primary strictures; above all, the Santa Casa does not kill."

"Dear God . . . you cannot be thinking that we should *use* this powder as part of the questioning?"

"And why not?" Sadrinho stood and began to pace in front of the window. "So many die before our work is done. Even when their spirit is willing and on the brink of confession, the flesh proves weak. The silence of death too often condemns them to eternal punishment."

"And you believe this substance will give us all the time we need for saving souls? Might we not instead be losing our own in exchange for those we rescue? Might the Santa Casa come to seem another Circle of Hell to those who return to us? Or because of the hard self-examination we require of our guests, might perdition seem more bearable, and thereby preferable to them? Once a lost soul has met demons of the underworld, are they even capable of redemption through an unnatural second or third life?"

"There are those who believe, Padre, that the lost can redeem themselves even out of Hell. Think of it!" said Sadrinho, eyes shining. "So much to be learned. We may discover the very architecture of the Afterlife. Think how the world will benefit from such knowledge."

So, you see yourself kissing Pope Clement's ring, do you, Sadrinho? And being praised throughout Christendom for your remarkable "discoveries." Immortality for your name. And, perhaps, immortality for your own earthly flesh? You should, instead, consider the fiery stake, and the smell of brimstone. "If God had intended Man to have this knowledge, would not His Son have revealed it at His Resurrection?"

"The Bible shows us there is a time and a place for all things, Antonio. Perhaps now is the time, and this is the place for this revelation to be made to mankind."

Gonsção leaned back in his chair, wondering what he could do to deflate Sadrinho's mad pride. "Well. There may be something in what you say. But the point is moot. Senhor De Cartago is dead again, and you have no other informants who can tell you where the substance may be found."

A victorious smile crept across Sadrinho's lips. "Ah, but we do, Antonio. Why do you think Brother Andrew dared our displeasure by bringing the powder into the Santa Casa?"

"I have been wondering that."

"For the young *inglês*, as he said. Brother Andrew knew that Senhor Chinnery had information that must not be lost. That is why he risked himself to take the *inglês* from our grasp."

"Ah. Yes." Gonsção remembered the *inglês*'s words to De Cartago: "I have told them nothing. . . ."

"Thanks to Brother Andrew's encouragement, the young *inglês* has made a full confession."

Gonsção felt his spirits sink further. "Had he anything of interest to confess?"

"Oh, yes. He was not the innocent he seemed. Apparently De Cartago had begun initiating him into the secrets of the cabal."

"Indeed? And Senhor Chinnery was willing to tell you the source of the powder?"

"He says he will do better. He will guide us to it."

Gonsção blew air out his lips. "And you believe him?"

Sadrinho's smile did not falter. "I have reason to. Has the young man not admitted that he is a merchant of drugs and poisons? Doubtless he seeks the powder for his own use. The roll of parchment we found within his clothing appears to be a crude map with alchemical symbols and the Sanskrit word 'Kṛṣna.' I am told there is a river of that name in the interior. Zalambur, De Cartago's associate, was known to make journeys as far as the Mughul court of Emperor Akbar, as was the Lady Aditi. Oh, yes. I believe the young *inglês* knows."

"Even if he does, what would keep him from escaping or leading others into a trap? These cultists seem willing to die for their erroneous faith."

"Senhor Chinnery has suffered the strappado, so escape will be beyond his strength for some time. As for a trap"—Sadrinho shrugged—"it will be up to those who accompany him to discourage such treachery."

"Surely you are not planning on following this man yourself, Domine? That would be highly improper for one in your position. You must not abandon your duties to go chasing pagan mysteries."

Sadrinho leaned forward again. "Of course. I knew you had the wisdom to understand the situation clearly. I cannot leave my work. That is why you must be the one to go, Antonio."

"Me?" Gonsção sensed the door of a trap shutting behind him. "That is impossible."

"But why? You were sent by Cardinal Albrecht all the way from Lisboa to learn the truth behind the downfall of Coutinho and de Albuquerque. You cannot simply ignore this last, and most important part of the puzzle."

"I can, if I deem it impractical and dangerous. My orders do not give me leave to wander far from Goa—"

"But they do not forbid it, either, Antonio. I have read again the missive from His Eminence, and he merely asks me to give you all assistance in getting to the root of the problem. Well. We now know the shape of that root and we must simply go and dig it out. Your superiors in Lisboa could not have foreseen all possibilities. And I do not think His Eminence would appreciate your narrow interpretation of his wishes."

You sly dog, thought Gonsção. *You think you have found a way to rid yourself of my meddling presence. If I die in the attempt, I am out of your way forever. If I succeed and return, I will bring you the seeds to your future greatness. Would Cardinal Albrecht understand if I refused? Or would he, upon learning of the powers of this substance, become as besotted with its possibilities as you have?*

"However," Sadrinho went on, "should you feel you are truly not strong enough for the task, I have already made plans to send another."

"Another?"

"Yes, I was hoping you would be a mature, guiding influence for him. I am going to send Brother Timóteo."

Gonsção stared at the Inquisitor. "You cannot be serious. He is just a boy."

"Boys must become men at some point in their life, Antonio. And Timóteo is reaching the age where he should have some experience of the world, and see the people to whom he may someday minister. I fear we have kept him too closeted here in the Santa Casa. He is bound up with books and childish memories. Besides, who knows more about this cabal we are investigating than you or me? Timóteo has read the records, after all."

Ah. Is this, at last, the punishment for that transgression? "What is to keep the *inglês* from leading the boy astray, or harming him?"

"I am not a fool, Antonio. I have asked Governador da Gama to arrange for us a detail of *soldados* for escort. Timóteo will be protected."

And how well might an innocent slip of a boy deal with rough, unruly soldiers? Who will protect him from them? "I see."

"I have also sent word through the city markets that our expedition wishes to join up with a trading caravan to guide us as far as Bijapur. We will offer protection in exchange for an introduction at the court of Sultan Ibrahim 'Adilshah."

"So. Timóteo is to travel in the midst of pagan merchants, and pay respects at a Muslim Mughul court?"

"Antonio, have you so little faith in the boy? I have no doubt he will make them all Christian in short order."

"What if they disapprove of his proselytizing? What if they tempt Timóteo toward sin, or apostasy? Will he have no one to go to for guidance?"

"As it happens, I have asked the good Brother Andrew to go and he is quite willing. He seems as eager to find the powder as we are, though his reasons are obscure. However, he speaks fluent Persian as well as Portuguese, so I felt his assistance would be quite valuable."

It was all Gonsção could do not to laugh with disbelief and say "You are mad." "Domine, you have seen that this so-called good Brother is acquainted with the *inglês*. For all we know, they have conspired together in order to create an avenue of escape from Goa. How could you trust these men? I must protest, Domine. You may be placing Timóteo in grave danger."

Sadrinho opened his hands like the wings of a butterfly. "That is why I hoped you would accompany him."

Gonsção narrowed his eyes. "Surely there are others you can send."

The Inquisitor lifted his gaze to Heaven. "Antonio, you have allowed your feelings to cloud your judgment. How many persons should we trust with this knowledge? Is it not true that in the Santa Casa, the fewer who know, the better? Do you wish to spread this secret throughout the city? What if the wrong persons learn of it? The 'Adilshah, or the Mughul Emperor Akbar? Or the Dutch? Or the Jesuits, God help us. Think what might happen if the incorruptible body of Francis Xavier is made to rise again."

Gonsção suppressed a shudder. "If your surmise is correct, one of those may already know of it. What of Domine Pinto? Can you not send him?"

Sadrinho sighed. "He wishes nothing to do with this case. He refuses to see its importance. Besides, he has his hands full with heresy in Diu and Pernem. It would be as improper for him to leave his work as for me to leave Goa. No, it must be you, or else Timóteo leads the expedition as the sole representative of the Santa Casa."

Timóteo is a good and obedient boy. If his quest succeeds, he would not have the strength of will to do what I now see must be done. "I am beginning to understand you, Domine. This is a larger concern than one outpost of the Santa Casa, one group of apostates and pagans. If the Muslims were to learn of this powder, they could bring forth infernal armies of resurrected dead against our colony, or the entire Christian world. And who knows what evil pagan sorcerers would do. It is a problem too great for a mere boy to handle."

Sadrinho leaned forward and nodded. "I knew you would come to understand, Antonio."

"Yes. You have convinced me. I will go." *Not to bring you more of the powder, however, but to destroy its source.*

Sadrinho clasped his hands and held them toward Heaven. "Glory to God. I knew He would inspire you to see the light."

"Yes," Gonsção murmured, "I believe He has."

The Inquisitor stood and went to the study doors, opening the one on the right. Brother Timóteo stepped in.

How well arranged this dance is. Sadrinho knew I was going to eventually agree.

"God be with you, Domine," said Timóteo. "And you, Padre. I have put Senhor Chinnery's confession in its proper place and I have told Brother Marco to write the letter to the *governador* that you requested."

"Very good, Timóteo. Now, Antonio, I must go see that provisions are acquired for you. This project must get under way as soon as possible. Please stay, Timóteo. Feel free to converse in my absence. There are things you and the Padre ought to discuss." Sadrinho left, shutting the door behind him. Timóteo blinked, looking uncomfortable. "You wish to speak to me, Padre?"

Gonsção felt some disquiet himself. "I hear the *inglês* has confessed."

The boy's smile was bright as the sun. "Is it not wonderful, Padre? How amazing is the Lord's work."

"Truly, He works in unknowable ways. Has Domine Sadrinho told you what he intends for you?"

Timóteo tilted his head. "Another task, Padre? Am I to be advocate to a new guest?"

Gonsção sighed. *The Domine even leaves the giving of the news to me.* "No, Timóteo. We are to go on a great journey, you and I."

The boy's eyes widened. "A journey, Padre? Across the sea? To Lisboa or Roma?"

Laughing sadly, Gonsção said, "Alas, no, my son. Not by sea and to nowhere so grand. We are to go into the wilderness of India. The journey will be perilous and what we will be seeking may be a great evil."

"Evil, Padre?"

"The *inglês* you helped has said he will lead us to the source of the powder that brings the dead to life. Dominc Sadrinho believes it may be of priceless value to the Santa Casa. I am not so certain. And the *inglês* may try to lead us astray."

"No, no, Padre! Senhor Chinnery is a good man. I know this. If he says he will lead us there, I believe him."

"I hope your faith is well placed, Timóteo. But in any case, we will face many dangers. Beyond Goa, there are few who honor the Santa Casa, or even know of Our Lord."

"I understand, Padre."

"Do you want to go on such a journey, my son? Domine Sadrinho is determined to send you, but I will try to protect you if you choose not to go."

The boy looked down at his sandals for a long moment. He looked up again and said, "If it is in the service of God and the Santa Casa, then I must go. We will be like the knights on the Crusades, or those who searched for the sacred Grail, yes?"

Gonsção smiled and laid his hand on Timóteo's shoulder. "Like the knights on Crusade, my son. I admire your courage and good heart. May they both survive the journey intact."

XXI

🌿 MONKSHOOD. This plant has but one stalk that grows from a tuberous root. Its leaves are dark above yet fair below, and it bears at its summit a cluster of purple flowers which have the shape of a monk's cowl. It is also named helmet flower or wolfsbane. Great care must be taken in the use of this herb, for from it is decocted a most deadly poison which afflicts one with palsy as it kills. The only antidote is made from slugs that have fed upon theriac. Legend says monkshood first grew from the spittle dripping from the maw of Cerberus, the three-headed dog which guards the gates of Hades. It was used by the witch-goddess Hecate to poison her father. Witches, it is said, chew upon monkshood leaves to benumb themselves, and bring visions of journeys to distant lands. . . .

Thomas sat on a cool stone bench in a courtyard of the Santa Casa. He leaned back against the wall behind him, eyes closed. The morning breezes flowed over him, exotic birds chattered and sang in the tree boughs overhead. Thomas tried not to think of the pain.

His arms hung useless, hands resting in his lap. *If rope were sensate, as are my limbs, is this how it would feel? Bound, twisted, and burnt at both ends?* His hands had been wrapped in bandages soaked in a strange-smelling balm. *I should inquire of Brother Timóteo what was used, for it seems to have virtue. The rope burns sting, but not so much as they might.*

The sounds of preparation for travel went on all around him: mules being saddled, carts loading, men shouting orders.

Thomas once more gave thanks to God for his approaching escape from the Santa Casa. And then wondered, with sorrow, if the Deity were listening. If his forced confession and baptism had been induction into the True Faith, then God might now be hearing him for the first time. If, however, Thomas had renounced what was the True Faith, then the ears of Heaven might now be closed to him forever.

A shadow fell over him and Thomas opened his eyes. A monk, face obscured within his brown Jesuit cowl, stood before him. *"Bom dia,* Brother," Thomas said, not caring that he mixed his languages.

The monk nodded. "Well met again, lad, and in better circumstance. 'Twould seem my faith was well placed in you."

Thomas frowned. "I am hardly well, Andrew."

"But you are alive and someday to be free, which is more than many who enter these walls could claim."

"Before aught else 'scapes your lips, Andrew, remember I have a question that wants answer."

Lockheart paused. "And you shall have it, when the time is right. But not here. Yon blackfriar who comes is yet wary of our intent. We must bide a bit."

At the sound of approaching footsteps, Thomas turned his head. It was the Dominican, Father Gonsção, his black cloak swirling about his white robe. *"Boa manhã, Irmão, Senhor Chinnery."* The blackfriar nodded at both of them and blessed Thomas in Latin, making the sign of the Cross. Father Gonsção appeared to be past thirty, with a face lined from experience not weather. His hazel eyes betokened some intelligence and probity, but Thomas wondered what cruelties they had beheld in the Padre's work. From the way Gonsção scowled at the preparations, Thomas gathered that the good Father was not at all pleased to be part of the expedition.

"How are you feeling, my son?" said Father Gonsção in Portuguese-accented Latin. He reached out a hand as if to grasp Thomas's shoulder, then stopped himself.

"I am better, Padre," said Thomas.

"I will pray the Good Lord heals your arms as well as he has healed your soul."

"My thanks. Your Brother Timóteo has some skill in the healing arts. I understood that he would be coming with us, yet I have not seen him." In fact, the boy had talked of nothing else as he had been bandaging Thomas's hands the night before; babbling about knights on Crusade, Arthur and the Grail, Jason and the Golden Fleece, Odysseus, Heracles, and Perseus. *As if this mad journey were some quest out of legend. What pity that I must disappoint him. For if I have my way, this expedition ends at Bijapur.*

"He is," said Father Gonsção, with a disapproving frown. "But this morning he is saying good-bye to his family. He will join us later outside town, where we are meeting the caravan that will accompany us."

Lockheart began to prattle at the Padre in Portuguese. Thomas could not follow much of it, but gathered that the Scotsman was offering unctuous, devout gratitude and assurances of future good behavior.

Father Gonsção accepted this with a perfunctory nod and quickly excused himself, heading back to where the loaded mules and carts were congealing out of chaos into a rough line.

"He is no fool, that one," said Lockheart. "He trusts us not. Much care should we take lest he divine our purpose." He looked back at Thomas. "Whatever that should be."

"Our purpose? My intent was to flee home at first chance."

Lockheart crouched on one knee beside Thomas. "Is

it?" he said softly. "Do you not truly intend to search for the source of the precious powder?"

Thomas sighed. "When I first learned of it, Andrew, I had thought to seek it, to bring some glory out of disaster. Now"—he looked at his arms—"I think it beyond me."

"Body and spirits can heal, lad. Your chances may be better than you think. Did the sorcerer tell you where the source was?"

Thomas regarded Lockheart a moment. "Aye, but not in close detail. Of course, there is the map."

Lockheart's brows shot up. "A map! Do you have it still?"

Thomas smiled at the Scotsman's open greed. "The Domine took it from me before I even read it. No doubt our good Padre has it now."

"Indeed? Then . . . what need has he of us?"

"The map is of little use without knowing how to hold it or what the symbols writ therein depict. De Cartago had to tell me what it shows. I wove a tale to the Inquisitor of how there were traps and riddles to be solved en route, and that although I could not predict what they would be, I have the knowledge to overcome them."

"Clever lad. So only you can interpret the map?"

Thomas paused again. "Perhaps. Though I have forgotten much of what De Cartago told me. I remember that Bijapur was a place of note. And from there, much is possible."

Lockheart narrowed his eyes a moment, then grinned broadly. "Well, then, we shall plan no further." He patted Thomas's knee. "Bijapur is our goal for the nonce. After that, we shall see where the Fates guide us. Come, 'twould seem they have your steed ready."

Thomas stood, with Lockheart's help, and let himself be led to a tall brown mule whose reins were held by a young blackfriar. With much awkwardness and pain, Thomas managed to flop onto the saddle and roll into a sitting position. He reached out for the reins, but the monk shook his head.

"By Christ," Thomas growled to Lockheart, "are not my useless arms enough to prove me trustworthy? Must I be led like a child?"

" 'Tis not the nature of the Santa Casa to show an abundance of trust. We must prove our meekness first. Be patient. Ah, here come the governor's men."

The gates to the courtyard opened and in rode twelve Goan soldiers. Their boat-shaped bronze helmets and polished breastplates gleamed, as did the rapiers at their sides.

"Only a dozen," murmured Lockheart. "The governor was not feeling generous. More good news for us, eh?" He patted Thomas's leg and walked down the line toward the heavily laden carts.

Thomas's mule snorted a sigh and shifted impatiently beneath him. Thomas watched the soldiers as they rode past on their nondescript steeds. Thomas was no judge of horseflesh, but these did not seem to be the finest of breed, nor had they had the best of care. The soldiers themselves, he noted, were all as lean and wiry as the man in the Aljouvar, Joaquim. In fact, one of the soldiers quite strongly resembled him. In fact, this one noticed Thomas and called out, "*Ay, inglês!*"

"Joaquim, by my soul!" cried Thomas. "What miracle is this?"

Ignoring the stares of the other soldiers, Joaquim sidled his horse over to Thomas. "Of which miracle do you speak, senhor? That I am here or that you are leaving this place as one of the living?"

"The first, my friend. I would embrace you with greeting, but my arms . . . are not what they were."

Joaquim nodded knowingly. "Just as well, my friend, for it would not do for my fellows to see me embrace a dreadful foreign heretic such as yourself."

"Heretic no longer, Joaquim. I have made confession in the Santa Casa."

"Ah, merciful Santa Maria. No wonder they let you live. So you are now simply a filthy *inglês* and almost worthy to be my friend," Joaquim said with a grin.

"I hope I may prove my worthiness in time," said Thomas. "But you have not answered me."

"But this is no miracle, senhor. When the Santa Casa calls for *soldados* for a long journey out of Goa, does our *sargento* send his best men? No, he sends to the stewpits and the jails, for undesirable men who are desperate. So they came to me in the Aljouvar and said, 'Joaquim, would you rather go on a mission for the Santa Casa or stay and hang for a thief?' It was a hard choice, senhor. But, as I am a brave man, I chose the difficult journey over an easy death."

Thomas laughed. "Grateful I am for your courage, Joaquim." He noticed Father Gonsção glaring at them from across the courtyard. *Alas, this meeting will doubtless not encourage his trust.*

Joaquim glanced at Gonsção. "The Padre does not seem pleased, Tomás. We will talk more later, yes?" Joaquim winked and rode over to where the other soldiers waited. They gave Joaquim curious looks, but did not seem angry.

His spirits lighter, Thomas sighed and relaxed in the saddle. *Hope is possible yet, if Providence brings me again into the company of such men.*

As the orb of the sun rose above the courtyard wall, final efforts were made toward departure; drivers tugged on the yokes of their oxen, carters checked wheels and axles. Father Gonsção at last mounted his horse, a stout grey. Lockheart was astride a black mule, and he rode with the Padre to the head of the line.

Whom does good Brother Andrew serve now? Thomas wondered. *Himself, God, or the Santa Casa?*

The soldiers arranged themselves: four at the front with Padre Gonsção and Lockheart, four at the rear behind the porters and carts, and four at the center, where Thomas rode. Somehow Joaquim had placed himself among these, and he brazenly rode up beside Thomas, taking the reins of his mule from the blackfriar.

"How is it you become trusted with my care, Joaquim?"

"We *soldados* know the effect the Aljouvar can have upon a man, senhor. I told them I knew all your tricks, that you had confessed them to me in the pit, and therefore I was best suited to lead you."

Thomas laughed. "How I wish I had been blessed with your quick tongue, sir."

"Do you attempt to call me a liar, senhor?"

"Never would I insult such a tender gentleman so. But I admire your skill in explaining how things must be. Tell me, have you news of the others? Is Sabdajnana free?"

Joaquim snorted. "He was freed not long after you left, senhor. His family ransomed him for a very great sum."

"I am glad. And Van der Groot? Is he still in prison?"

Joaquim paused, then said softly, "He has escaped the Aljouvar."

"Excellent news," said Thomas, also lowering his voice. "Is he headed home, then?"

"One might say so, senhor. There is a chance you may see him as we are leaving the city."

"Truly? Then I may be able to let him know we are well."

Joaquim gave him a peculiar stare, but said nothing more.

On a balcony above them, Inquisitor Sadrinho stepped out, black robe fluttering in the morning breezes. He held up his arms and blessed the expedition, finishing with exhortations to glory and Godspeeds. Thomas wondered how much the others in the expedition, the soldiers and carters and servants, had been told about their purpose, what they believed they were journeying forth to find. *How strange that my ruse has led to this turn in their fortunes. How many lives have I disrupted merely so that I can be free? May they not come to harm when I abandon them.*

At last, Father Gonsção shouted, *"Adiante!"* The cry was carried down the line like a swell on the sea. Whips cracked, men hupped to their oxen and horses, cartwheels creaked, and slowly the procession moved forward.

Joaquim clicked his tongue at Thomas's mule. It flicked its ears forward and began a sprightly walk to keep up with the taller horse beside it. Thomas grasped the front ridge of his saddle with both hands for balance, wincing with the pain.

It was not until they had passed through the gate in the walls of the Santa Casa that Thomas felt his muscles ease and his breath flow more freely. He had not allowed himself to believe in his escape until now. "Thanks be to God, this most glorious morning," he murmured.

Their procession passed through quiet streets, unlike the crowded avenues full of men and animals that Thomas had seen his first day in Goa. In fact, many doors and shutters were closed.

"Joaquim, is it a holiday or feast day? Is that why the town seems empty?"

The *soldado* snorted. "Look again, Tomás. Goans are not fools. They have been warned not to interfere with the progress of the beloved Santa Casa."

Thomas watched the houses they rode past carefully, and noted wary faces peering out from behind curtains and shutters. Small children were being yanked indoors by their mothers. Older children, hiding in shadows, made the sign of the fig at Padre Gonsção.

"They know we are leaving the city," said Joaquim, "or they would not be so bold."

A familiar large tree came into view, with men sitting under it. They looked up silently as the procession passed, and Thomas recognized a white-bearded face. He did not dare call out to Father Stevens, nor could he raise a hand to wave. Thomas merely nodded gravely at the old monk. Father Stevens gave a solemn nod in return, and seemed to mouth the words "Go with God."

The houses along the street gradually changed from wealthy Portuguese town houses, to walled homes of prosperous Hindu and Arab merchants, to simple Hindu thatched huts that smelled strongly of cattle dung. Thomas gauged by the sun that they were heading north and east. They passed through a gap in a crumbling stone wall and emerged onto a wide east/west road. To the north was a brown river so broad that the far bank was a dim, dark line on the horizon.

Small temples dotted the near bank, and just beyond them boatmen poled long, narrow craft filled with fish and flowers and bright-colored fruit on the placid water.

"Ah!" said Joaquim, "there is Pedro. You see him?"

"No. Where is he?" Thomas looked up and down the road, seeing only slim Hindu women carrying baskets.

"Back there, on the wall."

Thomas glanced back at the crumbling wall and the sight chilled his heart. Three corpses hung from spikes, facing the river. One was little more than a skeleton papered with skin. Another wore rags over his drying brown flesh. The third was fair-haired, dressed in Van der Groot's doublet and breeches. Birds were pecking out what was left of his eyes.

"Dear God," whispered Thomas, looking away. Two of the soldiers crossed themselves. Others chuckled and made sly jokes. "Why didn't you tell me he was dead?"

"I told you he had escaped the Aljouvar, Tomás. There is no surer escape than death."

XXII

OLIVE: This much-venerated tree is evergreen, with yellow wood and an oil-bearing fruit, green or black. They are said to live to a great age. Infusion of the leaves soothes the spirit. Decoction of the bark reduces fever. The oil of the fruit will heal burns, and swallowed it helps digestion. To the ancients, it is sacred to Athena, and the Romans made crowns of olive leaves to signify conquest and a peaceful reign. In the East, the olive is a symbol of peace, accomplishment, increase, and safe travel....

Padre Gonsção heard commotion behind him and turned in the saddle. Some of the *soldados* appeared to be joking with each other about the criminals hanging on the city wall. With a sigh, Gonsção faced forward again. *Timóteo leading such men. How could Sadrinho even have thought it?*

He wished he had Brother Timóteo's enthusiasm for the journey. Or even that of Brother Andrew, who prattled on beside him about the strange temples and curious plants and animals. The farther they rode from sights familiar, the heavier Gonsção's heart became. *How could I have been talked into this?* Then he remembered the greed on Sadrinho's face, the horror of the risen sorcerer. *How foolish of me. My discomfort is nothing to the worthiness of destroying the evil we seek.*

Two miles farther down the road, they came to an open area of flattened red dirt, ringed with tall coconut palms and banana trees. Camels knelt in the shade, lazily chewing grass and watching the expedition approach with large, dark eyes. Their turbaned drivers with dark, weathered faces sat beside them, chewing betel or conversing quietly. The caravaneers did not stand as Gonsção rode into the clearing, or call out, or even take much notice of him.

Brother Andrew looked around. "It appears our caravan is here. Do we wait only on Brother Timóteo?"

"No," said Gonsção, dismounting. "We are to be joined by the caravan master."

"He is not one of these?"

"She," Gonsção corrected, "is a widow of the Marathas clan. She inherited her husband's business. But I see no woman's palanquin has yet arrived."

"What?" said Brother Andrew, sliding off his mule. "Did she not have the good manners to fling herself upon her husband's pyre?"

Gonsção frowned. "You have a strange sense of the amusing, Brother. That barbaric practice, I am told, has been outlawed in Goa."

"Then she made wise choice of home and hearth. Forgive me, Padre. I am in strange humor today."

"We must regard this widow with respect," Gonsção said, leading his horse to tie it to a palm trunk, "as it is her family's wealth that in part supports this expedition, and her noble connection which will get us audience with the Sultan in Bijapur."

"I shall govern my tongue with care in her presence."

"You will not enter her presence, Brother," said Gonsção as he watched the rest of the expedition roll into the clearing. "I am told Brahmin ladies keep themselves apart from strangers almost as strictly as Muslims. She likely will not speak to us at all, except through her servants. I will expect you and the rest of our party to adhere to that custom."

"You may rely on me, Padre."

"I hope so. Ah. You'd best see to our young Senhor Chinnery. He appears to be having trouble getting off his mule."

Thomas lay on his stomach across the saddle, face burning with exertion and shame. He dared not move, fearing a fall onto his head. His arms flapped at his sides, useless as a baby bird's wings.

"Ho, there, lad! Bide a moment. Here I am."

Thomas felt Lockheart grab the back of his shirt and the waist of his trousers. With a mighty tug, Thomas was pulled off the saddle and into Lockheart's thick arms.

"Why did you not call for someone, lad? Where's your Goan horseman?"

"Off to piss, methinks," Thomas gasped, trying to stand. "This is idiocy, Andrew! I can be no use this way."

Lockheart glanced over his shoulder. "Come, then, I will do the deed before the good Padre can blink his eyes."

"Deed?" Thomas was hustled by Lockheart around the mule and to a large rock out of sight of Padre Gonsção. "What deed do you speak of?"

"You're better off kneeling, lad. I'll be swift, I promise." Lockheart crooked one leg around Thomas's ankles, sweeping them out from under him. As Thomas fell forward, Lockheart caught him with a hand under his chest. His right forearm was caught in Lockheart's large right hand. With a mighty twist, Lockheart shoved the shoulder back into its socket with a sickening crunch.

Thomas screamed. The pain was as intense as the strappado.

"Courage, lad. One more."

"No—"

But Lockheart ably grasped Thomas's left arm. Again came the twist and the grinding of bone. Thomas could only gasp as tears leaked out of his eyes. He leaned back against the rocks, eyes closed, his shoulders and arms throbbing with pain.

He heard running feet, and when he next opened his eyes, he and Lockheart were surrounded by soldiers with their swords drawn.

Padre Gonsção pressed his way through the soldiers and stared at him and Lockheart. "What are you doing?"

"You asked me to help him from his mule, Padre. The only help for him, however, was to set his shoulders right. Otherwise, he would need help on and off the whole journey."

Thomas felt the pain in his shoulders subsiding to a roaring ache. Without thinking, he raised his hands to touch them and marveled that he could move his arms again.

The Padre narrowed his eyes in suspicion and crouched down beside Thomas. "Why did he scream?"

"I had to hurt him in order to help, Padre. As one must in the setting of a limb that is broken, or severing a rotting one. Or ensuring a confession, perhaps? As you see, he recovers. A little suffering can, at times, be as good for the body as it is for the soul."

Thomas said, "It is all right, Padre. He merely . . . surprised me. I have heard of the method, though this is the first time I have seen it done. It will aid my recovery."

"There, I have helped you in your trade as well by teaching you another healing art."

"One I am not likely to employ myself," said Thomas, grimacing and rubbing his upper arms.

"Very well," said Padre Gonsção. "Take care, my son. We

are relying upon you." Glaring at Lockheart, Gonsção stood and walked away.

The soldiers drifted away also, some staring at Thomas with amusement, others annoyed that they had been roused for nothing.

Joaquim lingered a moment longer, eyeing Lockheart speculatively. "You, Irmão, have been a soldier, yes?"

"Among other things," said Lockheart.

Joaquim smirked at Thomas and strolled away to join his fellows.

Thomas rested his back against the rock. Lockheart sat down heavily beside him. "I suppose I should thank you, Andrew," Thomas said.

"Thanks are not needed, lad. Although methinks the Padre had wanted to keep you weak. He'll not thank me, I am sure."

"So. You've been a soldier. And a wool merchant. And now a doctor. As well as a false monk."

"And many other things besides, although this robe is more apt than many other things I've worn."

"And what garb weareth the man who sent you after me?"

Lockheart sighed and leaned his head back against the stone. "Garments most familiar to you, lad. 'Twas your own father sent me to watch over you."

Thomas stared, dumbfounded. "Now you prove yourself a liar, Andrew. As I have said, my sire cares not one whit for me."

"And as I have said, oftimes a sire's care is not visible. When he learned you were set upon so long a voyage, I was hired to follow and protect you."

"Wherefore did you not speak of this 'ere now? Could my father have not introduced you so to me before the voyage?"

"Come, now, what would you have said at such a meeting? You doubtless hoped to prove your manhood on that voyage. How would you have taken your father's gift of a nursemaid? Would you not have railed like the Furies? Would you not have spurned my company as if I were a leper?"

"True. You have the right of it. It angers me now that my father should have so little faith in me."

" 'Tis not want of faith, but surfeit of care. You are important to us, Tom. More than you know."

"What sort of nursemaid is it who would deliver his charge to the arms of pirates and the bosom of the Inquisition?"

Lockheart stared at the ground. "A most foul and cowardly one, I confess, although even that abandonment might seem an act of kindness, were all the truth to be known. Our voyage seemed at an end, my duty a failure. In a moment of weakness, I decided to escape my fate, and leave you to your own, howsomever I could. But the Divine Powers would not be thwarted and you followed, a proper chastisement. But you must allow that I have made amends since. Without me, you would have never left the Santa Casa."

"Without you, I should never have gone there at all."

"All things have a purpose, Tom, though beyond our ken they may be. Mayhap you are meant to find the fabulous Elixir of Life and Death. Mayhap it seeps from the fabled philosopher's stone itself. Do not all heroes of legend suffer trials of strength and courage before they are permitted onward to their intended goal?"

"You begin to speak like Brother Timóteo. Do not distract me with stories, Andrew. Have you proof that 'twas my father who hired you?"

"Only this." Lockheart pulled out from the neck of his brown robe a silver medallion on a chain. Thomas held it gently and examined it. On one side was stamped a stag rampant over a crescent moon. On the other was a female figure in Grecian clothing, standing between two lean hounds.

"Indeed, my father had a medallion such as this." The images brought up shreds of memory, of childhood or of dreams, wavering dimly like seaweed just below the ocean surface. A taste of sweet wine and honey, voices chanting too soft to be intelligible, a crescent moon shining over treetops, dogs baying at the hunt.

"A token of his good faith in me."

"Or you have stolen it. Does Master Coulter know about you and your appointed task?"

"Nay, 'twould seem he and your sire . . . are not of agreement. So he was told nothing."

"Hm. I have never heard my master speak ill of him. His good wife, Dame Coulter, has betimes been disapproving."

"Mayhap 'twas her meddling your father feared, then."

"I know not why she should meddle, as it was she who set me on our ill-fated voyage. She said 'twould cure my nightmares, and so it did, until we reached India."

Lockheart regarded him curiously, but said nothing.

Thomas handed the medallion back to him. "I am still not convinced whether you are a friend or the best whoreson liar ever to leave Scotland."

Lockheart raised his hands from his knees in a shrug. "Then we must let time and events give you answer."

There came a distant blast of horns from down the road. The camels in the clearing raised their long noses and whuffed the air. The drivers stood, dusting off their long robes. The *soldados* stopped their gambling and conversation and stood.

" 'Twould seem the caravan master approaches," said Lockheart.

Thomas peered down the road and saw two dark-skinned Hindus carrying the long trumpets which had sounded not long before, two more camels heavily laden with trunks and boxes. Behind them was a great palanquin borne by eight men, covered with a tent of purple cloth with ties and tassels of gold. Behind that walked four serving girls in scarlet saris and gold hoops through their noses, talking in animated gestures with vermilion-stained fingers.

"A person of wealth," said Thomas.

"Indeed, and she pays our way, so the Padre wishes we stay clear of her, lest we offend her noble sensibilities."

Thomas nodded, then saw a momentary flash of sunlight on silver, and a movement—a slender arm reaching out from the palanquin, tossing something away. The gesture was familiar. His heart nearly stopped in his chest. *Could it be?*

Aditi wiped her hand on her skirt after tossing out the half-eaten betel cake. *I must stop this chewing. It is a foul habit. My teeth are already becoming stained.*

But her spirits had needed calming ever since the *puja* at the Mahadevi's temple. Her disquiet had become worse when the servant she had sent to Padre Stevens returned with the news that the young Tamas had been imprisoned in the Orlem Gor. Not knowing what De Cartago had told him, Aditi had nearly become frantic with worry and powerlessness.

Then had come the news that the monks of the Orlem Gor sought a caravan leaving for Bijapur, and backing for a minor expedition into the Deccan. In her heart, Aditi knew the reason. She convinced her supporters, despite their hate for the Orlem Gor, to give that backing and send her as the caravan master. It was, she had realized, the task she had remained in Goa for, as if Gandharva had somehow known. It was *dharma;* whatever else, the monks of the Inquisition must not find the Mahadevi.

The swaying of the palanquin stopped and Aditi peeked out of the side curtain. The camel drivers in the shade of the palms were rousing their groaning beasts. These men knew their business and she was not concerned about them.

She called quietly to one of her serving girls.

"What is your wish, Sri Aditi?"

"You are not to speak that name. I am Sri Agnihotra now. Look about and tell me how many soldiers you see."

"Forgive me . . . Sri Agnihotra." The girl glanced around, walked away for a moment and then returned. "Not many. I see only twelve."

"More than I would like, but I will manage. How many monks?"

The girl bustled away again. On her return, she said, "One in black and white robes, one in brown."

"Only two. That is good fortune. And did you see a pale young man with yellow hair?"

"Yes, Sri Agnihotra. He is over there, by the rock."

"Ah." Aditi peered out at where the girl pointed. She saw him and felt a strange tugging within. *He is more thin and pale. But what did I expect? The Orlem Gor is never kind, and they surely did all they could to pry his secrets from him. I must find out what he told them, and see that they learn nothing more.*

Beside Tamas, she recognized the untrustworthy Lock-heart, in the guise of a monk. *This becomes more interesting still. Does he also seek the* Rasa Mahadevi?

The serving girl returned. "Sri, the priest from the Orlem Gor, Padre Antonio Gonsção, sends his greetings, and asks that we delay our departure a little longer. He says they await one more of their party. Another monk."

"Another monk," Aditi sighed. "Again, not as I would have hoped." She glanced out again at Tamas. "While we are delayed, ask the yellow-haired one to approach the palanquin. If you are questioned, say that I have never seen one of his appearance before and I am curious."

The serving girl bowed. "As you wish, Sri Agnihotra." Aditi closed the curtain and settled herself back against the cushions. She could not find a comfortable position and her hands seemed determined to tremble. For once she was glad for the ruse of being a noble, secluded woman. *What can be keeping that girl?*

At last, she heard the servant's voice outside the palanquin. "I have brought him."

Aditi dared not open the curtain to look. "Is no one else near?"

"No, although the Padre watches us from a distance. He did not wish to permit it."

Tamas mumbled something in what may have been an attempt at Portuguese.

"Turn him so that the Padre cannot see his face."

She heard the girl giggle and speak cajolingly to him. "It is done, Sri Agnihotra."

Softly, Aditi said in Greek, "Tamas, it is I, one whom you have met before."

"*Nai,*" he replied in a husky voice, so near the curtain. "I thought it might be you."

Aditi reached up her hand and then lowered it. "Are you well?"

"I live, and my body is healing."

"Ah. We must not speak long, but I wished you to know. I have come to help you. Whatever your goal. Again we are travelers on the same path, Tamas."

There was silence for some moments. "My hope is to escape, Despoina. When we reach Bijapur. Any aid you can give shall be most welcome."

Aditi felt her spirits lighten. "I will do all I can. But the monks, will they continue on without you?"

Another pause. "Without me, they have nowhere to go. We must stop speaking. The Padre approaches."

"Very well." Aditi began to laugh loudly and to speak in broken Latin. "What strange thing you are, yellow-hair! You amuse me. You bring happy to bored old woman me."

"Domina," said a new voice, whom she presumed to be the Padre. "Forgive me for this improper intrusion of your privacy. Forgive our delay but I have heard the last member of our party will be here soon. I must take this man and help him prepare for the journey."

"All forgiven, Padre. Where find this creature you?"

"He is a Brittanian, Domina. Please pardon us. We must get ready."

"Go, go. I will enjoy laugh much at him in future."

Aditi heard the two men walk away, murmuring to each other. She leaned back on her pillows again and sighed. *"Without me, they have nowhere to go," he said. This is not good. He is their only guide. The priest will keep close watch on him. And it means he has something to tell them. He has taken no vow to be silent. So long as he lives, there is the chance that the Orlem Gor will make use of him. Ai, Mahadevi, why do you give me this task?*

She lightly touched the ivory hilt of the knife in her *ghagra*'s waistband. She wondered how it would feel to use it, to feel his hot blood spurt upon her from the wound in his neck, at the very moment his male organ spurted another warmth between her loins. The thought excited and disturbed her. *Life and death at once. Truly I am my foster Mother's daughter.*

Led away on the arm of Padre Gonsção, Thomas felt a strange elation. Just upon learning that Aditi was near. He justified it to himself by thinking of her offer of help. Such an unexpected ally was a providential gift. *And at such danger to herself. I was not wrong to trust in her mercy.*

"What did she say to you?" asked Padre Gonsção.

"Um, nonsense mostly, Padre. She . . . she thought I was very strange-looking and wished to know what I was."

"Highly improper," Gonsção grumbled, leading Thomas to his mule.

"Perhaps away from the constraints of her family, she feels more at liberty."

"You are not to pester her."

"No, Padre, but if she wishes to speak with me again, should I insult her by refusing?"

The Padre paused, clearly unhappy with either choice. "We will see. Up you go."

Thomas allowed Gonsção to help him onto the mule, even though, after Lockheart's treatment, his own arms had become more capable. With a nod, the Padre went off to his horse.

Thomas sat, the warm sun on his back, watching the caravan reassemble with him at its center: recalcitrant camels led onto the road, men directing each other and their animals with shouts and gestures. He was feeling better than he had in a long while. Life was not without hope. He had the use of his arms restored to him, however weak and sore. He had refound unexpected friends. *Even Lockheart, if his tale be true, is but a reluctant guardian and not a complete scoundrel.*

If, by chance, Providence put in his path the source of the miraculous powder, well and good. But ahead lay Bijapur, a city of which he knew nothing, save that his life would turn there. And signs were that the turning would be for the better.

Brother Timóteo swatted the flank of his burro with a bamboo switch, hoping to catch up to the procession of the Marathi lady. He did not want to keep Padre Gonsção and the whole expedition waiting just for him. Indeed, he would not have been so tardy, had he not had to go to the Leilao bazaar.

His mother regularly sent him little bits of money that he never spent, as the Santa Casa saw to all his needs. He understood now that his thrift had had another purpose, unknown to him before.

For today, after tearful farewells to his mother and sister, he had been able to go to the morning market, where among the spice merchants and horse dealers, there were metalsmiths. There he had bought what now hung in a jute bag beside him.

It was a silver-backed mirror, in a wide brass frame. The metalsmith was a Christian, so there were crosses embossed in each corner of the frame, and roses and lilies down the sides.

Timóteo did not know how he would explain his extravagant purchase to Padre Gonsção. He did not want the Padre to think it was for vanity; Timóteo did not care about, nor particularly like, his own appearance. Perhaps he would say nothing, until it was needed.

The mirror was only for protection, after all. Timóteo had read the trial records. Timóteo had been well taught by his grandfather. And a mirror was what you needed when facing a gorgon, wasn't it?

Timóteo kicked his burro into a reluctant trot, eager for the journey of his life to begin.

AUTHOR'S NOTE

In the late sixteenth and early seventeenth centuries, the Portuguese colony city of Goa was as splendid as many of its European contemporaries, such that it became known as "Golden Goa." One traveler went so far as to call it the Rome of the East. It was the first European colony on the subcontinent of India, taken from the Sultan of Bijapur by the Portuguese in 1510. The rich trade possibilities in India quickly made the colony a hotbed of mercantile intrigue between the Portuguese, Arab, Dutch, Danish, and eventually English and French nations.

It was also a battleground of faiths, as an outpost of the dreaded Inquisition was established there in 1560. Its original purpose was to harass Nestorian Christians, who had lived on the west coast of India for centuries, and "New Christians," Jews who had ostensibly converted yet retained their former customs. However, the Goan Inquisition rapidly earned a reputation as the most corrupt in the world, focusing on those with money and property to confiscate. It was also the longest-surviving arm of the Inquisition, operating into the mid-1700s. The detailed descriptions of the Santa Casa are based on the memoirs of a Frenchman who was imprisoned there in the early 1600s.

Thanks to the sources available in the Ames Library of South Asia, a subdivision of the Edwin O. Wilson Library at the University of Minnesota, I was able to learn the names of the Inquisitors Major in Goa in 1597 (although their appearance and personalities as I describe them are purely fiction) as well as the Governor (who was, indeed, the grandson of the famous explorer Vasco da Gama). It was there I also learned of the shameful recall of Governor Coutinho and Viceroy de Albuquerque on charges of heresy and sorcery and had that wonderful feeling of "Aha!" when a historical detail happens to fit perfectly into one's story.

The expedition of *The Bear*, *The Bear's Whelp*, and the *Benjamin* was a real voyage, headed by Captain Benjamin Wood, sent from England in 1597 with a letter from Queen Elizabeth I intended for the court of Cathay (China). The ill-fated voyage never reached its destination, disappearing at some point after its encounter with Raleigh and his fleet in the Canaries. However, in the collection of historical documents, *Purchas, His Pilgrimes*, there is a letter dated 1601 from a Goan Portuguese captain, describing an encounter with a small group of Englishmen, the last survivors of a shipwrecked expedition on the Indian coast. Most of their crew had been lost to disease after sacking Portuguese ships. This might well have been the ill-fated voyage of the *Benjamin* and the *Whelp*.

(The only one of the survivors to finally make it to Goa, where he was thrown into prison, was named Thomas.)

Garcia de Orta, the Portuguese herbalist, is also an historical figure, who lived the last thirty years of his life in India, traveling throughout the Deccan. He was well regarded in Goa, where he often used his herbal remedies to heal the poor without payment, and he often worked at the Jesuit Misericordia, which was described by travelers as one of the finest hospitals in the world.

It was by odd chance that de Orta came to befriend Luis vas de Camões. The poet had been driven out of Lisbon due to a hopeless infatuation with a handmaid of the Queen. Broke and blind in one eye from a fight, Camões was taken in by de Orta, much like a stray cat, and in his household Camões wrote *Os Lusiados,* now the national epic poem of Portugal, and a fine piece of historical fantasy in its own right.

The Jesuit Father Thomas Stevens was one of the first Englishmen to set foot in Goa, and his letters back to his homeland have been credited with stimulating England's interest in trade with India. He learned several of the local languages and was the first European to write a grammar of an Indian language, as well as writing the *Christian Purana.* He was known to give assistance to Englishmen in Goa, although he was not always successful in shielding them from the authorities' ire.

Saint Francis Xavier, known as the Apostle of the Indies, was a Jesuit monk whose tremendous impact on Christianity in the East is better recounted by others. He died en route to China, and his body, amazingly preserved in quicklime, was eventually returned to Goa, where it lay on view for many years. However, this led to bits of the body being pilfered for relics, and the Jesuits finally sealed him into a glass coffin at the end of the 1600s. In the mid-1800s, the Jesuits began a cycle of displaying Saint Francis Xavier's body every ten years.

All other characters are fictional, although I have tried to depict them and their world as accurately as my research would allow.

Little is left of "Golden Goa." It declined rapidly in the late seventeenth century, with the rising influence of other European settlements in India. Nowadays Goa Velha, or Old Goa, is a collection of ruins (with a few of the churches still well maintained by worshipers), the rest having been reclaimed by the jungle.

In a novel of this scope (including the volumes to follow), the amount of research required and the years it took to bring it to fruition, the number of acknowledgments due is too great to list. Deserving of special acknowledgment, however, is Denny Lien, librarian at the Edwin O. Wilson Library, University of Minnesota, for service above and beyond the call of ordinary librarianship. His help in sifting through the mass of information available helped this book take shape so many years ago.

Acknowledgment is also due my former writers' group, the Scribblies—Emma, Will, Pam, and Steve—for helping me in the early stages of this work to hammer it into something resembling a novel.